SIX DEGREES OF STUPIDITY

Greg Moodie

ABOUT THE AUTHOR

Greg Moodie is an artist and writer with an impressively ludicrous CV and a poor recollection of everything on it. He has published a weekly comic strip every Monday since 2013, sometimes within the pages of the *The National*, Scotland's newest daily newspaper.

The author of three comic compendiums, *Greg Moodie Versus The Union*, *Election Dissection* and *Striptease*, he also penned *Borrowing Burns*, a semi-fictional or "factually dubious" account of the making of his series of Tam O' Shanter murals, and *Cool Scots*, a psychedelic reimagining of Scotland's rich and varied past.

Six Degrees Of Stupidity is his second novel, but the first in print. He regularly threatens to publish its predecessor, *The Unbearable Stupidity Of Being*, and it's even rumoured he was foolhardy enough to start a third, *Stupid Animals*.

Technically Dundonian, Moodie graduated in Fine Art from the city's Duncan of Jordanstone College of Art "sometime before the invention of fire" but believes that, like Vegas, what happened there stayed there.

He currently resides in The Enchanted State of Torphichen (population 570), a conservation village and imaginary island sanctuary in central Scotland. He won Torphichen Citizen of the Year in 2016 "for bringing disrepute to the community".

Published by Greg Moodie
Copyright © Greg Moodie 2021

A catalogue record for this aubergine is available from the
National Library of Scotland and the British Library.

ISBN 978-1-9993627-4-4
IngramSpark edition

Design, layout, cover and illustrations by Greg Moodie.
Author photograph by Arran Mcmillan.

www.gregmoodie.com

VOTE YES

CONTENTS

1. THE ADVOCATE FOR SELF-IMPORTANCE (page 1)

2. THE CURE (page 7)

3. AN EAGLE DOESN'T CATCH FLIES (page 12)

4. MARTINI: THE BREAKFAST OF CHAMPIONS (page 15)

5. THIS IS YOUR CAPTAIN CALLING (page 23)

6. PROJECT X (page 29)

7. BIGGER THAN A CANOE (page 34)

8. A CAUSE FOR ALARM (page 40)

9. THE LITTLE HITLER (page 45)

10. FORTUNE TELLING BY BEARD READING (page 63)

11. DRY LAND IS JUST A FIGURE OF SPEECH (page 84)

12. PARALEGAL ACTIVITY (page 103)

13. SMOKE ON THE WATER (page 130)

14. SIX DEGREES OF STUPIDITY (page 153)

15. THE LONGEST DAY (page 178)

16. THE PROMISED LAND (page 215)

17. I HEART DARKNESS (page 220)

TONY BOAKS

LAFLAMME

GUY LESNIDE QC

SUAVE GAV

THE ADMIRAL

MR BEARD & CORKY

1.
THE ADVOCATE FOR SELF-IMPORTANCE

I'm thinking about having my doorbell removed. It makes a pleasant enough sound but all too often heralds the arrival of something disagreeable. For a while I tried ignoring it but I suspected this particular doorbell had some kind of inherent magnetism that drew the disagreeable towards it and made pressing compulsive. I set out to try and understand its subliminal appeal by pretending to be disagreeable myself. It was difficult to get a frame of reference for this until I imagined being one of my clients. Then I began wondering instead how to make it deliver a small electric shock.

I recognised The Advocate For Self-Importance immediately. His finely chiselled features and rigid jaw had accompanied many a newspaper headline. I wondered if his popularity with the press was due to the squareness of his jaw complimenting the lower half of picture frames. But it wasn't so much his appearance that I recognised, as the general aura of self-satisfaction that accompanied it. It had exuded throughout the numerous TV news reports I'd endured and now here it was exuding on my doorstep.

He was completely absorbed in his phone, and whatever interest he had in me seemed to end at my doorbell. Despite my presence he continued to press it and I began to regret not having pursued the electric shock idea. Between the doorbell and the phone I felt he had enough to occupy him and made to close the door, but this caught his attention and finally the ringing ceased.

"I'm on the phone," he said to me, as if I had been the one bothering *his* doorbell. I could tell that within minutes I'd want to punch him.

I returned to my knotted ball of string – something I attempted to disentangle periodically as a means of avoiding work – and against my better judgement left the door ajar. The consequence of this was that The Advocate For Self-Importance and his phone conversation followed me in. After several minutes the conversation showed no sign of abating and I wondered if perhaps I had been in the wrong house all along.

Unable to give the ball of string my full attention, I had no choice other than to wait. (For The Advocate, the verb 'to wait' didn't conjugate in the first person. It was said that even time, which normally waits for no man, would have to sit around twiddling its thumbs whilst he completed his current engagement.)

"Lovely to talk to you," he said to the caller fortunate enough to command his attention for so long, "but I've had forty-five missed calls whilst we've been talking and now I'm with my design interfacer. I've an important matter to attend to." He brought the phone to a position where he could terminate the call, then caught sight of the mobile screen and returned it to his ear adding, "Forty-six."

Apparently considering my hospitality a fundamental right, he slumped in an armchair expectantly. He could be as expectant as he wanted as far as I was concerned. I'd long since given up on hospitality.

"Apologies," he began. "It is an addiction."

"Being annoying?" I said. I wouldn't normally insult potential clients freely like this but I felt secure knowing that he wasn't really listening.

"I was in Madrid last week and the network ground to a halt because of my calls. I wanted to tell them their system was quite shoddy as it had only been a moderately busy week. But of course the line was never clear for long enough. Eventually I bought a relief phone to ease the strain." He produced a second phone and both began ringing at once.

"It's tough being popular," I said. Thinking I should try to bring the conversation around to what he was doing in my house, I added, "Can I help you?"

"Indeed," he replied, setting the phones to one side. "Doubtless you've seen my face in connection with one of the many high profile cases in which I've acted." I knew only that he was an attention seeker of enormous magnitude and told him so. He thanked me.

"Media visibility may not play a large part in the lives of ordinary legal professionals, but for me it's vital. Being on television, radio and appearing in print means in effect I can be in several places at once. This helps raise awareness of the many little people my work touches. Were it not for me they would have nobody to represent their interests, nobody to cast a light onto their sad little lives, nobody to hold a mirror up to their hopelessness." Nobody to swear about at night, I thought, but I decided to keep this to myself, as I didn't want it mistaken for flattery.

"I put everything into my work. It is all consuming, all encompassing. It filters through to every moment of my waking life then permeates my non-waking life. My non-waking life informs my waking life. My waking life is already overcrowded, so at times I'm forced to research cases in my non-waking life."

"You're all singing, all dancing," I said. "I get it."

"At the moment, the whole world wants me and I owe it to them to deliver. But herein lies the problem. Even if there were an entire channel devoted to my sayings and doings, it would not be enough. I would have to be beamed across all networks at once in order to be fully effective. However magnificent I may be, commanding the utmost admiration and godlike awe from all corners of the globe, I am limited to being just one man."

I felt sure his phones, which had continued to ring throughout this monologue, were on the cusp of melting. Eventually he succumbed to half of the ringing and with a sigh answered phone number one.

"LeSnide," he said. It sounded like a sneeze but was evidently a name. Seconds later he was pontificating at volume in my hallway. I picked up the relief phone from the table. The caller display said 'Mother'. At this point it occurred to me that he may have paid his many callers to ring at regular intervals throughout the day in order to reassure him of his greatness. This caused me to do some pontificating of my own. Not only did I want the doorbell removed, I wanted it surgically implanted in his back passage. Once implanted, I would instigate the electric shock idea. Whether this would stop him ringing it however was a moot point.

With LeSnide currently attending to one of his little people and the relief phone tailing off and resuming repeatedly, I thought I should field the call. But there weren't any fields within throwing distance so I decided to answer it instead. The caller was 'Dave'.

"Are you there?" said the plummy voice at the other end.

"Yes?"

"I'll be up next week. Are we still on for tennis?"

"Tennis?" I replied, unsure how best to decline. Tennis was my least favourite sport, ranking some way behind cheese rolling and extreme ironing. There were several reasons for this:

1) Only the overeducated play it. 2) Nobody looks good in white. 3) Cucumber isn't really sandwich material. 4) You never know when Cliff Richard might show up. I could go on but that would involve talking about tennis.

"Hello?" said the caller.

"You know me," I said, choosing an alternative approach. "I love tennis."

"Good," he replied. "I took your advice, by the way."

"What advice?"

"The back to work scheme for the over sixty-fives. You know, wheel them out, give them a silver-seeker's allowance instead of a pension."

"Oh that," I said. "I was really drunk when I said that."

"You were?" said Dave. "Well it's going down a treat. Not with the over sixty-fives obviously, but the people that matter love it."

"That's nice. Look, I have to go. I'm with this incredibly gifted design interfacer by the name of Boaks."

"Ah."

"He said to tell you you're a knob."

"I see," said Dave. "Well, any more good ideas let me know. See you next week."

He rang off just before LeSnide returned to the fray. I was concerned that he might have heard me using his phone but I needn't have been. LeSnide's self-absorption was absolute. He practised it like a martial art and would not be distracted by inconsequential external events.

"What was I saying?" he asked, as if I was sure to remember his last magnitudinous utterance.

"You were about to tell me what you're doing in my house," I said.

"Ah yes," he replied. "There is only so much of me to go round." This was remarkable. He managed to recall the exact point at which he'd broken off and at which I'd first considered verbal abuse. He was a self-absorption tenth dan.

"If I have been bequeathed a great gift – and I have – the question must be how to apportion that gift in order to maximise its efficacy. It's all very well being outrageously talented and in perpetual demand, but if my public are unable to access this talent due to mere physical laws then I have failed them. Having given this a great deal of thought in recent weeks, it strikes me that there may be a very simple solution to the problem."

He paused and I wondered if striking him was indeed the solution.

"In short," he said finally, "franchise."

"Franchise?" I said. "You want me to be a franchisee?"

"Clearly, *franchisees* would have to be vetted by the *franchisor* and, as the *franchisor*, it is safe to say you are not *franchisee* material. However, I imagine a design interfacer such as yourself could establish an appropriate design interface for the franchise brand." It seemed a long way round to ask for a logo, but it was actually a relief as I felt sure being a franchisee would involve tennis.

I wondered if I should suggest a couple of weeks in a rest home prior to project initiation, as it was clear that the man's grandeur had gone beyond delusional and into the realm of the supernatural. Two weeks in a rest home might be just what I needed to help me forget.

"Not that I don't appreciate your plight," I said, "but unless your name's Hugo Boss, a man isn't really a brand."

"Is too," he said defiantly. "I'm a very sellable brand. Try googling LeSnide. I'm so popular you won't get through." I wanted to tell him that wasn't how Google worked, but actually I had no idea how it worked. It may well be that people the world over were bringing the internet to a standstill through incessant self-searching. I suspected there would be no problem if he could just stop googling himself.

I had only a matter of minutes to weigh up the pros and cons of accepting a commission from someone who could put Narcissus in the shade. On the one hand, a man who was a couple of writs short of a decree could be a difficult client. On the other, a man who needed industrial supplies of booze in order to ease the pain of being alive had to fund those supplies. But was there really enough booze in the world?

I also had a growing concern for the ratio of hinged to unhinged within my client base. It was already dangerously favouring the latter and one more would tip the sanity scale deeper into deficit. I might as well start designing my own brand of straitjacket.

I thought I should let the decision rest on whatever this kook said next.

"I'm thinking of a coat of arms," he declared finally.

This practically broke the sanity scale altogether and should have clinched it. But the mere thought of drink sent me into a misty-eyed reverie and clouded my judgement. Abandoning my misgivings about his stability, I forgave his appalling liberties and crimes against modesty, and welcomed The Advocate For Self-Importance into my increasingly barking client base.

2.
THE CURE

I met LaFlamme at the botanic gardens. "It's a fecund paradise," she said. Her language was quite shocking at times.

We were on a semi-furtive mission to procure a cutting from a particular herbaceous perennial, the name of which continues to escape me despite The Admiral's constant reminders. The Admiral had been researching a supposedly highly effective hangover cure which depended on the leaves and stem of the plant.

Early tests with a garden centre variety were hampered by our collective inability to keep anything in a pot alive apart from fungus, and it was decided that growing a little one from scratch might bring out a parental instinct that would help discourage him from dying.

"Mental torment," I said. "Mental torment. Mentalent. Mentalor. Mentament."

"What are you doing?" said LaFlamme.

"This is how I remember the name," I replied. "I start with mental torment then combine the words in different ways until it comes back to me."

"How do you remember mental torment?" said LaFlamme.

"Mental torment comes naturally to me. Talmanent. Talmator. Talmanentator. Talmanentalatertater."

"Tormentil."

"Tormentil," I said, nodding. "I'd have gotten there eventually."

"Maybe," said LaFlamme, unsure I was capable of retaining any kind of knowledge.

We found an uncharacteristically useful piece of graphic design in the form of a signpost. It read 'Herbaceous Perennials'. This led us to a winding path on a shallow incline towards an extensive rockery. When the incline turned steep, my own incline was to turn back, but LaFlamme was two paces ahead of me and I was blinded by her milky-white calves.

As the slope levelled out we rounded a corner and LaFlamme stopped abruptly, forcing the top of my head to collide with her back. It had long been my dream to collide with LaFlamme but this wasn't quite what I had in mind. I peered round from behind her elegant frame to find a well-groomed middle-aged gentleman with fine, thinning hair. He had secateurs in one hand, a cutting in the other, and an expression of complete guilt on his face. He froze in a half-turned position, as if playing statues and unsure whether to make the full hundred and eighty or return to base. Either he too was blinded by the full beam effect of LaFlamme's legs or he was up to no good.

"Phlobaphenes," he said. It was an unusual opening gambit.

"Do you work here?" asked LaFlamme.

He hesitated before replying in a painfully hesitant whine, "Yes?"

"Why are you wearing a suit?" I asked.

"I try to be presentable at all times?" he said, again offering his reply in question form as if testing how much we were willing to believe. "It shows the plants due respect?"

When I stepped out from LaFlamme's shadow, something I'm unable to do often, I recognised the man. It was gourmet, bon viveur and martini devotee, Suave Gav, who I'd met at a winemakers convention. (I was only there because I designed a flyer for one of the exhibitors and thought there would be freebies. Suave Gav was altogether more serious. He was taking notes.)

"Armstrong, Gavin," he said, extending his secateurs. "I believe we may have met previously." At this recognition, he relaxed a fraction and attempted what sounded like levelling with us.

"To be perfectly honest, we extract phlobaphenes and triterpene alcohol from the old potentilla erecta here in order to produce a rousing Bavarian liqueur called Blutwurz." At least this wasn't a question. And it was certainly plausible that the plant he was interfering with could produce a rousing Bavarian liqueur. Less plausible was the idea that scholarly botanic types called it potentilla erecta. But they did. Go ahead, look it up.

"Potentilla erecta?" said LaFlamme. "That does sound rousing. Does it have any special powers? You know – improving the circulation, causing hot flushes, shortness of breath, panting, drooling?"

"Oh yes," said Armstrong. "Its health benefits are well documented. A compound prepared from the roots and bark has been used to treat a number of ailments from headaches to pimples. It's often used in herbal medicine as an astringent due to its tannin content."

"Anything else?" asked LaFlamme.

"Well," he replied, "prepared rather differently, it can give you a thumping great erection." This was evidently the answer LaFlamme was looking for and she chuckled with delight.

I stepped towards the herbaceous bush and viewed its accompanying signage. 'Potentilla erecta,' it read. 'Common name: tormentil.' So this was the elusive shrub The Admiral asked us to track down for his dubious and very likely fruitless experiment. It was nothing to look at. Its straggly, low-lying leaves seemed banal and its weak yellow flowers uninspiring. I wondered if it might feel much the same about me. Skinny, it would say, not very tall individual with pale skin and a heavy frown that won't be forgiving in middle age. Probably ought to quit moping and take some exercise.

But whatever we made of each other's appearance, it was a multi-talented organism that could both cause a hangover and cure it, not to mention having the combined powers of Aspirin, Clearasil and Viagra. It was a wonder there wasn't a line of impotent, spotty migraine sufferers all queueing up for a hair of the dog.

I wanted to ask Suave Gav tactfully what his interest was in the miraculous little bush – was he also on the hunt for a hangover cure? (Tact has never come easy to me; it seems to require more intelligence than I can usually muster. But on this occasion I managed not to blurt out the question and asked instead, "Do you have a headache?" Given the plant's effectiveness in the trouser department, it could have been worse.)

"No no," said Suave Gav. "I'm just enthusiastic in the kitchen, especially the bar, and I like nothing better than a flaming Bavarian liqueur of an evening. Although let me tell you my friends, the potentilla can be fierce. Many is the time I've taken a sundowner or two and woken the following day to wonder if I would live to take another." He winced.

"Are you aware of its use as a morning-after potion?" I finally let out.

Suave Gav sharply drew in breath and gazed in obvious wonder at the cluster of bushes before him.

"Can it be true?" he said, apparently oblivious to the possibility. "Nature's larder is surely the greatest of God's gifts, and I have always felt my duty on this earth was to exploit all that it has to offer. But I have yet to encounter a compound which can fully counter the devastating effects of overconsumption. If indeed such a preparation exists, then children we may be standing at the gates of the promised land. Where may I ask did you hear mention of such a thing?"

I was about to explain how The Admiral picked up the tip at one of his *Dungeons & Dragons* nights (where assorted dweebs sit around in bobbly cardigans quaffing vigorous dark ale and talking in JavaScript), when LaFlamme coughed demonstrably and said, "We didn't. Just a rumour. Should probably keep your pants on for now."

"Blutwurz preparation requires only the roots of the potentilla erecta," mused Suave Gav, "but it may be that other compounds, perhaps utilising the leaves and stems, could nullify the undesirable after-effects of the glorious aperitif."

"Do you always talk like that?" said LaFlamme.

Suave Gav fumbled for business cards and handed one to each of us. "Clearly you are people after my own heart," he said. "Are you interested in salsa?"

"The dance?" asked LaFlamme.

"The condiment," he replied. "A group of us dedicate our Friday evenings to experimental cuisine – vegetarian, of course. This week the focus is on the many complex varietals of chutney."

"Experimental chutney?" I said.

"I like it," said LaFlamme.

"Then you must come. I'll be unveiling a new batch of our Bavarian speciality." He waved his cutting and left.

I looked at the business card. 'Armstrong, Gavin,' it read. Even on business cards he insisted his name be displayed back to front, like in an old phone directory. I'm sure he would never have adopted this practice had his name been Richard Little.

3.
AN EAGLE DOESN'T CATCH FLIES

You might know them as 'barristers' or 'attorneys', but in this part of the world they're called 'advocates'. They're like lawyers but even more so. I have no idea what they do. Nobody does. They spend a lot of time explaining that they're not lawyers, so I know they're definitely not lawyers. They wear wigs and gowns though and there can't be many jobs you can do that without at least raising eyebrows.

LeSnide is one of them. When I first saw him I thought his chin was going to take off. Then it started moving around and I got quite concerned until I realised he was talking. I was mesmerised. It was some TV news profile and they introduced him as Guy LeSnide QC and pronounced his name 'ghee' like he should be holding a baguette.

I didn't think at that point he might be off his trolley, just that he had the self-confidence of ten people and their combined chin acreage too. I was at The Admiral's at the time, and The Admiral got distracted and looked up from his soldering long enough for his words to register. (It's quite easy to distract The Admiral, hence the number of soldering iron burns in the table. I told him he should leave the iron in strategic positions so it looks like a deliberately charred effect. He did, and let me tell you the man's got no design sense.)

Anyway, The Admiral said, "The Advocate For Self-Importance," and I realised then it was an official title. It seemed apt as LeSnide was explaining how he was terribly in demand and that that was his cross to bear. Then he went on to list his extensive achievements, first chronologically, then alphabetically, then by their magnitude.

So it's not that I didn't realise I might be opening the gates of vanity hell when I agreed to work for him. However, I could not have known just how dedicated he was to his own brilliance. That became clear at our second meeting, which took place amidst a cacophony of ringing devices.

"I googled myself again this morning," he said, "and discovered that I'm a god."

I sighed in a resigned fashion. Graphic designers only ever sigh in a resigned fashion, as resignation is such a big part of what it takes to be a success in the design industry.

"One of the lesser gods admittedly, but a celestial being nonetheless. Probably akin to Aeacus or Dionysus. At this very moment people are worshipping my graven image all over the world and there's nothing I can do about it. It's a living nightmare."

"I only asked if you wanted coffee," I said.

"I don't know how they even obtained my graven image. Obviously I send out signed eight by tens regularly to random samplings from the electoral role in order to maintain a consistently high profile. But I wouldn't have expected these to fall into the hands of common worshippers."

It's difficult to express how much I disliked my new client. I'd gone from wanting simply to administer small electric shocks to devising whole systems for inflicting more extensive pain. So elaborate were my fantasies that I wanted to write to my former teachers and tell them to take back their accusations of lack of imagination.

"All the more reason to be here with a design interfacer," said LeSnide. "We must guard the LeSnide brand by controlling the image projected across the globe."

"Are your eight by tens not suitable graven image material?" I said.

"They are, but imagine how much more powerful our coat of arms would be as a worship base."

"Okay, you might need to explain to me just what you mean by a coat of arms."

"Heraldry," he replied. "Blazoning. Armorial bearings. Tinctures."

"I'm glad we've cleared that up," I said, none the wiser.

"To include the LeSnide motto."

"Which is?"

"*Aquila non capit muscas*," he replied.

"Nice," I said. "What does it mean?"

"Latin. Translates as 'an eagle doesn't catch flies.'"

"I still don't know what it means."

"Me neither," said LeSnide. "It was just something my father used to say as he practised his tuba."

By now, the mortals at the end of his two devices had run up a dozen missed calls between them and the incessant ringing was starting to wear me down. These were not ideal working conditions. Ideal working conditions didn't involve work.

"Can't you put them on silent?" I asked.

"Silent?" he replied, vaguely offended. "Then I wouldn't hear them. People would be calling and I wouldn't know anything about it."

"I admit it's a novel idea, but I believe modern phones include such a feature for this very reason."

I gathered from LeSnide's response that having phones which refused to ring was something of a calamity for chronic attention seekers. He didn't waste any time with the idea and instead, with two immensely irritating call devices ringing throughout, detailed his requirements for a LeSnide heraldic crest. *Ad absurdum.*

4.
MARTINI: THE BREAKFAST OF CHAMPIONS

I wasn't sure what an experimental chutney session would involve, other than maybe chutney, but LaFlamme and I thought crackers might be a safe addition. On the way up to Suave Gav's top floor suite in the Lafayette building, cocktail jazz filled the elevator and LaFlamme started eating the crackers to block out the sound. When we stepped into the lobby the cocktail jazz was there too. This was bad news for the crackers. By the time we reached Suave Gav's door, there was a trail of them back to the elevator. It was a little messy but would at least be handy for finding our way back.

Suave Gav was delighted to see us and invited us into the lounge. He even looked pleased when we presented him with a half empty box of crackers. "We were experimenting with them on the way up," said LaFlamme, grabbing a last handful.

The room was impressive with its velvet drapes, flock wallpaper, billiards table and fully stocked bar – Suave Gav had his priorities right. He introduced us to his wife Ethel and friends Dick and Jane. Collectively the group appeared to have stepped directly out of a Doris Day movie. The men wore dress suits with bowties, Suave Gav topping his own ensemble with a chef's hat and apron. The ladies wore elaborate gowns styled no later than 1959 and had reality-defying hourglass figures and beehive hairstyles. Even the air seemed tinged with a Technicolor haze that twinkled like the crystal chandelier above us.

"Martini," said Suave Gav, handing us stem glasses. "The breakfast of champions."

"Hear hear," said Dick, chewing an olive.

"This one is a watermelon variation based on one of Jane's original designs. I've been working with it for a while now. The idea was to substitute my daily sundowner with a lighter, summery alternative and even, dare I say it, make it a little healthier with the addition of fruit. Unfortunately, today my hand slipped as I was pouring the gin so all pretence of it being a health shake went out the window."

"Nevertheless Gavin, old boy," said Dick, "it's a triumph."

"There is a virgin version, darling," said Ethel. "Perhaps our guests may have preferred a lighter alternative given we're so close to the peak of summer."

Suave Gav spluttered. "Good god woman, have you lost your mind? I didn't give up my Friday evenings to join the Temperance Society."

The martini was indeed a triumph but LaFlamme and I were having some initial difficulties with the stem glasses. Even after working with them for several minutes we remained unsure how they should best be gripped. Normally we drank from tumblers – a practical move as The Admiral is prone to boisterousness – so this was a challenge. Eventually LaFlamme held hers from above, the base resting on her palm. I cupped mine with both hands like a goblet. Neither seemed satisfactory and I considered either drinking very fast or asking for a mug.

"To think," said Suave Gav, demonstrating the correct method by holding his glass at the stem with just the thumb and index finger, something that must have taken years to perfect, "some would choose to adulterate this finest of man's inventions with the common potato base vodka."

"Yuk," said Jane.

"Utter debasement," said Dick. "Surely you want your martini to taste of something."

"Now now," said Ethel, "we've been over this many times."

"Sorry darling," Suave Gav replied. "But martini is an art form and if you'll allow me a moment's immodesty, I regard myself as the Michelangelo of said form."

"Michelangelo?" said Jane.

"Actually, probably not Michelangelo. He tended to use male models for his female figures, which explains why parts of the Sistine Chapel look like a women's rugby team."

"Lordy," said Dick, fiddling with his cocktail stick. "Why would he do that?"

"Because he was a raging poofter," said Suave Gav firmly.

"Really, dear," said Ethel.

"Sorry darling," he repeated. It had been so long since I encountered that particular term, I flinched slightly and wondered if I'd inadvertently strayed into a dodgy '70s sitcom.

"Poor chap did his best with some of the most beautiful women of the age, and drew them with great accuracy. But he was never happy with the drawings and always reworked them; adding muscle tone, trimming those fulsome breasts so they looked more like well-honed pectorals, fleshing out their waists and tightening their little bottoms. Soon they all looked like wrestlers."

"Beauty is in the eye of the beholder," said Jane.

"Indeed," said Suave Gav. "And Signor Buonarroti's eye could only detect beauty in the most butch of womankind. Not that I have anything against confirmed bachelors, or butch women for that matter. But I shouldn't imagine in reality the creation of Eve involved quite such devotion to the Charles Atlas programme." It was a bizarre rant and unfortunately showed no sign of ending anytime soon.

"Rubens, on the other hand, was never one to shy away from female flesh. He used female models for everything. Big plump ones, the bigger the better. Even if he were only painting a still life, he'd nevertheless insist on a fat girl lolling around the studio feeding her face with pies. Poor fellow. Drove him mad eventually."

"So you're the Rubens of the martini?" said LaFlamme, tossing her cocktail stick over her shoulder.

"I don't see why not," said Suave Gav. "It has a nice ring to it and I can't see there being many other contenders for the title."

"I like a nice fat girl," said Dick.

There was a quaintness to this group that I couldn't quite fathom. Their views appeared to be those of a much older generation, a generation who say what they want and make everybody laugh because they're old. And yet it appeared they were at the forefront of contemporary cuisine. There was nothing old about their cooking.

The chutneys came thick and fast; onion marmalade with white wine and herbs, hot and sweet cranberry relish, pineapple ginger salsa, chestnut and ginger in red wine vinegar pâté, and were served with Suave Gav's own specialty breads – olive, onion, cumin rye, raisin and fennel – alongside numerous dips, spreads and Dick's selection of 'baroque' cheeses. One thing was sure. These weirdos liked food.

LaFlamme, who can be difficult at dinner parties due to her low boredom threshold, behaved remarkably well around our hosts. I think she was genuinely confused.

"How do you get your hair to sit like that?" asked Jane. It seemed we were something of a novelty to them.

"I iron it," replied LaFlamme.

"Ooh," said Jane excitedly. "Do you have tongs?"

"I have an ironing board," said LaFlamme.

When Suave Gav said he had a question to ask the group, LaFlamme and I gazed up at him like ten-year-olds at a birthday party. This may have been the martini or a delayed reaction to the discussion of lolling fat girls.

"Bavarian summer," he said, "or Alpine winter?" There was a collective intake of breath from the gathering. "In other words, flaming or on the rocks?"

Without hesitation Dick and Jane began chanting, "Flaming, flaming, flaming."

"In that case we're heading for the après ski," said Suave Gav, retreating behind the bar. "Whilst I make the final preparations, perhaps Tony might like to recant to the group his most fascinating insight into our beloved bloodroot." I wasn't sure what this meant in English but I was sufficiently emboldened by the brandy and olive mustard to address the gathering.

"Well," I began, "a friend of ours heard about this plant. It's called turniptil or something."

"Tormentil," called Suave Gav.

"I don't know if it's true but these guys who play *Dungeons & Dragons* know a lot about science on account of having had nothing better to do at school than learn things. I mean it's not like they were going to chase girls or anything. If people who played *Dungeons & Dragons* chased girls, we probably wouldn't have computers now."

"Point," said LaFlamme. "Get to it."

"So it's too early to say if it is actually effective as a hangover cure." For some reason this suddenly gripped them. "But if you're anything like me you'd probably try chewing old elastic bands if you thought it would help you get up in the morning."

The group appeared stunned. Even the virulent cocktail jazz had ceased. The only sound was Suave Gav whistling softly, one ear still cocked towards the conversation.

Dick split the silence. "Did you say hangover cure?"

"Yes," called Suave Gav from the bar. "He did."

"And your friend," said Dick, taking a notepad and pen from his jacket pocket. "You have a number for him?"

"Now Dick," said Suave Gav, "there's plenty time for that. Let our guests enjoy a little Alsatian hospitality for the moment. Lights please, Ethel." Ethel rose and dimmed the main lights, leaving us in a glow of candlelight. Suave Gav emerged from the bar, underlit by a ghostly blue haze. "Ladies and gentlemen," he announced. "I give you – Blutwurz à la flamme."

We all applauded although I wasn't sure why. My mind was perhaps not at its sharpest after a few hours working with a succession of experimental martinis. I guess I just thought it was great that somebody had invented a drink with 'LaFlamme' in the title.

Suave Gav laid a tray of asymmetrical serving dishes on the table; a cross between miniature soup bowls and saucepans, with small protruding stumps for handles. Each contained a deep, murky substance with a soft blue flame rising from the surface. The liquid gave off a strong medicinal odour, sweet with strong hints of menthol and spices. If nothing else, it would clear my sinuses.

"Do you have any marshmallows?" asked LaFlamme. The others laughed but I could tell she was quite serious. Suave Gav took his seat and continued.

"Flambé is of course an important part of the Bavarian summer," he said. "It both improves the flavour and reduces the alcohol content."

"Aren't you concerned about reducing the alcohol content?" I said, like a true lush.

"Ordinarily I might be," he replied. "But as its original content is around sixty per cent proof and burning for five minutes reduces it to only around fifty, it's not something we get too concerned about." No wonder these people were interested in a hangover cure.

I eyed the potent brew nervously. Already intoxicated by its odour, I wasn't sure I actually needed to drink it. But drink it I did, LaFlamme too. It was warm, with a tanginess that you might find in unripened citrus fruit. There were hints of pepper, mulberry, bramble, tobacco, and just the faintest suggestion of liquorice. Not that I tasted these things. It's just what the gastronomes said.

At this point, the gentlemen in particular seemed eager to press us for further information on our own experiments with the unusual root. We didn't have much to offer but that didn't stop LaFlamme saying the prototype cure was at an advanced stage of development, that an announcement would soon be made in the press and even implying that government funding was being made available. They probably thought we were keeping our cards close to our chests, but in reality any cards we had were likely to have been soaked in Blutwurz and accidentally set alight.

I felt distinctly giddy by the time the entire beverage was downed, but giddiness turned to alarm when Ethel turned up the house lights. I was shocked to be surrounded by a sea of black teeth. I would have to drink red wine all day before achieving a similar effect, and don't think I haven't tried. But this was a single serving.

LaFlamme, her lips dark, had drifted off and was lightly snoring, the empty miniature soup bowl still clutched in her hands. This wasn't a comment on the evening; merely something LaFlamme did when light was low. It was a good thing to remember for times when she was obstreperous. A bit like having a budgie hood.

As Suave Gav continued to discuss the positive health effects of the bizarre bloodroot concoction, I was curious that nobody seemed inclined to acknowledge its rather more obvious teeth-blackening effects. But I was feeling no pain and besides, it was getting late. I nudged LaFlamme and she snorted awake. LaFlamme pointed to my teeth in a befuddled manner but clearly thought twice about mentioning it.

As we prepared to leave I thanked our hosts for a most interesting evening of experimental vegetarian cuisine and complimented them on their formidable food science. However, there was a gasp of shock from the quartet when I said quite innocently, "Thanks too for the blutwurst."

The room fell silent. It was as if I'd said something inappropriate to the host's wife.

"Tony," said the demure Jane under her breath, "it's pronounced *blootvoortz*."

"I'm sorry," I replied. "What did I say?"

"You said *blootvoorst*," said Ethel, in the faintest whisper.

"Blootvoorst?" I said again, to even more horror.

"Please," said Ethel.

"Steady on, old man," said Dick, removing his pipe from his mouth. Suave Gav fainted away into an armchair.

"Darling, are you all right?" said Ethel, racing to mop his brow. Jane began to loosen his collar.

"I'm... sorry," I repeated.

"You weren't to know," said Ethel. "Gavin's terribly sensitive to that word."

"Blootvoorst?" I said yet again. Suave Gav broke into a sob and Dick ushered us rapidly to the hall as if my next utterance might shatter his fragile casing.

"Easy mistake to make, Boaks," said Dick.

"But..."

"Don't give it a second thought," he said. "Are you sure you have to leave? We'll probably play *Twister* shortly."

On the way home, I left LaFlamme at her flat and continued the quarter mile path to my own. She called the moment I arrived. She said she'd consulted a Bavarian dictionary she kept on hand for moments like this and discovered that Blutwurz, meaning 'bloodroot', was a traditional liqueur from the Alsace region and that blutwurst, meaning 'blood sausage', was a foul affront to vegetarians everywhere.

"It doesn't say that," I said.

"Does," replied LaFlamme.

"Okay," I said, "I made a mistake. But what a reaction. You'd think I tried to force feed him foie gras."

"Do that next time," said LaFlamme. "It'll take his mind off the blood sausage."

5.
THIS IS YOUR CAPTAIN CALLING

LeSnide had broken all records. From the moment I met him to the moment I knew I disliked him was a mere five seconds. Even the previous titleholder had been in the room two or three minutes before I wanted to hurt them.

Nevertheless, having accepted the commission to design his coat of arms, I was committed to delivering and pressed on until it was complete. I did what I could to incorporate the imagery LeSnide suggested, but had to continually remind him that a coat of arms should boil down to a very simple design and that it probably wouldn't be practical to include the heroic battle scene he described. Nor would a self-portrait on the cross or any of the other martyrdom scenarios we discussed have been appropriate. However, I conceded to his request for a modest depiction of himself carrying the world on his shoulders. Above this was his family motto, something to do with an eagle that swallowed a fly.

It wasn't the most fun job I ever had, but ultimately the client and I both agreed it reached a reasonably successful conclusion. Shortly I would issue an invoice and then look forward to being remunerated for my efforts. In the design industry that's as close as you get to fun.

As a consequence I spent the weekend eating cake and abusing American presidential candidates on TV by way of celebration. I don't necessarily need a celebration in order to abuse presidential candidates but it all helps. When the phone rang, apart from hardly being able to move for cake, I was almost happy to answer – a rarity and a sure sign that I had completed a commission. But as always, the happiness was tainted by the fear that the call may herald a successor.

"Mr Boaks," said the man's voice. "I'm Captain Priscilla Pantling from the Faculty of Advocates."

"Hello Captain," I said. It was probably too early to start calling him Priscilla.

"I'm the advocates' clerk here," he continued. "I'm responsible for the diaries of all the counsel members."

"That's tremendous," I said. "We should diarise."

"It concerns Lord LeSnide."

"*Lord* LeSnide?" I said. "Are you sure he's a lord?"

"No, actually," said Captain Pantling. "But he insists I address him so. Probably because I'm a captain."

"Are you sure you're a captain?" I asked. "I know a guy called The Admiral and as far as I'm aware he's never been to sea."

"Mr Boaks, it's rather an urgent matter," the Captain continued. "From LeSnide's diary I note two meetings with a 'design interfacer', which include your name, number and the word 'lackey' in brackets."

"That's me," I sighed.

"You undertook some work for counsel?"

"Yes."

"May I enquire as to the nature of the work?"

"Heraldry," I replied. "Blazoning. Armorial bearings. Tinctures."

"A coat of arms?"

"How did you know that?"

"Did you find him behaving in any way unusual?"

"He had a hugely inflated sense of his own self-worth, but I made allowances for this because he was a lawyer."

"Technically not so, but certainly Guy LeSnide is one of our most eminent legal minds."

"Yes, he told me many times," I said, "and I've only met him twice. What seems to be the problem?"

"It appears that the constant demands on his time may have clouded his judgement. He was on a routine trip to the Court of Session where he was evidently arguing against what he termed 'the wilful misrepresentation of his height' by the much taller counsel opposite. The court record shows him insisting he was at least seven feet tall and 'a giant in any man's terms'. Court was adjourned whilst a measuring tape was sought. However, the shorter counsel failed to return and indeed failed to report back to the faculty."

"He's gone AWOL?" I said.

"Yes. I was hoping you could shed some light onto his whereabouts."

"That's not possible. I haven't invoiced!"

"As it was not faculty business, I have no record of your agreement with counsel. I'm therefore unable to assist in that regard."

"This is disastrous."

"Yes, we are quite concerned about him. Episodes such as this are all too common in the legal profession. I probably should have seen the signs."

"If you were a real captain, you would have," I said, furious.

The advocates' clerk said he would do his best to keep me informed as to LeSnide's whereabouts and rang off. I returned to my ball of string in order give my fury some time to subside. Here I was, having been suckered into working for a man who was close to madness but still capable of commissioning a design. What were the chances he would topple into the abyss before paying for it?

An hour later, Captain Pantling called again and said he had good news. I waited for him to tell me he was transferring funds into my bank account and that the matter was settled. Instead he still seemed to be under the mistaken impression that I was concerned for LeSnide's well-being.

"Some weeks ago," he said, "counsel thought it would be helpful to us if we were able to track his every movement. He installed specialist tracking software, which monitors the locality of his mobile phone, on one of my deputies' computers. Naturally nobody ever thought to try it until now."

"And?"

"It seems that following his Court of Session appearance he headed towards Hilderton Marina and from there chartered a canal boat, taking it some way up the Kenneth & Keith into deepest Wester – an area accessible only by water. He's been there ever since."

"Did you try calling him?" I asked.

"Of course," said the Captain.

"Did you say 'this is your captain calling?'"

"Alas the novelty of that particular greeting wore off some years back, and anyway a connection could not be established. But no sooner had we discounted this particular method of communication than counsel himself called the faculty, apparently asking to be sent shoes."

"He's shoeless?"

"Yes. He said he discarded his shoes and socks but then had come to believe they were of great value after realising he could be cloned from them."

"That's my client all right," I said.

"He said shoelessness in itself was not a problem as he had engaged one of the local tribes as his foot soldiers. These poor indigenous people – many of them little more than savages, and some junior lawyers – now transport him in a sedan chair and bow to his every utterance."

"Hmm," I said. "Is that so unusual in the legal profession?"

"I admit," he replied, "a great deal of enforced idolatry exists in legal chambers. Resistance can be troublesome. But this, I think you would agree, is extreme."

Aware that the word 'mad' was politically incorrect and had long since been consigned to the past, I tried to enquire as to LeSnide's mental health in a manner that would show I was a sensitive and caring individual, and not one who used such belittling and negative terms. But that was too difficult so I asked if he'd gone mad.

"It's not a word I care to use," said Captain Pantling, "as it's not for me to judge a man's sanity."

"He thinks somebody might clone him from his shoes," I replied. "I think you're on safe ground."

"The faculty medic did mention a *personality disorder.*"

"A *personality disorder*?" I said, repeating the Captain's emphasis.

"Yes," he said. "A *per-son-al-it-y dis-or-der.*" This time Pantling made inverted comma gestures with his hands. I'm not sure why he felt the need to spell it out as if I had learning difficulties or partial hearing. I was perfectly capable of grasping the combination of syllables, even if I didn't know what they meant when stuck together.

"Isn't that just another term for mad?" I asked.

"Again," he replied, "I will refrain from using that word. But essentially yes, a *per-son-al-it-y dis-or-der* is a rather ill-defined class of personality types which deviate from the norm."

"He's ill-defined," I said. "I always thought so."

"You do get *borderline personality disorders*," he said, "but I'd suggest in this case there's nothing borderline about it. Counsel is at the epicentre of his disorder, even though as you suggest the disorder may be rather vague."

"Vague," I said. "Ill-defined." I still preferred mad but knowing Captain Pantling was uncomfortable with the term, I made an effort to modify my language. "Surely if you know *where* he's being ill-defined, you can monitor his movements and bring him back."

"Which brings me to the reason for this call," said Captain Pantling – the man had been speaking for a lifetime and only now decided he had a point. (Even at my wandery best I can only ramble incoherently for a few minutes before either giving up or accidentally stumbling across a completely different point.)

"As you know," he continued, "members of the legal fraternity work only for the betterment of mankind. Their rewards are modest for what is in fact a vast contribution to society. When one of our fraternity therefore has a lapse of judgement and abandons select garments in a public place, the whole fabric of that society risks collapse." I told the Captain if I lost my socks and shoes, society would probably just expect me to move on to the next step – to stop washing and start volleying random abuse at passersby on the high street.

"But you are an exponent of the arts," he explained. "Rather than discarding your socks and shoes, it's more likely they would walk off on their own accord due to the fortifying effects of several years' dust. Should you have met with a similar fate to the counsel member, society would not mourn your sanity's passing because it was so utterly predictable." He certainly nailed that one good and proper, but he still hadn't come to the point. I failed to see the connection between myself and a mental non-lawyer.

"In short Boaks, we need Guy LeSnide returned to civilisation. And I believe your interest in being remunerated for your work with counsel to be sufficiently strong to elect to send you to Wester in order to return the errant senior member. We can supply a suitable narrowboat and will of course cover your expenses. Since we have already pinpointed the location of the insufferable one, it should not be such an arduous task."

"Insufferable?" I said. "Why do you want him returned if you don't like him?"

"Boaks," he explained, "I should not have lasted long as advocates' clerk were it necessary to 'like' faculty members. Indeed when I studied at advocates' clerk school adequate provision was made for coping with self-righteous despotism, as sufficient interest in being a despot is one of the main prerequisites for entry to the bar. We ask for his safe return only because of his fee-earning capacity, which is frankly greater than the sum of all other counsel combined."

Captain Pantling explained that an invoice signed by LeSnide would act as a purchase order and was all he required to process payment. He even offered to forego the statutory thirty day grace period and settle immediately. It was a nice touch and certainly sweetened the deal, but even before this I'd come to the conclusion that I would have to track him down – there was no question of allowing a client to escape without settling a bill, even if they were falling between a dozen forms of indefinable madness.

"If this is acceptable to you," he concluded, "I shall make the necessary arrangements. First however, I must request that you undergo a physical examination with the faculty medic. Wester is dangerous territory. It has been known to corrupt the finest of minds, and yours could be affected too."

6.
PROJECT X

The stress and anxiety caused by being stiffed had at least distracted me from other matters and when Suave Gav called, ostensibly to offer an apology for fainting after I mispronounced 'Blutwurz', I was pleased to have something different to fret about. I had been feeling rather sheepish about my faux pas but I would never have expected even the most rabid vegan to pass out at the slightest mention of blood sausage.

"I should think my parents had a sadistic streak," said Suave Gav. "No animal was sacred in the Armstrong household and no animal part was off the menu. The beasts of the field would cower when we passed. Not that anything we ate ever resembled animal flesh – which was a blessing, for had my five brothers and I known the origins of the various delicacies Mamma dished up we would surely have mastered the art of hurling from an early age.

"The main justification seemed to be that it was 'economical'. That is, once the rich had done with the finer cuts of an animal, the remains would go to waste were it not for the Armstrongs. 'I see,' I said to my father. 'But if they hadn't slaughtered the beast in the first place that particular problem wouldn't have arisen.' I thought this was a keen observation for a five-year-old, but it landed me a clip around the ear.

"It was somewhat strange given that my father was a man of means. He had a successful glass blowing business, Armstrong Blows, and this afforded us the luxury of private schooling. But he had seen poverty in his youth and 'waste not, want not' became not just a motto, but a challenge.

"I don't blame my parents. They did an otherwise excellent job of rearing my multitudinous siblings and I. In fact anyone who knows me will confirm that I am a near perfect physical specimen, despite such early gastronomic torture. But I hope what I have said goes some way towards explaining my sensitive disposition in this field."

"Yes," I said. "I'll be careful not to mention... that word again."

"The thing is," said Suave Gav, "all of this is neither here nor there when there is a matter of far greater consequence for you and I to discuss." I wondered if there was something else I had said to offend him but mercifully this didn't appear to be the case. "Since our meeting at the herbaceous perennials, I've done some research and even conducted a few preliminary experiments."

"Chutney?" I said.

"Hardly," he replied. "I refer of course to our precious bloodroot. If you were not simply pulling my leg with your talk of gastronomic wizardry resulting in a cure for overindulgence, then I should very much like to compare notes."

"I see," I said. "Well, The Admiral's your man."

"Admiral, you say? Seafaring sort?"

"No, he just grew sideburns once."

"We all make mistakes," he replied. "Can I suggest a kitchen confab? Ingredients discussed, recipes exchanged, vol-au-vents optional? Purely in the interests of science, you understand."

"Well as long as we're expanding the boundaries of scientific knowledge," I said, "I don't see why not." He was an oddball but at least this time he wasn't a client.

The Admiral said he was only too happy to confer with a fellow gastronomic engineer on what we'd been calling Project X. (We didn't call it Project X because it sounded cool or enigmatic, it was just the twenty-fourth such project we'd attempted. We were two projects away from starting again at Project A or finding another alphabet to abuse.)

When I explained to him that Suave Gav wasn't actually an engineer but merely a hardened drinker with a vested interest in dealing with troublesome mornings after, The Admiral realised we were in *Lorenzo's Oil* territory. "All the better," he said. "We must make our own miracles."

Suave Gav was punctual, early even, and carried a heavy briefcase handcuffed to his wrist. "It's quite all right," he said. "I haven't been followed." Without delay he unlocked the cuffs, discarded his jacket and opened the case, unpacking an apron, funnel, several small jars with cloth coverings, test tubes, various twigs and roots, a syringe and finally a sheaf of papers bound together by elastic bands. He was certainly taking this evening seriously. By contrast, The Admiral produced his notepad of equations and a ceramic jug with a cork in the top.

Our guest was fairly open with his findings, at least for one whose findings arrived handcuffed to him. He outlined the extent of his research at length, pinning diagrams to the wall and highlighting with a laser pen. It was the nearest thing to a lecture I was ever likely to see.

He explained the struggle he'd had in trying to produce an elixir from the branches of the mental torment plant and made the last week's endeavors sound as if they had taken a lifetime. Clearly he'd given up his day job or abandoned sleeping in order to devote the maximum number of hours possible to the task. He was committed. And if he wasn't, he probably should be.

"As you know," he said, "we're dealing only with anecdotal evidence here. As yet there have been no formal studies. But the consensus seems to be that it's essential the elixir be produced from the area as close to the roots as possible. After a proportional five per cent or thereabouts of the plant's height, it's entirely ineffectual. Too close to the root however, and you're essentially making Blutwurz. A couple of millimetres either way mean the difference between creating a hangover and curing it."

"Precision and craftsmanship," said The Admiral, nodding in agreement. "A surgeon's eye."

"Exactly," replied Suave Gav. "It really requires a botanist, chemist and philosopher to sit down together and agree on where the stem ends and the root begins. But therein lies the art."

The Admiral appeared semi-familiar with much of this, continuing to nod sagely at appropriate moments, but that didn't necessarily mean he was keeping up. We'd been in similar situations before only for him to quiz me later on the issue. If The Admiral has to ask me to explain something, we're in trouble.

By now Suave Gav was more than a little curious as to the contents of The Admiral's ceramic jug and in fact had been edging towards it for some time. The Admiral consulted his notes.

"According to this recipe," he said, "what we should have here is a refreshing beverage that removes all traces of alcohol from the system, leaving the previously inebriated quite sober."

"Could I drive after taking it?" I asked.

"According to the instructions, yes," he replied.

"That's funny, because I couldn't before." The Admiral congratulated me for what he called 'a prehistoric jest'.

"What's this?" I asked, spotting another set of ingredients and instructions on the opposite page of his notebook.

"That's a recipe for a rousing Bavarian liqueur," he said, about to expand on this until the meaning of his words seemed to sink in. I was reminded of what went wrong with Projects A to W. Brilliant though he was, The Admiral was easily distracted and in this case a second potentilla erecta recipe may well have caught his eye. I could see him weighing up the ceramic jug, wondering which recipe he'd followed – the one to get drunk or the one to sober up. Was it an antidote or just a dote?

Suave Gav had begun gnawing at one of the twigs he'd brought with him. His teeth turned dark. "Apologies," he said. "It's only a minor compulsion." It wasn't normally the sort of behaviour we would expect from someone we called 'suave' and I made a mental note to rethink his moniker.

"Well gentlemen," he continued, "I think we can clear up any doubt by employing some of my tried and trusted methods. May I?" He reached for the jug and poured a vial-full into a test tube. He first checked for colour, tipping it towards the edge of the tube before deciding it was too dark to see any. He swilled it around and thrust his nose to the tip. As he did, I thought I saw his saw his hair, which admittedly looked rather thicker than it had previously, ripple. He dipped a litmus paper into the liquid and nodded as he watched it change colour. He dipped his pinky in and delicately dabbed it to his tongue. Finally he surprised us by producing an elegant lighter and setting the liquid aflame.

"There you have it," said Suave Gav somewhat disparagingly.

"Ah," said The Admiral. "Success." I wasn't sure what kind of success The Admiral had in mind as I shouldn't think a hangover cure would ordinarily flambé quite so easily. It was in fact a forty per cent proof hangover cure. If he'd been trying to make us look like complete idiots, it was a huge success.

"This is what we drank the morning after the night before," I said. "Just the other day."

"Correct," said The Admiral.

"But we felt better afterwards."

"Hair of the dog," said Suave Gav, swaying slightly as he packed up his kitbag. "Effective. Very. But not a cure. I could lie in a darkened room for ten hours. Also effective. Very. Not a cure."

"I met the bank manager that day," I said. "Maybe that's why he wouldn't give me any money."

"Bank managers tend to be reluctant to issue loans to drunks," said The Admiral.

"I didn't ask for a loan," I said. "Just some spare change."

"Gentlemen," said Suave Gav, now distinctly weaving, his teeth black and his toupée slightly askew, "you are wasting my time." He headed for the exit but tripped over the rug, falling headfirst onto the floor and sending his toupée and kitbag flying.

"Please," he said, replacing his toupée and dusting himself down as if nothing had happened. "Do not embarrass yourselves further."

7.
BIGGER THAN A CANOE

Today I had my appointment with the faculty quack, Dr Seward, a peculiar old duffer with a monocle and more than a hint of the Third Reich about him. It wasn't just that his methods felt like interrogation. He was wearing an SS uniform.

"Faculty am-dram," he explained. "I've been in regalia for days."

"Regalia," I said. "Is that Puccini?"

"Alistair MacLean. *Where Eagles Dare*. It's a minor role but I intend to shine. I always think the method approach helps one become the character."

"Sharp uniform," I said, suspecting his motivation was less to do with method acting and more to do with wanting to dress up as a Nazi at work.

"It's the first rule of drama," he replied. "Always give the villains the best costumes. You know the theatre?"

"I know *of* the theatre," I said.

"It's obviously gone downhill since the invention of the mobile phone. I imagine Chekhov never foresaw a day when the audience had more lines than the actors. But who am I to stand in the way of progress?" He produced a set of callipers and advanced towards my cranium. "Do you mind?"

"Go right ahead," I replied.

"So we're sending you to Wester?" he said, measuring my skull's diameter. "A queer place. It used to be a centre of excellence for the theatre, although it tended to be of the populist music hall variety. Died out many years ago. Nothing much left now. Many sally forth, few return. They do things differently there." He made some notes on a clipboard.

"Now I must ask you some personal questions, which you may find impertinent. You're not under any obligation to answer, but should you refuse we have more persuasive methods at our disposal."

"What?"

"Just kidding. Do you have any legal qualifications?"

"Not that I'm aware of," I replied.

"Wester has had some trouble with legal types in recent years. It may be unusual to hear such a thing from the faculty medic, but a rogue element has been giving the profession a bad name. You should avoid them if at all possible."

"I've always tried my best."

"Do you know your IQ?"

"It's pretty high," I said. "Somewhere in the nineties."

"During your excursion up the Kenneth & Keith you may become convinced it is much higher, and feel the urge to voice your new found intelligence to anyone who will listen. Asking you to resist such an urge may be futile but it's as well to mention it, as the waterways and pedantry go together like the judiciary and paraphilic infantilism."

"I don't really like horror movies," I said.

He eyed the soft stubble on my chin.

"I see you have light and somewhat sporadic facial growth. How often do you shave?"

"Face or back?" I said.

"Your shaving habits may be subject to change on the waterways. I recommend you stock up on toiletries and on no account let your depilatory customs slide. The consequences could be disastrous." This wasn't particularly concerning for me as, despite my little jest, I still had the facial growth of a fourteen-year-old, and not necessarily a male. Whilst this might have bothered me at twenty, at thirty it seemed incredibly good fortune. Now I counted my blessings during each of my thrice weekly encounters with a blade.

"Do you own your own teeth?"

"I'd hate to find out they belonged to someone else," I said.

He produced what appeared to be a battery powered dentist's drill and cranked it up fully.

"Is it safe?" he asked.

"What?"

"Just kidding." He dispensed with the drill. "Look after them. Teeth are apt to soften during the narrowboating process." I couldn't imagine what might cause teeth to go soft or even what it would be like to have soft teeth. I pictured a mouthful of jelly stumps and ran my tongue along the top set just to check their density. I suppose if they did turn to marshmallow I could rent another set. LaFlamme would have too much fun with this.

The old thesp seemed ready to pack me on my way. I asked if he was satisfied I had the necessary psychological strength required to amble up the Kenneth & Keith stopping at every other canalside pub to swill vigorous dark ale and eat my own weight in fish pie. He said it was no laughing matter and that I would have to 'get up to speed' with the dietary customs immediately.

"Narrowboating is not child's play. It requires a strong constitution. It's essential that you acclimatise by building up a tolerance of gastropub cuisine and cask ales prior to departure. You may otherwise experience something akin to toxic shock.

"The faculty is procuring a vessel especially for this trip and it will be a couple of days before the necessary preparations and paperwork are in order. I suggest you use the time wisely and begin training immediately. And remember..."

"*Achtung?*"

"Exactly," said the medic. "Be careful."

I decided to take Dr Seward's advice and call LaFlamme to help me get into shape. Having watched *The African Queen* it occurred to me that if I could persuade her to accompany me on this expedition, the close proximity might create the sort of conditions where sexual tension could lead to actual sexual sex. This was obviously a long shot but my infatuation with LaFlamme was chronic. I feared that unless love was reciprocated soon my overworked heart would develop a hide.

The problem was that LaFlamme was bound to see through such an obvious ploy. She would no doubt realise an invitation to join a heavily perspiring infatuate in a confined space, whilst appealing, was not engineered in order to play *Monopoly*. It would take considerable effort to persuade her that there was more to this than my gratification, but I only had to imagine the possible consequences of things going my way to convince me it was worthwhile. At this point I thought I should stop salivating and picked up the phone.

"A narrowboat?" said LaFlamme. "Like a canoe?"

"Bigger than a canoe," I replied.

"Like a yacht?"

"Smaller than a yacht."

"Like a raft?" I could hear her having difficulties visualising such a fantastical vessel so I explained as best as I could that a narrowboat was a kind of houseboat favoured by Cary Grant types who have the ennui with modern life.

"When do we leave?" she asked. It was a much more straightforward negotiation than I imagined.

We agreed to meet at The Rowan Tree, the closest thing we had to a canalside pub in that it had a cold water tap outside. Over fish pie and a pint of Old Geriatric, LaFlamme asked me a string of cryptic questions.

"Is this a suitable juncture for you to consider taking such a trip?" she said.

"What?"

"Are the planets aligned in such a way as to guarantee a successful outcome? Will the current celestial atmosphere continue for the duration of the trip?"

"What are you talking about?"

"I have to write horoscopes for *Toady* magazine," she replied. "That's the way they talk. Do you know anything about it?"

"I know it's drivel," I said.

"Yes but do you know the star signs?"

"Some of them. Capricorn, the guy with the horse's body, The Twins, Grumpy, Sleepy, Dopey."

"Good," said LaFlamme. "You can help me."

"Don't you have to be psychic to do this?"

"I *am* psychic," she replied.

"No, you're not."

"When I asked if you knew anything about it, I knew you'd say it was drivel." I couldn't dispute it. Maybe she was psychic.

I asked LaFlamme what possessed her to take on a job like that. She told me it allowed her to write six months' worth of material in advance, meaning she only had to deal with her employers twice; once on commission and once on delivery, something we agreed was awesome.

"Don't you have to respond to up-to-the-minute movements of the stars and stuff?" I asked.

"You think the planets are going to do something unusual?" she said. "They have this stuff mapped out decades in advance. Anyway they asked me to put a spin on it, so I was thinking of trying something different."

"Like?"

"I could do a horrorscope – where I only predict bad things."

"I don't think *Toady* readers want to hear bad things."

"I could do a hopelesscope – where I predict good things that might happen if you weren't so hopeless. It doesn't matter. The point is I can knock these out in our rare moments of sobriety and the money will keep us afloat for the whole trip." It struck me that it might be better to knock them out in our less rare moments of total drunkenness, but it was LaFlamme's call.

"So this LeSnide character," said LaFlamme, "what kind of magic does he do?"

"He doesn't do magic," I replied.

"Didn't you say he was an alchemist?"

"I said he was an advocate."

"What's the difference?"

"I don't know. Maybe he'll explain when we bring him down with a dart gun."

By the time The Rowan Tree called last orders the continual drinking had left me with mild repetitive strain in my right arm, and the fingers of my right hand were freezing due to almost constant contact with cold glass. When we hit the street, despite being close to midsummer, the midnight air was chilly and I lost some of the feeling in my hand.

"I've got green fingers," I said, waving them at LaFlamme.

"You?" she said. "I gave you a parlour palm and it fried in a week."

"The crispy one?"

"Yes," she said, "the crispy one. You know crispiness is not a natural state for plants, right?"

"I was sure I watered it," I said in my defence, which admittedly was weak. "I watered something that night. Anyway that's not what I meant. I can't feel my fingers."

"That's Raynaud," said LaFlamme.

"What's Raynaud?" I replied.

"Your fingers."

"My fingers are Raynaud?"

"Some guy called Raynaud invented cold fingers," she said. "If it wasn't for him, your fingers would be warm right now." She brought my hands together, placed them between her palms and rubbed vigorously. It was oddly maternal and oddly erotic at the same time. I imagined a Freudian would have a field day if I let one anywhere near me. If this was what training was all about, I liked it.

8.
A CAUSE FOR ALARM

I was a little tender following the previous night's training session but remembered the faculty quack Dr Seward warning this might happen. "What do you do if you fall off a horse?" he asked. This was clearly part of his intelligence test and I'll be honest it kept me guessing for some time. I suggested a bike and even questioned whether the journey was necessary at all. Eventually he said, "You get back on again." The metaphor was obscure to me as I'd never spent much time in the country (once I mistook a sheep for a puma in the Pentlands). Eventually I gathered he meant I would have to suffer some more.

I told The Admiral I needed him to assist me with my training schedule and that he could act as coach. He said he was happy to help and as he hadn't had a drink for a few days he could probably do with getting into shape himself. But he reminded me that The Rowan Tree was out of bounds for him due to an unfortunate incident last year when his polymer bouncy balls became unruly. Why he thought it was appropriate to demonstrate how to make bouncy balls in a city centre bar is still unknown, though I have to say it was one of our more memorable nights out.

The Admiral said The Malt Loaf often had a puddle of water outside after sufficient rain and could easily pass for a canalside pub, so we decided the training session would be held there instead.

I stopped in for him on the way and he showed me a new contraption he'd cobbled together from discarded pieces of circuitry and an old record player. In essence it was an alarm clock. At the specified hour the device would spring to life, activating the turntable and lowering the stylus arm onto the record. Result – you woke up to the gentle sound of a Chopin sonata or koto music from Japan. He hadn't tried it yet but assured me it would be a hundred per cent effective. I doubted whether the invention would ever be commercially viable, what with its need for discarded pieces of circuitry and an old record player, but The Admiral countered that my use of the word 'viable' was pejorative, whatever that means.

We left in pursuit of fish pie and vigorous dark ale and spent several hours testing degrees of vigour. We discussed Project X and how we could progress the hangover cure to a stage where it might actually cure hangovers and not simply embarrass us in front of eccentric potential collaborators.

"The Armstrong chappie certainly gave me some pointers," said The Admiral. "I've never seen a man so dedicated to a cause."

"Suave Gav's need is great," I said. "I suspect he's an inebriate of distinction. What was he chewing?"

"Many plants and roots contain opiates which can be released through chewing. The effect can be akin to morphine. Of course they can be equally addictive."

"So that's why he's so keen on nature's larder. The man's a raging substance abuser." I downed my drink and ordered another round, thinking it terrible that some people had to get off their faces all the time.

"The thing is," said The Admiral on my return, "we're going to burn up a truckload of tormentil plants if we're going to see this through. A couple of specimens aren't really going to suffice."

"Don't you have an allotment?"

"I do," he replied. "I shored up my maris pipers earlier."

"Couldn't you shore up something useful? Maybe something that could cure hangovers?"

"I think a plot devoted to potentilla erecta could raise suspicions amongst the allotters, don't you? Even lettuce is exotic to some of these people."

"What about those cannabis farms where they put heaters and lights in the attic so the plants grow really quickly? Couldn't we do that with the mental torment plant?"

"Tony," said The Admiral, "in case you haven't noticed we don't have an attic, and if we did we'd probably prefer to use it as a cannabis farm."

"Suppose so," I said.

"However," he continued, "there is something we may be overlooking. Tormentil surely grows in the wild and if it's happy to do so in this country then simply finding a suitable location ought to be our priority. From there we can either hire a van to gather a sufficient number of them or conduct our experiments in situ. Perhaps once you've found this LeSnide character he could help us locate such a place."

"Why would LeSnide be able to help?"

"Didn't you say he was an augurer, a diviner or suchlike?"

"He's an advocate."

"Ah," said The Admiral. "An advocate."

"He doesn't have any special powers."

"Perhaps then you could remind me why you must see him?"

"He owes me money," I replied. "There's no question of letting a client use my work without paying for it. I am not a charity."

"You could probably get charitable status if you wanted," said The Admiral. "It would save you the trouble of finding him. It's just a question of filling in a few forms and proving you do charitable acts for the public benefit. You'll need at least three trustees but they shouldn't be too hard to round up."

"I don't want to be a charity."

"Well, it may not be strictly necessary for you to have charitable status in order to donate your designs for free."

"I don't want to donate my designs for free," I said. "That's why I'm taking this trip. If I was happy to donate my designs for free I could be at home, poor and working on one now."

At midnight The Malt Loaf barman called time. The Admiral stood, briefly, then sat down again. He stood a second time and buttoned his cardigan, badly, leaving an extra button dangling at the bottom. He sat down once more and suggested we try again, heartily, only that this time I should go first. It seemed fair so I stood, abruptly, knocking over both chair and table and blaming him in a misguided attempt at dignity.

There was a limit to how far we would get in such a condition and with The Admiral's flat being nearest, it was decided it would be far enough if I could reach his sofa. En route to the sofa The Admiral explained he had an early start, as he had a couple of days' work at the hospital devising a way of keeping tags on runaway patients. He said it would be an opportunity to test his new alarm clock and were it not for runaway patients he would have no use for such a gadget.

"I'm going to make doubly sure I don't sleep in," said The Admiral, his last words of the evening as he set the device for 7:00am and left me muttering incomprehensibly about kotos.

I slept as if consigned to a morgue but was awoken by the gentle stirrings of Motorhead's 'Ace of Spades' at a level likely to have been set at The Admiral's last party. It was a testament to his electronic ingenuity that the device actually worked but it didn't work for long, as a high velocity boot was soon heading towards it from the direction of the sofa.

It was no use trying to sleep now. Soon The Admiral would be up crashing about, and this was not a figure of speech. There would be breakages.

I lay back on the sofa and drifted. I wondered what I should pack on our canal journey. Being a Capricorn I was usually prudent in such matters. (Caution is a good thing when it comes to holidays. For example, you're far less likely to fall out with the person accompanying you if you don't go in the first place.)

Then I began to wonder about astrology. Was it really drivel? I always thought so but look at me – Capricorn the goat – prudent, cautious and stubborn. Sometimes I even have little straggly hairs on my chin. I *am* the goat. I mean, why wouldn't your date of birth provide you with a whole range of predetermined personality traits? If you'd emerged from a warm hospital into a January blizzard, you'd be cautious too. Buggered if I'll do that again.

The Admiral was getting ready to deal with his runaway patients. Showing my trademark caution, I asked for his advice on packing. He was a regular at the Munich Beer Festival so he suggested I take a first aid kit. He rummaged in his bathroom cabinet. Various items crashed into the sink below, one of which he handed to me. It was a long white tube of something called 'Cryofreeze'.

"Take this," he said. "It's relieved a great deal of pain for me in the past. Apply to the affected area and numb's the word."

"Numb?" I said.

"You won't feel a thing," he replied. "Cryotherapy is the new aspirin."

"Do I rub it on my head if I get a headache?"

"Only if you've been hit with a frying pan."

"What if it's a saucepan?" I said. "Or a griddle?" He told me I was being facetious. I didn't see what politics had to do with it.

On the back of the tube it said, 'Do not use in combination with a heating pad.' I asked The Admiral what this meant – if I applied Cryofreeze then added a heating pad, would I start to melt? He said he thought my brain had already started to melt and that it might be too late for Cryofreeze. Now I thought *he* was being facetious.

I pointed to his broken record player and said, "Look at the time. Shouldn't you be at work?"

9.
THE LITTLE HITLER

The five-hour drive to the marina was a challenge, partly because of LaFlamme's innovative driving technique and partly because last night's training session left me feeling like a hundred and fifty pounds of tenderised meat.

On arrival we had to deal with the marina troll, a hirsute lady in a waterproof hat. First she asked us for a driver's licence. It never occurred to me I would have to be able to drive before taking responsibility of a forty foot, twenty tonne floating bungalow, but the troll assured us it was just for ID purposes. Luckily LaFlamme had a licence. No one would ever say that LaFlamme knew how to drive, but she had a licence.

Then the marina troll showed us a model of a lock and explained that we would need to know how to get the boat from one side to the other.

"You open the gates," she said, demonstrating with the model, "drive the boat in, close the gates, open the paddles, the water goes up. You open the gates on the other side and drive out."

"What's the point?" said LaFlamme.

"The point?" spluttered the troll. "The point is to get to the other side."

"Surely we could get to the other side quicker without the obstruction," I said.

What she should have said is that water cannot travel uphill. It's all very well ambling along level countryside in a man-made waterway, but what happens when you meet an incline? I suppose they could have dug deeper into the hill until the water came out the other side, but remember – laziness, not necessity, is the mother of invention. Instead of wasting time digging they sat down and came up with something that would move the water, and hence the boats, to a higher level. That's what locks are for. Needless to say it was The Admiral who explained this to me, as Victorian mechanics are like a form of pornography for him.

I marvelled at the ingenuity behind this tremendous feat of engineering and the fact that science for once had been useful. However, it didn't bring me any closer to understanding how to operate such a device once we encountered it.

"Don't worry," said LaFlamme confidently. "I've got it."

"You do?" I said. I didn't believe her but I was eager to get past the troll and let our journey commence.

We were shown to our boat, 'The Little Hitler', and clambered aboard. It was surprisingly spacious. I could almost stand up straight without stooping, something I found difficult generally. There was a kitchen, bedroom, shower room, and sitting room that converted to a second bedroom with twin bunks. It was far from salubrious but compared favourably with my flat.

LaFlamme had just finished marching end to end declaring the lodgings satisfactory when a swarthy looking man stepped aboard with a set of keys. "Are you the driver?" she asked.

"Well, I can get you started," he replied. I told him not to get LaFlamme started, as he would regret it.

"Have you driven one of these before?" he asked.

"Many times," replied LaFlamme. "We're frequent flyers."

"Then I'll keep it brief." He started up the engine. It surprised me to see that the driver positions himself at the back of the boat and has to stand to see above the hull in front of him. It seemed perverse, like having an HGV truck with the saloon at the back, but I suppose it's nearest the fridge.

He took the boat around the marina and ran through a set of operating procedures, demonstrating how to steer by manoeuvring a large rudder thing – called a tiller – in the opposite direction from the one you want to turn, and how to brake by employing a burst of full throttle. Dr Seward had warned me they did things differently down here.

"Documentation is here," he said, opening a kitchen cupboard and producing a stack of papers along with a chunky tome. "Let this be your bible." It was a well thumbed copy of a turgid guide called *The Waterways Code*. "Please study it," he said. He'd have a better chance getting me to study a bible.

"I'll get right onto that," said LaFlamme, who had long since stopped paying attention and was looking for a minibar.

Our guide brought the boat neatly to a stop at the towpath and hopped out at a convenient point around five hundred yards out of the marina. He left us with keys and a map of Wester. It was dense, but then so was I.

LaFlamme insisted on driving. Given that she'd paid no attention to the demonstration, I wasn't entirely convinced of the wisdom of this move. But there were plenty of other things to be done in the cabin so I went below and began by laying out the map on the dining table. I marked our departure point and established that we would be travelling in a westerly direction. Good navigation was going to be vital. But that was enough for one day.

In the kitchen I got to grips with the cupboard spaces, noting where the dishes, pots and pans were stored. I connected the fridge, which had a small ice compartment, just big enough for our needs in these fierce temperatures. I stacked the groceries, mostly just bread, cheese and gin. We would be sustenance light as we planned to rely on canalside inns for the more substantial fare.

After a short time I began to wonder why, despite hearing the engine running, we didn't appear to be moving. When I returned to the deck I found LaFlamme facing the back of the boat with one hand revving wildly on the gearstick, the other on the tiller. She seemed content, as though she thought we were actually sailing. But seeing the taut ropes securing us to the towpath I knew there was a limit to how far we'd get.

"We should probably cast off first," I said, proud of my nautical terminology.

LaFlamme stopped revving. "I thought it was a bit slow," she replied.

I hopped out and untied the rear rope, one of a trio of two-inch thick tethers securing us to the bank. By the time I'd untied the middle rope, the back of the boat was well adrift. I was beginning to see the error of my ways – I would have to untie the front rope and jump aboard there before the whole boat drifted out. That seemed straightforward enough, but once aboard I realised the front cabin doors were locked from the inside. There was no walkway from stern to bow, only the slenderest verge around the boat's side, barely wide enough to accommodate a single foot.

I called to LaFlamme across forty feet of rooftop. "I'm locked out."

"I like you over there," said LaFlamme. The boat was now at a ninety-degree angle to the waterway and LaFlamme's revving was butting the hull into the canal wall.

"You need to turn the tiller thing," I called.

"Which way?" she called back.

"Left," I said. The front of the boat began to veer away from our direction of travel. "The other left."

Slowly, very slowly – a floating bungalow doesn't go anywhere in a hurry – it changed direction. But instead of righting itself and moving forward we began rotating in a loose circle, colliding with the bank intermittently. LaFlamme began to flap, but I wasn't sure what I could do on the other side of the cabin surrounded by murky canal water of an unquantified depth.

I clambered onto the rooftop and began sliding my way across in the manner of a lateral Spiderman. I probably could have made it all the way across too, but the boat's rotation had gathered momentum. This time when we collided with the bank, it rocked violently and I lost my balance. Now there was no issue with the water depth being unquantified. I could confirm it was chest height.

"We have shows at 2:00, 3:00 and 5:00pm," said LaFlamme to a couple on the towpath who had stopped especially to witness this display of buffoonery.

By the time I'd climbed back on board, LaFlamme summed up our general mood with the words, "I can't believe you didn't get a chauffeur."

However I was eventually assured that everything was under control. Yes we were travelling in reverse, as she was still intent on making the back of the boat the front, but at least we were moving in the right direction.

The Little Hitler made its way up the Kenneth & Keith, regularly colliding with the bank and other boats. According to *The Waterways Code* we should have been driving on the right but in keeping with the temperament of both the boat's namesake and its skipper, we ploughed down the middle and made everyone else adjust accordingly. We discovered quite quickly that it was difficult to damage a narrowboat. They generally just bounce.

Once we had passed through Hilderton's industrial belt, the Wester countryside revealed itself to be quite exquisite. Its lush green fields and mature woods rolled by and I began to feel like maybe it wasn't all a massive mistake. There were even a few moments when the motion didn't make me nauseous.

LaFlamme was single-minded in her stewardship, at least until she realised there might be some effort involved in stewardshipping. Interpreting her whining, I thought to offer her a refreshment. We were meticulously prepared for the journey, having packed both a first aid kit and gin.

"Do you have any sunscreen?" I asked LaFlamme, handing her a glass. LaFlamme never went anywhere without sunscreen and passed me her Factor 99. "That's awfully high, isn't it?" I said. "I thought Factor 50 was complete sunblock."

"After 50," she said, "it starts beating the sun's rays into retreat. At 70 it starts talking back. At 99 it sends out a threatening letter."

"Why does it have Retinol in it – is it for skin with attention deficit disorder?"

"You're thinking of Ritalin," replied the skipper. "Which is not a bad idea – help the skin stay focussed on being gorgeous." LaFlamme didn't need to focus on being gorgeous. If she were any more gorgeous they'd have to put up health and safety warnings.

Content that I was now giving the sun as much grief as it was giving me, I relaxed on deck behind the determined LaFlamme and began to drift off, only occasionally disturbed from my meditation by howls from passing boats.

Who knew how long it would take to reach the heart of Wester, especially travelling in reverse and in almost continual collision? What were we likely to find on the way and would we be sober enough to deal with it? Without doubt we faced a long and arduous task, fraught with danger on several fronts.

For example:

The wildlife appeared hostile. I felt sure I saw an alligator slip into the water at one point, although LaFlamme insisted it was a duck. I wasn't about to approach in any case, as ducks frighten me just as much.

The heat was intense. I thought I could take respite from the sun by retreating below deck but it was easily five degrees hotter there. I returned rather sharpish to the mere baking heat above, where there was at least a breeze.

Supplies would have to be maintained. As well as continually replenishing our gin stocks, we would be stopping at canalside inns – but here, timing was everything. Some of the inns appeared to be many miles apart and according to *The Waterways Code* mooring by 8:00pm was essential. I couldn't tell if this was simply etiquette or whether there were waterways police to enforce it. But should you find yourself miles from an inn at curfew time you would risk almost certain drought.

Something else was troubling me and it took a little while for it to sink in. Everywhere I looked there were... beards. All the men had them and the women had distinct tufts on their upper lips and excessive underarm hair. It was not a good look, even for the men. Was it a collective act of defiance? Something in the air? A lawyer thing? I don't remember the legal establishment being particularly beardy. The only things that really united them were camelhair coats and cocaine. It was something we would have to watch carefully because where we came from, beards were strictly taboo.

And what of our mission itself? Although finding LeSnide was going to be a lot easier due to his tracking device – I was to receive regular updates from Pantling – it was unlikely to be a joy once we did, as the man was stark raving ill-defined. Even though all I had to do was jog his memory about the work I'd completed and get a signature, this may end up being more difficult than it sounded. How might he react? He may have no recollection of our meeting. He may quibble over the amount. He may insist that being a resident of Wester – arguably no man's land – he was exempt from VAT, although I've found debating with the VAT man to be most unsatisfying.

Then there was the question of returning LeSnide to the relative civilisation of the faculty. What if he objected? If he'd engaged a tribe of indigenous peoples and junior lawyers as his foot soldiers, they may turn against us. It could lead to violence, or worse, lawsuits. And even if he agreed, how would I survive being in a confined space with him?

At least the Captain and I had agreed on a payment process. Normally, getting money out of clients is in itself a long and arduous task fraught with danger on several fronts:

It begins with an invoice, which contains your details, a description of the job, the cost and your payment terms – strictly thirty days. The client ignores this and takes at least sixty days, during which time you issue two reminders and a statement and call to explain that, much as you love your work, there are other things you love more such as not having to speak to them.

Thereafter the client may, even in these times of instant electronic banking, choose to issue a cheque – a form of fiscal scammery which allows a bank to use your money for a week without the slightest justification. If they take this route, they're also likely to post it and will ensure to attach a second class stamp to draw the process out further. It becomes an exercise in postponement, and some have it down to an art.

One client told me over the phone he was writing a cheque there and then.

"How do I know you're not just making scribbly sounds?" I said. He started scribbling louder.

"I tell you what," he said. "I'll take a picture and email it to you." Sure enough I got the email and the picture did indeed show a man scribbling enthusiastically in a chequebook. But generally I've found banks unwilling to lodge email attachments in lieu of actual money, so I had another month of swearing.

"What's going on ahead?" said LaFlamme. We were about to enter a dense wooded area where there appeared to be very little light. It was even difficult to discern any tangible shapes ahead and felt as if we were approaching a void. I'd also become aware of drumming, which usually meant drummers, and that was rarely a good thing.

"According to the map," I said, "we should be nearing a bar shortly."

"Hallelujah," said LaFlamme.

"But this doesn't look like civilisation."

The further we travelled into the wilderness, the more insistent the drumming became. Although ominous, it had also been vaguely reassuring that the drums hadn't stopped because in my experience when the drums stop, the bass player takes a solo.

But as the light faded and the water below turned turgid and swamp-like, the constant beating became unsettling. I didn't need any further reminding of Cozy Powell. Fleeting shapes appeared in glimpses of shadowy light. Eyes shone brightly out from the heavy facial growths surrounding them. We were being watched.

As a Capricorn I felt it my duty to tell LaFlamme to exercise caution. As an Aries (obviously LaFlamme was a fire sign) she felt it her duty to ignore me. When the canal veered around a tight corner, the light all but disappeared. And that's when the assault began.

"Drive on the right!" cried a lurking beard before disappearing into the undergrowth.

"Indicate!" cried another.

"You are in violation of bylaw 158!"

Many of these savages were frothing at the mouth. It occurred to me they might be lawyers.

"Take cover!" I said to LaFlamme. "Once we get through this stretch, the canal widens and 'The Hirsute Lady' shouldn't be much further." LaFlamme ducked down and pushed the gearstick into full throttle. It took a few seconds to have any effect but soon we were tanking along, even if tanking along in a narrowboat means the equivalent of a brisk walk.

It was our first encounter with a hostile local tribe and we considered it a narrow escape. Their comments were cutting, displaying a level of pedantry that I hadn't witnessed since the time I watched *QI*. Were these people professors of the art of boating? Or were they just self-righteous, nitpicking busybodies who didn't really know what they were talking about? Did being around canals and canal boats instil a love of rules and regulations in locals that made them need to tell everybody else what to do? I suppose only time would tell. But they missed the most obvious problem with our presence on the canal – we were travelling in reverse. In comparison being told the oil needed changed and we were likely flooding the engine was minor.

We were both relieved when we finally cleared the woods and reached the safety of The Hirsute Lady.

Still shaking from the experience, I jumped onto the towpath and grabbed a rope from the hull, reeling it in towards the bank. There were moorings in place and all we had to do was attach our three ropes. This sounded simple enough but what kind of knot holds a floating bungalow? I took the middle and rear ropes and pretended they were giant shoelaces, even placing a foot below each to help me visualise. The result was spectacular in terms of footwear but whether it would secure the vessel was open to question. LaFlamme took the front rope and tied a simple double loop in it. She said it was called a constrictor. It would probably be more effective than my knots but didn't look nearly as nice.

"I wouldn't do that if I were you," said a cardiganed beard smoking a pipe. He looked as if knots might be his thing.

"Are you the knot king?" replied LaFlamme, in no mood for more unsolicited advice.

"Well it's just..."

"I didn't think so. You know who taught me this knot? Don Knotts. He knew knots. He knew lots. And when is a knot not a knot?"

"Umm..."

"I'll tell you when. When it's not."

This was sufficiently mystifying for the beard to shrug his shoulders and leave us alone, saying something about a shocking disrespect for the noble art of knot tying. But I chastised LaFlamme for deliberately antagonising the natives. We had a long road ahead of us and there could be trouble if word should spread that we were devotees of the cult of Don Knotts.

The Hirsute Lady was a quaint old girl entirely covered in ivy – even the buildings here were hairy. We were apprehensive about entering following our crash course in waterway pedantry but once inside, the atmosphere was convivial. The staff and regulars were reasonably welcoming, although they obviously lived in fear of barbers.

"Fish pie and gin for two," ordered LaFlamme.

"Ice?" asked the barman.

"Tony," whispered LaFlamme. "They serve their fish pie cold. What do I do?"

"Ask them to stick it in the oven for a bit," I said.

I saw a blackboard with the words 'cask ales' in decorative handwriting and some wildly named beers below. The Admiral told me to always look out for cask ales and never pass up the opportunity to try the week's special. I related this rare nugget of his wisdom to LaFlamme when we took a seat at a nearby table.

"Get a couple of pints then," she said.

"But you just bought gin."

"I'm on holiday. Get on with it."

"I can't," I said sheepishly. "The special has a funny name. It's embarrassing."

"Don't be ridiculous. Do you trust The Admiral?"

"When it comes to beer, yes."

"Well then?"

I returned to the bar and asked for two pints of Get Knotted.

It was borderline four o'clock by the time we headed back to The Little Hitler. We were pleasantly merry and ready to take command of the high seas once again. My attractive shoelace knots had predictably come undone, leaving the boat adrift at a ninety-degree angle and blocking the movement of many other boats behind. But LaFlamme's knot remained secure, which made me think perhaps this Don Knotts bloke knew his stuff.

It was only when LaFlamme hopped aboard and I set to untie it that I realised why the cardiganed beard had tried to intervene – a twenty tonne boat pulling on a constrictor knot will tend to make it rather tight. Now it was going to take an axe to set us free.

Several beards gathered on the towpath and muttered disapprovingly. I considered asking for advice but feared I might suffocate under the deluge.

Our options were limited. As far as I could see, we could either take up residence in The Hirsute Lady or send out for the axe. I was on the point of the latter when LaFlamme said, "Tony get in." She had disengaged the rope at the boat end and cast it into the water. The boat began drifting from the bank. I made a leap from the shore and would have made it were it not for the rope, which got tangled around my foot and sent me head first into the water. The beards may have been knowledgeable but no one really knew the canal like I did.

When I re-emerged, LaFlamme was saluting the bystanders as they shook their heads in despair.

"That probably wasn't such a good idea," I said.

"Who needs three ropes?" she said.

"We can't just abandon ropes every time we cast off. We're going to run out pretty quickly."

"We'll get the advocate to conjure up some more," she said, apparently still under the misapprehension that an advocate was some type of wizard. She would be deeply disappointed when he started boffing on about tax law.

Once aboard, I spotted an envelope on the open deck and my heart sank further. It was addressed to 'Occupants of The Little Hitler' and had come from the offices of Stickler & Zealot LLP, 'Correcting You Since 1924'. I read it aloud.

Gentlemen,

It has come to our attention that you and your crew have been in violation of both *The Waterways Code* and *The Boater's Handbook* in reference to the Kenneth & Keith canal. Ordinarily we should point to specific sections of both guides and detail the violation(s) in question. However in this case it will save time to point to the sections you have not violated and thence you can address the inverse.

Namely:

1) *The Waterways Code*. Section III (36) 'Sound Signals'. We

believe you are not guilty of abusing the use of the horn, but suspect this to be because you are unaware of there being one.

2) *The Waterways Code.* Section III (37) 'Speed Limits.' We believe you are not guilty of abusing the maximum speed of four miles per hour but this is likely to be because you have been travelling in reverse.

In other words, the entirety of Section I – Boat Handling, Section II – Boating Safety, Section III – Rules of the Road (minus the aforementioned exclusions), Section IV – Good Boating Behaviour, and even Section V – More Information, appear to have been flagrantly flouted since the sad day of your arrival in Wester.

It goes without saying that *The Boater's Handbook*, being only a slim volume, has been violated thoroughly from cover to cover. We take this matter most seriously and our threatening letters even more so. Should you continue to flout the waterway regulations we would have no choice but to take action on behalf of our client(s).

Yours sincerely,
Morry Stickler LLB KnoB

"Gentlemen?" said LaFlamme, as if it were the only point that registered.

The letter was certainly troubling, but not as troubling as it would have been had we not just quaffed several pints of Get Knotted. Who were Stickler and Zealot? And who was their client? Had they been instructed by LeSnide? Was it possible they were LeSnide's foot soldiers, protecting their leader from an attempt to have him removed? Had they just seen our boat handling and decided it was best for everybody if we go home? Given these hostile conditions I was beginning to think we should find our own LLB KnoB, or at least somebody who could tie a knot.

We moored for the night in a remote wooded area bordering open fields. It seemed a safe bet; in the event of another attack it was neither too exposed nor too confined. There were still bearded types walking their dogs and taking the evening air so it was evidently not too far from dwellings.

I was less than confident about our moorings, having had difficulties at our last pit stop. I didn't want to go to sleep on the edge of open fields and wake up in the Belgian Congo, and we certainly couldn't spare another rope. At the risk of being told everything we knew about boats and boating amounted to the sum total of bugger all, we decided to stop the next dog walker and ask for advice. As it turned out, it looked like the next dog walker was carrying his dog in his arms.

"Hey beardy," called LaFlamme, gesturing to the man. The beard approached the boat and it became clear it was not a dog he was carrying at all. It was a doll, a little wooden man-doll of the type that might have been employed by a Victorian ventriloquist.

"How did you know my name?" he said in his odd Wester accent.

"Your name's Beardy?" I said.

"Timothy Beard," he replied, "at your service." Once again, LaFlamme's psychic ability was confirmed.

He introduced the doll, who incidentally was the first clean-shaven person I'd seen in some time. "This is Corky."

"Charmed," said the doll. I cast a nervous sideways glance at LaFlamme but she didn't appear fazed. I reminded myself of Dr Seward's words. I think if he'd said that Wester 'differences' extended to talking wooden men, I may have decided settling the LeSnide account wasn't such a big deal.

"You look like a man who knows knots," said LaFlamme.

"Why indeed, young miss," said Mr Beard.

"Yes yes," said Corky wearily. "We're all aware you're the knot master. He's the ass master too, you know."

"We only have two ropes and Tony doesn't like the Belgian Congo," said LaFlamme. "What's the best way to tie them?"

"Well it's a thorny question," Mr Beard began. "Some say the mooring hitch, some say the clove hitch and some say round turn and two half hitches. Some say round round round she goes, where she stops nobody knows."

"Heavens above," said Corky, raising his eyes skyward. "He's going into one of his routines."

"There's the bowline loop. Or if it's a bollard, you can't beat a spliced loop twice round."

"Tie them up, you imbecile," said Corky.

"Righto then," said Mr Beard. He put Corky on the towpath but they continued their rather terse exchange nonetheless. They were like an old married couple.

"I'd say the mooring hitch," said Mr Beard. He took one of the ropes from the roof of the boat and began tying it to a mooring pin. "She's a cruel mistress but I wouldn't have it any other way. The bowline's sticky and the clove hitch can slip. You often need to back it up with a couple of halfs if you want to keep it in check."

"If only we could keep you in check," said Corky. "Or in shackles. Stocks, perhaps. Take you to the village square and pelt you with expired *légumes*."

I said I'd like a word with my associate in private and took LaFlamme to one side.

"What's up?" she said

"Are they French or something?" I asked.

"I think they might be hobgoblins."

"Hobgoblins?"

"Yes."

"I knew it was one or the other."

"If they're hobgoblins, they'll stick around and do good deeds for as long as we leave them favours. Let me try something." She turned to face the odd couple on the towpath and said, "Would you gentlemen like a drink?"

"Does Pinocchio have a wooden arse?" replied Corky.

"Hobgoblins," said LaFlamme under her breath. "Gin's their favourite treat."

As LaFlamme proceeded to fill four glasses I watched Mr Beard demonstrating the mooring hitch, an ingenious quick-release knot that involved looping three parts of the rope around each other and slipping the end through the middle. He repeated it several times for my benefit. So far I'd gotten the hang of the quick-release, but tying it again was a mystery. I asked if there was a clip-on version.

"Pull the rope over the pin," said Mr Beard, "leaving some slack to form a loop. Then pull it through the loop and form another loop." I thought I was going to faint.

"We have to do this every time we moor," I said. "Do you know how many bars we need to visit?"

Corky watched LaFlamme intently as she returned with refreshments. His head remained static but his eyes followed her every move. "Didn't we meet in Marienbad?" he asked her. "Last year?"

"I've never been to Wales," said LaFlamme.

After just the smallest taste of gin, Mr Beard was of a mind to do some basic maintenance on The Little Hitler and set about checking the gauges, something that I admit did not upset us greatly.

He asked what brought us to this neck of the woods and I told him we had been sent to track down The Advocate for Self-Importance.

"Is he going to grant your wishes, do you think?" he said.

"I don't think it's a question of granting wishes," I said. "That's not really what advocates do."

"What do they do then?" said Mr Beard.

"I have no idea," I replied. "Nobody does. But I expect to come away suitably enriched."

"I met a sorcerer once," said Corky.

"Now Corky," said Mr Beard, "that's a long story."

"At least it's not stultifyingly dull like one of yours," said Corky.

"I'll just check the gearbox oil," said Beard.

"Check your pants while you're at it," said Corky.

As Mr Beard set about the gearbox, the pair continued their low-level antagonistic banter. They made an unusual team and I wondered why they had chosen to be around one another. Mr Beard seemed a simple soul with a dowdy appearance and down to earth, countrified ways. Corky on the other hand was immaculately dressed in dinner suit and bowtie, and was altogether a more debonair character. He spoke with a refined English accent and it wouldn't have surprised me if he had been privately educated. Although I never caught sight of him drinking, the level of gin in his glass did indeed go down. Whilst Mr Beard drank, Corky spoke freely and openly and was in fact quite eloquent, holding forth at length on subjects as diverse as politics and literature.

"You know, I do wonder what has become of the comic novel," he said at one point. "It seems the entire genre has deteriorated into vulgarity. The only possible exceptions are the Wodehouse contenders, but they tend to be turgid in the extreme. I'd almost prefer the vulgarity. I would have written my own tomes twenty years ago had I known things would get so bad."

Each time their glasses neared the empty stage, both became distracted as if ready to move on. At one point LaFlamme held back on a refill just to see what would happen. Mr Beard gathered up Corky, stepped onto the towpath and continued the maintenance of the boat exterior, checking the ropes were secure and the window frames intact, their mutual sniping ongoing throughout. I suppose eventually they would have wandered off and returned to their normal lives, or whatever passed for normal life in Wester, but then LaFlamme would refill their glasses and we'd hear the distant muttering edging closer as they stepped back onboard and took up some other routine tasks.

Following a hefty replenishment, Mr Beard asked if we had operated the bilge pump since we moored. We asked him what it was. How could we know about the bilge pump? We were still driving in reverse. He said he would need to lift the hatch on deck in order to tackle it and we had best move to another part of the boat. This suited me fine – although they were undoubtedly useful to have around, the incessant bickering was tiring.

LaFlamme and I moved to the front of the boat where we could unwind with our drinks and dangle our legs over the side. The early evening air was balmy. A light haze rose from the water as the sun began to dip behind the trees. This was more like what we were expecting from a boating excursion: a floating gin palace that was fully maintained by experienced help. I asked LaFlamme what we would do if we ran out of gin. She suggested tethering them. But that raised the whole issue of knots again and we couldn't very well ask them to tie their own.

Ahead of us was an expansive stretch of reeds and amongst them I saw a chicken standing on one leg. LaFlamme assured me it was a heron.

"Why is it standing on one leg?" I asked.

"That's what herons do," she replied.

"I'm not convinced it's a heron."

"Why would a chicken stand on one leg?"

"Why would a heron?"

"Thermodynamics."

"What?"

"Well," said LaFlamme, "it's hard to say for sure without having the mind of a chicken or heron. I mean you're probably better placed to answer the question. But they think it's a thermoregulatory function. Standing on one leg keeps the other leg warm."

"Does it work?"

"You should try it."

As my legs were lightly chilled from dangling over the side, I thought I could give it a go. I stood in the tight triangular floorspace of the boat's nose, an area only a few feet across, and pulled my right foot up behind my tailbone. Unfortunately my left foot being wet, I lost my footing and seconds later was once again able to confirm the depth of the canal water. I could also confirm that what I spotted was indeed a heron as it took off at a speed that would be most unusual for a chicken.

On hearing the commotion, Mr Beard and Corky ambled along the towpath to the front of the boat.

"Everything all right?" said Mr Beard.

"I was looking for something," I replied, hauling myself out of the water for the third time.

"I say," said Corky. "I think this one's been beaten with the stupid stick."

"Well," said Mr Beard, "everything seems to be shipshape." LaFlamme looked at their glasses, mindful of not having refilled them for a while. "But there's one last thing. Corky always ends with a song."

If I'd been asked how to make today even more irritating, I doubt I would have had the imagination to suggest a little wooden man serenade us. I was tired. It had been a long day and I'd spent more time in the water than Captain Nemo. But with the sun now set, the sound of crickets filling the air and steam rising off my clothes, I resigned myself to hearing out the little man.

"What are you going to sing tonight, Corky?" asked Mr Beard.

"'Show me the way to go home'," said Corky.

"All right then," said Mr Beard.

It was a peculiar old number, probably intended to be sung in an upbeat style rather than the slow maudlin approach favoured by the posh little man who had by now soaked up a skinful of gin.

> Show me the way to go home
> I'm tired and I want to go to bed
> I had a little drink about an hour ago
> And it's gone right to my head
> No matter where I roam
> On land or sea or foam
> You will always hear me singing this song
> Show me the way to go home

With this, Mr Beard and his companion began wandering along the towpath, their voices trailing off into the distance.

"Did I check the gearbox oil?" said Mr Beard.

"For the third time, yes," said Corky. "You're an oily little man."

"Ah."

"It's a wonder I don't slip through your fingers."

"Righto then."

"You're like the Duke Of Oil."

"Okay."

"I should call you Slick."

I was close to exhaustion. But as LaFlamme and I prepared to bed down in our respective berths, she had one final challenge for me.

"Do you snore?" she asked.

"I'm not sure."

"Well I do," she said. "Like a foghorn. You won't hear any boats during the night. When they hear me they stay put."

"I'm not too concerned," I said. "My bedroom's above a busy street. If I don't hear the sound of attempted murder at night, I get jumpy."

I was just beginning to drift off when I felt the boat begin to rattle. 'Snoring' hardly does justice to the sound emanating from the buzz saw operator on the other side of the flimsy partition. I'd heard quieter jackhammers. It was like the most exaggerated, over the top impression of someone snoring I'd ever heard. I resigned myself to it being a long night.

10.
FORTUNE TELLING BY
BEARD READING

I managed a full three or four hours last night. Cursing under my breath, that is. As well as my fellow passenger's inability to sleep without waking the dead, I had a group of particularly rowdy owls to contend with. The overall effect was like being at a large scale sporting event.

At some stage I must have tuned them out because I don't for a moment believe any of them simmered down. I awoke to the sound of a passing engine, the wake of which caused The Little Hitler to gently bob up and down as if we were at sea. I was at sea – vaguely hungover, not remotely rested and unsure what I was doing there.

LaFlamme was already up and skimming a book in the kitchen area of the cabin. LaFlamme didn't read books, she only ever skimmed them. This didn't seem to impair her understanding and if questioned could supply in-depth answers to any questions regarding their contents. She was some kind of genius with the printed page. A genius and a half, or maybe even two geniuses.

I sat up and glanced over the small collection of reading materials resting alongside a few well-used board games in a rainy day cupboard: Enid Blyton, *Three Men In A Boat*, the *Big Ladybird Book of Waterways*, a few copies of *Cosmopolitan*, colouring books, some mighty tome on art, *Architecture Now*, *Collins Concise Dictionary*. (I never understood why

63

they called it the 'Concise'. Was there an Inconcise? Collins Vague and Rambling? Maybe there was a special Collins Editor's Day Off edition.)

I suppose even the Concise would give me a chance to extend my vocabulary, which The Admiral said was 'limited'. I said it was only limited by the number of words in it. He said I was 'preternaturally asinine', which may or may not have been true. I don't know the first thing about dinosaurs.

Then it occurred to me that the Concise might not be long enough for this journey, which after all could take some time. I might get to the letter Z before we arrived and have to start on the colouring books. Or this little number, something called *Hosier's Guide to Westerchestershire*.

"Where's Westchess… Westerchesh... Wessershessersher?" I said.

"They abbreviated it to Wester," LaFlamme replied.

"Why?"

"Because they knew you'd sound like a dribbling idiot when you tried to pronounce it." I was relieved. I didn't need any help sounding like a dribbling idiot.

"What are you reading?" I asked. She showed me the cover of a book called *Magic and the Twelve Signs of the Zodiac*.

"Research," she explained, scanning the pages.

"What does magic have to do with the zodiac?" I asked.

"That's what I'm trying to find out," she replied. "I don't know anything about the zodiac."

"You know something about magic?"

"There's magic in my genes. The Great LaFlambé was a relative."

"Who's The Great LaFlambé?"

"He was a big music hall star in the twenties. The other twenties. I don't know much about him except he was French and he was a great magician. He was more than a great magician, he was a great uncle – my grandfather's brother."

"You never told me this," I said.

"I ration what I tell you, Boaks," she replied. "It's for your own good. If I told you everything I knew, a) it would take forever, and b) you'd get confused. I'm very careful not to overfill your little dome needlessly. Everything you hear is on a need to know basis."

"Thank you," I said, trying to figure out if it was a good thing.

"What's important is that you continue to be pretty somewhere on my horizon and amuse me with your bartending skills and occasional acrobatics." LaFlamme said this kind of thing to me all the time. But I didn't feel *emasculated* because I hadn't looked it up yet.

She handed me a copy of *Music Hall Luminaries* and said, "Read this." It was bookmarked at an entry for The Great LaFlambé.

Visionary magician and showman, The Great LaFlambé is mostly remembered for his flamboyant stage style, his apparent way with fire, and the unusual and untimely manner of his demise. Up until 1921 when a trick that went wrong resulted in his burning to death on a London stage, he was one of the highest paid performers on the variety circuit. His legendary act was booked for up to ten years in advance.

Born Claude Balls LaFlambé in Bordeaux in 1890, he began his theatrical career as a stagehand, developing his routines whilst studying the performers of the day. The greatest of these was the renowned flatulist Le Petomaine, and it was after hearing Le Petomaine's gusty impression of the 1906 San Francisco earthquake that LaFlambé was inspired to take to the stage. It was some time before he wanted to take to that particular stage but there were many others where Le Petomaine had not played. LaFlambé went on to forge an illustrious career that many say was only held back by having died.

A close friend of fellow magician Harry Houdini, the pair were known rivals and their semi-friendly competitive sparring occasionally resulted in problems for both. Houdini often doused LaFlambé in water, severely limiting LaFlambé's pyrotechnical abilities; LaFlambé regularly locked Houdini in his hall cupboard, challenging the escapologist to make his way out unassisted.

Some of LaFlambé's routines were theatrical classics of the time. For example, *Ashes to Ashes*, *The Rising Sun* and most famous of them all, *The Combustor*, in which he conjured up fire telepathically. Unfortunately on its ultimate performance *The Combustor* was conjured up on stage curtains, and whilst management considered this excellent theatre, they thought differently when they had to build a new one.

LaFlambé initially escaped the theatre but returned when he realised he'd forgotten his umbrella, something he was rarely seen without. His last words were reportedly 'It is possible to be too successful'.

"This is incredible," I said to LaFlamme who was filing her nails. "He was your great uncle?"

"Mm," she replied. "He was like Liberace, only with magic."

"I thought only lords set fire to curtains. And he didn't need matches? That's some trick."

"It's not a trick," said LaFlamme. "It's magic. And it's my birthright."

"What?"

"It should have been hereditary. These types of conditions are passed down, you know. But something's missing."

"You've tried raising fire with your mind?" I asked. LaFlamme nodded. "And?"

"All I ever get is a temperature. I'm hoping the alchemist can help."

"He's not an alchemist," I said. "He's an advocate."

"Any kind of wizard will do," she replied. Despite having no idea what core skills advocates employed, I felt sure telepathic combustion was not amongst them. I was getting discouraged. I considered asking LaFlamme to be less generous with her information rationing.

I couldn't imagine why she would feel so strongly about the matter. There weren't many practical applications for telepathic combustion unless you were a Boy Scout. Couldn't she buy a lighter? I suppose some people have more of an affinity with fire than others.

I had a school friend who loved to start fires. There was no telepathic element to his brand of combustion, he just had an endless supply of matches. One day, in a break between *conflagrations*, he told me if you wrote the word 'WHY' vertically it would look like a woman in a bikini. He demonstrated by scrawling the letters on a page he tore from one of my notebooks.

It should have been hugely titillating for a ten-year-old but I had a little trouble grasping the concept from his primitive sketch.

"Look," he said.

"What?"

"WHY."

"What?"

"WHY."

"Why what?"

"A woman in a bikini."

"Why what a woman in a bikini?" By this time he'd set fire to the paper in exasperation.

Years later, The Admiral showed me the same trick and was quite beside himself with glee. He was twenty-five at the time. I still didn't understand it, until he began drawing the shape of a woman in a bikini on top of it. He took such care over this that I thought he was spending too much time at his *Dungeons & Dragons* sessions and tried to have them cancelled. Finally, after many layers of detail, the visual joke sank in. But by now I was altogether more worldly and sophisticated. I told him it was way too big for a bikini, that he was a rubbish drawer and a big fat fatty.

As it was borderline 10:00am I thought I should get up before succumbing to *atrophy*. LaFlamme suggested I try the shower. She said she'd been feeling less than gorgeous earlier, popped in and emerged radiant and glowing. It sounded good so I took her advice. The shower was certainly *revivifying* and remarkably effective given the cramped enclosure. I couldn't stand up under it – I had to stoop and point the showerhead in the right places and predict when LaFlamme might next turn on the kitchen tap. I did emerge radiant and glowing but only where I had been scalded.

Afterwards I wiped the steam from the mirror until I could see something that vaguely resembled me. It took a while but that was because I kept trying to rub away my stubble. I had a few days' soft growth emerging – nothing too worrying, but I recalled Dr Seward warning me to shave regularly. Thought I should probably tackle it before it reached the deeply unappealing fluffy stage.

It was only then I realised I'd forgotten to pack a razor. There was plenty Cryofreeze in my toilet bag should I want to make any part of my body numb, but nothing to remove pesky facial hair. I asked LaFlamme if she had one.

"*Moi?*" she said and continued in what sounded like impeccable French, something about a bicycle and a boy called Jean. Either they were going to the seaside with the pen of the boy's aunt or he'd lost the loaf of bread he'd just bought at the butcher shop. I don't know. It's all very well for two-year-olds to pick up language but for adults it's pretty much impossible.

I didn't even know LaFlamme could speak French. But having discovered she had a French magician in her family it made more sense. At least more sense than trying to buy bread in a butcher shop.

I never saw the point myself. Surely the only reason for learning French was to live in France, refuse to speak English to tourists and delight in their frustration. Admittedly this would be fun but I would not be tempted. Not for me the language of the great ice hockey players and Edith Piaf – someone I felt sure made up words as she went along. If I were looking for a novel way of tormenting my frontal lobes for several years only to be thoroughly discouraged when trying to hold a meaningful conversation with native speakers, I would choose Spanish. Why? Because in virtually half of the world I could get little fried doughnuts simply by uttering the word '*churros*'.

LaFlamme poured two glasses of gin. Given the hour, it was wildly ambitious, even by our standards. I was about to reach for one anyway when she slapped my hand. "Not for you," she said, taking the glasses and placing them on the deck.

I returned to the bathroom and took a comb through my hair. It seemed a little thicker than normal. I put this down to the salty Wester air, although I noticed the shampoo said 'for increased volume'. I made a mental note not to use it on the rest of my body in case I ended up a bloater.

Shortly I heard a familiar voice from the deck. "Morning plebs!" My heart sank to another new low. It was Corky.

"Everything still ticking along?" said Mr Beard. LaFlamme climbed the short steps from the kitchen. By the time I joined her and looked up to the deck, the gin levels had dropped and Mr Beard was fiddling with the gauges.

"How's my little simpleton?" called Corky. "You needn't have washed just for me, you know. Although obviously we're all very grateful you did.

Pee-yew!" I was beginning to dislike the little man and was *perturbed* by his reappearance. Was it sensible of LaFlamme to refill their glasses so early in the day? This was a *rhetorical* question, as it was unheard of for the words 'LaFlamme' and 'sensible' to ever appear in the same sentence. Although I was happy for the hobgoblins to ensure The Little Hitler was seaworthy, I would be happier when they finished their gin and moved on.

"I had the most marvellous dream last night," said Corky. "I was dining at my club when little Josephine appeared."

"Josephine?" I said.

"Baker of course, do keep up. Bendiest limbs in Paris. The girl was practically elasticated. Had to wear a girdle just to hold herself together. I said 'Josephine dear, would you like some champagne?' I was standing next to a champagne fountain, you see, glass upon glass filled to overflowing. I've never been so happy. Then I woke up and realised I'd left a tap running. It was probably just as well because little Josephine could be a terrible bore after champagne. And of course it loosened her up even further. Never needed a taxi. She'd just fold down the street like a Slinky."

Much as I love hearing other people's dreams and the interminable rambling nonsense detailed therein, I thought I could make better use of my time below deck and ducked back inside just as the engine started up. I was none too pleased with the idea that LaFlamme was going to allow the goblin people to travel with us and was considering a private word when my phone rang.

"Good morning Tony." It was Captain Pantling. "I believe you are still several days from counsel. Last night he attended a hostelry where I'm told he was toasted as guest of honour."

"Toasted?" I said. "Like in *The Wicker Man*?"

"I should imagine they were toasting his health rather than his flesh." This certainly seemed more likely but it led to me fantasising about LeSnide being shut in a huge straw man along with a bunch of goats and chickens. Torching it wouldn't be necessary; maintaining a constant discomfort would do.

"Today he has returned to his enclave. How is everything else?"

"Fine," I said. "But I forgot to bring a razor."

"Beg pardon?"

"My razor. I didn't pack it."

"That's most unfortunate."

"Is it such a big deal?" I said. "I mean obviously being beardy's a slippery slope in that soon I might start listening to jazz and smoking a pipe. But nobody else here seems to bother. I've only seen one clean-shaven guy since we arrived and he's made of wood."

"I see," said Pantling. "I didn't think we'd have to have this conversation quite so soon."

"What conversation?"

"Tony," he began, "the people of Wester have some unorthodox views. Many of them believe in the ancient art of pogonomancy."

"Pog-no-what?"

"Pogonomancy," he replied. "Fortune telling by beard reading." I had the *Collins Concise* to hand and looked under P but there was no sign of pogonomancy. I suggested the Captain had made it up. He laughed.

"Language is continually evolving. Anything to do with divination by beard reading is unlikely to have survived into a recent *Concise*. You'd have more luck with Wikipedia."

"Is that the Vague and Rambling edition?"

"You should be aware that in the forthcoming days you may hear other archaic terms no longer in general circulation."

"For example?"

"Well, shortly you may become *chaetognathous*."

"Meaning?"

"Hairy jawed."

"And?"

"In polite company you might find yourselves discussing ornamental *capillamenta*."

"Meaning?"

"Chin wigs."

"Anything else?"

He paused.

"*Merkins*." I waited for a translation. "Pubic wigs." I realised we had come to a very curious and perverse place indeed, although I couldn't help wondering how a pubic wig might suit me.

"I'm afraid your dictionary can't help you now," he continued. "Best just get used to these terms and familiarise yourself with the various beard types. The Van Dyke, Maltese, Dutch Elongated and Hibernator are but a few. Have you read *Whiskers of the World*?"

"Not that I can recall."

"It's the hairy *Tao Te Ching*," said Pantling. "The definitive work. It discusses pogonomancy at length."

"Can you give me any pointers?"

"Well, in the 21st century we would consider it a pseudoscience, much like palmistry or phrenology, the study of the skull's surface. It stems from a period when beards played an important role in the social order. The ancients believed follicles opened the pores and cleared the mind, and that the more substantial the beard the more likely you were to be a great thinker; perhaps a poet or philosopher. It's no accident that the biblical prophets are always depicted bearded and indeed that our vision of God is a man with the ultimate Hibernator. A modern day remnant of this can be seen in the many faiths – Islam, Orthodox Judaism, Sikhism among them – which give the beard religious significance.

"The great and the good have always been barbed. Take for example kings throughout history, they positively embraced beardliness. And our authors have been permanently fuzzy." This much I knew. Writers appear to have been beardy since the beginning of time and even today continue to be amongst the worst offenders in chin hygiene. I asked Pantling if having a beard was a prerequisite of great writing.

"It may help some way in the authorial process," he replied. "I mean, how many clean-shaven scribes can you think of?"

"Only JK Rowling," I replied.

"I personally believe George Bernard Shaw could have written *Pygmalion* without vast swathes of cotton candy dangling from his chin. It would have been easier too, not having to disentangle his nib from the stuff every few minutes. But Shaw was drawn into the murky world of beard divination at an early age. He consulted a pogonomancer who saw literary greatness in his fledgling chinwear, and old GB was loath to interfere with it thereafter. In this case the pogonomancer turned out to be correct, even though Shaw's wife never forgave him.

"But don't forget, it wasn't just beards that our forefathers were passionate about. Hair styling in general was the mark of a civilised society, so it was understandable that hairpieces would become status symbols. You see it from the Romans to Queen Elizabeth, and in the first American presidents. Returning to the wordmongers, Shelley and Byron used to see who could tease out the greatest ornamental bouffs and often came to blows over them.

"And whilst it may be tempting to suggest the practice died out many years ago, here at the Faculty of Advocates I am confronted daily with evidence to the contrary."

"Wigs?" I asked.

"Exactly. Counsel members are bewigged throughout much of their working day and despite the seasonal discomfort most would never dream of casting them aside. Not everybody gets to wear a wig, you see. So from the standpoint of hair marking out important individuals, pogonomancy – believing that a beard's appearance can give insight into not only the wearer's character but to his fate – is not such a great leap."

"For a discredited art," I said, "you seem to know an awful lot about it."

"I can tell you about phrenology too."

"Now that you mention it, why *did* the faculty medic measure my head?"

"Boaks, in order to understand the Westerians we must know their ways. Had you been bearded, Dr Seward would certainly have attempted a reading, although he is a hopeless pogonomancer. His phrenological insight on the other hand is remarkable. I recall on one occasion after fumbling with my bonce for a matter of seconds, he told me I'd meet a tall dark stranger. Later that very day I was arrested for shoplifting."

"Impressive," I said.

"There aren't many practising pogonomancers in our part of the world but in Wester you're likely to meet many. They may be best avoided."

"How will I know them?"

"They'll plant your head in an electrical device and measure the odylic force of your beard."

"I see," I said. "I'll look out for that."

"But it's unlikely to happen against your will. In Wester good pogon-omancers are highly valued. Readings are expensive."

"Why didn't you just say I couldn't afford one?"

"Because frankly you might eventually find that no price is too high. A beard can become fascinating to the wearer, and the longer you have been without a razor the more fascinating it may be. You can end up believing it has powers; that your fate is in fact written in your beard. But once you start down this path you're discarding rational scientific thought in favour of an arbitrary system of rules dictated by ancient kooks. It's like believing in astrology. Or magic."

It was a lot to take in. I considered telling him about LaFlamme's system of rationing information and asking him to adopt it where I was concerned. Then I thought I might be able to pass some of Pantling's information to LaFlamme, have her store it for a while and feed it back to me in stages.

LaFlamme was making coffee. "Old Pantless says we're going to a place where they can tell your fortune by reading your beard," I said.

"So that's why you have one underway," she replied.

"Well no, it's because I don't have a razor."

"I thought you were joking."

"Why would I joke about that?"

"I agree it's a serious matter," said LaFlamme. "Are you telling me you're growing a beard?"

"I'm not *premeditatively* growing a beard, but circumstances may be conspiring against me in such a manner as to produce a beard regardless."

"Couldn't we adjust your circumstances to produce a different result?"

"In theory," I replied. "But in practice that would mean heading back to base to find appropriate tools for the job. Because by the looks of things, it's not going to happen in Wester."

"You're refusing to do anything about it?" asked LaFlamme.

"What do you suggest?"

"I don't know. Do we have a saw?"

"I'm not about to saw my beard off."

"What about hormones?"

"You might not like me with a beard, but I'm pretty sure you'd like me even less with man boobs."

"They're called moobs."

"Whatever, it's not a good look for me. And you're forgetting something – if we can't find a razor, we sure as hell won't be able to find hormones. It looks like I'm growing a beard."

LaFlamme continued to rack her considerable brain for a solution but eventually seemed resigned to my impending beardiness. "How long do you have left?" she asked, as if I'd been handed a death sentence.

"I don't know," I replied. "I've never accidentally grown a beard before. It could take weeks. I'm likely to be borderline beardy for some time."

I turned my gaze to the window and only then realised we were in unfamiliar territory. "Are we moving?" I said, although it was a particularly inane question even for me. The dense Wester landscape was hurtling past at a rate of knots, which in this case was probably around three miles an hour. It was a testament to Mr Beard's driving that I wasn't even aware we were on the move, but this journey was definitely not going the way I planned.

I wanted to open up to LaFlamme. I could tell her I'd changed my mind about LeSnide and the outstanding design bill, suggest we turn back and hole up somewhere that was *conducive* to drinking champagne from her navel. But this probably wasn't the moment. I was feeling weepy, and weepiness was not likely to result in the champagne/navel combination I craved, unless I wanted to try it with Corky.

I lay back on one of the dining area benches, which had doubled as my bunk the night before. Soon the gentle drone of the engine and my lack of sleep conspired with the heat and I found myself drifting off. Just as it only took the absence of light to send LaFlamme to sleep, any continuous droning sound – a vacuum cleaner, lawnmower, computer, The Admiral – was for me generally zed-inducing. In the case of the computer this was unfortunate because I already spent more time at my desk asleep than awake.

But if life has taught me anything, which is debatable, it's that after continuous droning there is no better alarm clock than silence. When the engine was cut, my eyes blinked open and I slipped off the bench, crashing to the rough-hewn carpeted floor. Mr Beard called down to us. We had reached a bar he called 'The Folly' and were moored directly outside. LaFlamme and I wasted no time in preparing to disembark, as we were still making the utmost effort to maintain our diet.

We left Mr Beard and Corky to deal with the gauges, ensuring their gin had been amply replenished. "I only drink to forget, you know," said Corky, his swivelly wooden eyes following LaFlamme. "But try as I might, I can't forget you."

'The Folly' turned out to be The Jolly Follicle, a splendid old Tudor style building with a wildly unkempt thatched roof. It reminded me of Dylan in his prime. Inside hung a couple of overhead fans suspended from the ceiling. This was a blessing because the air could have been cubed and sold to historians as an example of fetid canalside atmosphere. We ordered fish pie and gin and sat directly under one of them.

"Is there a special ale?" said LaFlamme. I scanned the beer taps and realised once again I might have some difficulty ordering.

"I refuse to ask for such a ridiculously named beer," I said to LaFlamme.

"Which one?" she asked.

"The one with the kilted bloke and the caber."

"Don't be such a pussy," she replied. "The specials are obviously the best beers in the world. The Admiral would be envious."

"But we just ordered gin," I said.

"Holiday," she reminded me.

I sighed and reluctantly made the trip back to the bar, ordering two pints of Big Tosser.

Returning red-faced with the drinks, I was suitably emboldened to then ask LaFlamme what we were going to do with the hobgoblins.

"There's plenty room," she said.

"We can't let them stay with us."

"Well, we can't just drop them off either. We're miles from where we found them. Besides, look how well they're managing the boat. They're like the help."

"But where are they going to sleep?"

"We could make the bedroom the servants' quarters. You and I could take the twin bunks." This would mean LaFlamme and I having adjoining beds in the converted dining area, something that thrilled and terrified me in equal measure.

"Okay then," I said, practically tripping over the words in my eagerness.

With the issue settled and an agreement to divvy up the potentially substantial final gin bill, I expected LaFlamme to be at ease. But something else was troubling her. "Is it my stubble?" I said.

"Obviously it's not ideal," she said, poking it with her finger. "Especially as it's more like soft fur than actual stubble. But that's not it."

"What is?"

"The future," she replied. It was most unlike LaFlamme to be concerned about the future, the past, or anything else for that matter. I wondered if she had succumbed to some local malaise. It could be cholera, a stroke, or even the early signs of dementia. I asked her if she was getting forgetful. She said she'd forget I asked.

"Not the future as such," LaFlamme continued. "Horoscopes."

"What about them?"

"I think they might be silly."

"You had to read *Magic and the Twelve Signs of the Zodiac* to work that out?" I asked.

"*Magic and the Twelve Signs of the Zodiac* was very instructive," she replied.

"So what made you realise they were silly?"

"*Cosmopolitan.*"

For LaFlamme to be one of the last people in the Western world to realise something so blindingly obvious was rare and definitely symptomatic of fever. I asked her if she wanted to lie down. She gave me such a withering look that I thought my shades might break.

"I mean," she said, "the moon's in the second house of our lady of the cups so you're going to find love? The solstice is approaching your ruling planet Saturn so you're entering a new financial phase with an accountant called Derek?"

"Did you really think *Toady* magazine wanted you to plot the movements of the planets and predict the future?"

"I didn't see the problem. I told you I was psychic. But I suppose this makes the job easier."

"How?"

"If it's silly, I can just make it up."

"Well duh," I said in exaggerated fashion. (I like to milk any odd fleeting moments that might highlight my intellectual edge.) "It's entertainment. People go along with it because it's fun. But really, astrology, phrenology, magic – it's all very, *very* silly."

"Magic is real," said LaFlamme. I waited for her to say she was only teasing or that it was real in the sense that it was unreal. Or something. LaFlamme had an answer for everything. But either she was very sick or she was serious. Now I was troubled too and, like Corky, began drinking to forget.

By the end of the afternoon I'd pretty much forgotten everything and that suited me fine. Outside The Jolly Follicle it had clouded over but was still stiflingly hot and as we stumbled onto The Little Hitler, Mr Beard looked upwards whilst eating sardines from a can.

"Rain ahead," he said.

"You saw a forecast?" I asked.

"I feel it in my beard," he replied. I thought it more likely to be sardines he was feeling in his beard, as he seemed to be having limited success getting them into his mouth. I wasn't even sure they were dead. He suggested we make progress before the eight o'clock curfew.

Setting off, I thought a rain shower might be just what was needed to cool things down. I was concerned that my heavy perspiration combined with the dehydrating effects of Old Tosser was going to leave me looking prematurely aged. I asked LaFlamme if she'd like some water.

"Only if you dilute it," she said.

"How do you dilute water?" I asked.

"You add the same amount of whisky."

"We don't have any. And anyway, you should be careful of dehydration. In these temperatures you can dry out pretty fast." She looked at my t-shirt. It was wringing wet. I'd have a better chance of drying in the rain.

By the time we moored it had grown dark; not the darkness of nightfall, but the darkness of an impending deluge from the skies. It was so murky inside the cabin we had to switch on two Art Deco tiffany lamps we normally only used after hours. There was a light peal of thunder in the distance and seconds later, heavy raindrops began pelting the rooftop, sporadic at first then building to something that sounded like a thousand Carl Palmers had decided to form a military band.

"I'm having déjà vu," said Corky, who had been oddly pensive all evening. "I remember a night like this many years ago."

"Is that so?" said Mr Beard.

"I believe it began in Granada," continued Corky, "where I'd been a guest of Pablo and Paloma."

"Picasso?" I said.

"McGlumpherty," he replied, raising his eyes skyward with contempt. "It rains so rarely in Andalusia. When it does, however, one might as well be standing below the Horseshoe Falls. I had just bid adieu to the little beady-eyed painter and his wife and begun the long drive north when the sky ahead turned the most appalling shade of mauve. It looked like heavy bruising. The ground was parched and cracking, clearly crying out for moisture, and I'd been sweating like chopped onion in vichyssoise since I left Paris, so I wasn't upset about a spot of rain. But it looked like I was driving into a solid wall of the stuff.

"I thought it might be thirty minutes away but I had the windows rolled down and could already smell that peculiar reaction rain has with dust. Most refreshing, I thought, until I was plunged into the thick of an artificial night and the lashing rain cut visibility to thirty feet. Luckily there was barely another car to be seen – there were very few cars on the roads in those days. Oxen were more common. I had to be terribly careful not to find myself on top of one at any moment.

"After a couple of hours, as well as the electrical storm raging above, I had the additional bother of *la noche*. It was so dark I thought my peepers had run out on me. By now I was on the plains and, there being precious little in the way of trees or other raised terrain, I became concerned that my little motor hurtling through the muddy wilderness would make a fine target for the wrath of God – especially as the driver was no angel and had long since given up on any future encounters with Saint Peter. The skies discharged their electrical tridents into the atmosphere with an alarming frequency, each followed by a thunderous roar. For a split second the landscape was bathed in vivid blue light and I caught a glimpse of the normally arid terrain.

"But when the vivid blue light also picked out a female form standing in the middle of the road, I had to swerve suddenly in order to avoid her. I lost control of the vehicle, careered onto the verge and thence into a field. When I finally came to rest I smacked my head against the windshield, but was otherwise unhurt."

"Lucky to be alive," said Mr Beard.

"Yes," said Corky. "But I was more concerned about what had caused me to swerve. I got out to see if there was any sign of the woman I had very nearly mown down. But the only light was a distant glow back in old Granada and I soon gave up any hope of seeing anything much at all. I hopped back into the car thinking if I could turn the headlights onto the road I might be able to illuminate the scene. But now the car wouldn't start.

"I was in two minds. The best course of action might have been to stay there and wait until morning, but as my eyes grew more accustomed to the dark I spotted houselights a few hundred yards ahead. I thought if it was a farm, I might be able to use their telephone or even get assistance towing the car out of the field. So I risked being struck down by one of the almighty's electric char sticks and stepped out.

"It was indeed a farmhouse and, other than a few related buildings, was completely isolated. I was soaked to the skin by the time I reached the front door and felt I had very little to lose. Well imagine how I felt when the door was answered by a beautiful young girl wearing a silk white nightgown. She introduced herself as Juanita. She couldn't have been more than twenty and had long blond hair, which was most unusual for the region. I'm terribly sorry to trouble you, I said, but my car's broken down and I wondered if I might use your telephone. It's no trouble, she said, come in. In fact she seemed quite pleased to have company and led me through to a rather sumptuous drawing room with a roaring log fire. This was surprising as despite the storm it was still a stiflingly hot night. But inside, the house had a chill to it that was quite pleasing to the senses.

"The little dear provided me with a fine cotton dressing gown, insisted I get out of my wet things and hung them to dry by the fire. Where are your parents? I asked. She said they had died long ago and she was all alone. I don't mind telling you I began to think crashing the car was a fantastic stroke of luck. When she asked if I was hungry and if I'd care for some wine, I had a mind to take up residence.

"She drummed up a fairly elaborate feast; cured Andalusian meats, smoked cheeses, bread and fruit. And over a carafe of wine, she spoke about her home – a splendid example of Moorish architecture – and the paintings, mostly Spanish romantics, which adorned its walls. We rounded the evening off with a brandy and I have to say I can't recall a more delightful evening. However, it was getting late and I felt I'd already outstayed my welcome. Then little Juanita said she had prepared a room for me and I would find it *muy cómodo*.

"Now, a man with my reputation might have been inclined to take advantage of this situation. But the *muchacha* seemed such a fragile and delicate thing, I felt it would have been quite improper. So I behaved like a perfect gentleman, thanked her for her hospitality and turned in.

"I was just drifting off when I heard the creaking of my chamber door, followed by a light patter of footsteps. Juanita? I said. Shhh, she whispered, and slipped almost imperceptibly between the sheets. We embraced passionately and I felt her naked skin warm next to mine.

"Well, innocent or not, she held nothing back."

"Now Corky," said Mr Beard.

"She rode me like a Castilian donkey, and let me tell you, her cup quite runneth over."

"Oh my," said Mr Beard.

"She must have been saving it up, poor thing. Needless to say after that I slept like a babe in arms. It was a deep, satisfying sleep; I must have been out for ten hours. But when I awoke I knew immediately something was wrong. The air was musty with the smell of decay and my skin felt powdery to the touch. When I opened my eyes I found the bedclothes were in tatters and the powdery sensation was dust. Half of the floorboards were missing and those that remained were dry and rotten. The window frames had no glass, the ceiling had collapsed and above that I could see the sky through a gaping hole in the roof.

"I jumped up, dressed and made my way to the drawing room. It was in a similar state of decay. There was no sign of a fire, no remains of a feast, certainly no paintings on the walls, Spanish romantics or otherwise, and crucially, no Juanita. I got out of there *inmediatamente*, and just in time too. As I opened the front door, one of the roof beams collapsed into the hall where I'd stood just a moment before. Once I saw the building from the outside, it was obvious no one had lived there in decades.

"An old man was passing on a horse-drawn cart. *Perdón señor*, I said, *conoce a la señorita Juanita*? He was rather taken aback and looked over towards the derelict house. Juanita had been dead for many years, he said. An only child, she blamed her parents for her intense loneliness after they were unable to provide her with a sibling. When they passed on, the solitude became intolerable and she took her own life. The house had been empty ever since."

"Now Corky," said Mr Beard, "you know fine that's a tall tale."

"Tisn't," said Corky. "It was the best shag of my life!"

I recoiled in horror but LaFlamme was nonplussed. When a heavy burst of thunder split the air, Mr Beard said it was time to turn in.

"What are you going to sing tonight Corky?" said Mr Beard.

"'Sweet and Lovely'," said Corky. Without any further explanation, he launched into this serenade from a bygone era.

> Sweet and lovely
> Sweeter than the roses in May
> Sweet and lovely
> Heaven must have sent her my way
>
> Sweet and lovely
> Sweeter than the roses in May
> And if she loves me
> There is nothing more I can say

Corky's delivery was once again slow and melancholic, but tonight there was an added sense of loss about it. It displayed an emotional depth that I would not have thought existed in one so otherwise unpleasant. By the time he reached the final line I believe a tear fell from his eye – remarkable given that he was made of wood.

As Corky and Mr Beard retired, LaFlamme and I prepared our twin bunks. I wasn't sure I would be able to sleep. The idea that the object of my dreams was in a state of undress three feet away was not an altogether restful notion for me. "If you get cold in the night," said

LaFlamme, "Corky can heat you up." This may have been her way of flirting but somehow I doubted it.

By 2:00am the rain had been pouring down consistently for hours. And as if the drumming on the rooftop wouldn't be enough to ensure I had another sleepless night, Mr Beard and Corky kept up a continuous bickering dialogue through the partition and LaFlamme's foghorn snoring was on a par volume-wise with the frequent rumbles of thunder.

It was too hot, too loud and altogether too freaky. I switched on one of the tiffany lamps and LaFlamme immediately stopped snoring, yawned and sat up.

"Morning," she said. It looked like she was thinking about heading for the shower.

"What are you doing?" I asked.

"Getting up."

"It's 2:00am."

"Then why am I awake?"

"Because there's a raging typhoon outside."

Lightning filled the boat, and the time between each flash and the ensuing rumbles had shortened considerably, a sure sign that the trouble was raging directly above my head.

"I feel weird," I said, sweating profusely and starting to hyperventilate. "I'm not sure a boat is such a great place to be in a thunder storm." I looked out of the cabin window. The water was charged with electricity, little blue sparks dancing across its surface.

"Relax," said LaFlamme.

"How can I relax?" I said. "We need to get out of here. We could be electrocuted."

"Don't be ridiculous," said LaFlamme. "Beardy would tell us if it was dangerous."

"What if he's asleep? Maybe I should ask him." I jumped up and knocked on Mr Beard's door. The dialogue within stopped.

"Mr Beard," I said, opening the door. I could see only an indistinct mound of covers, but in a flash of lightning Corky appeared in silhouette, perched quite still and upright on the edge of the bed.

"What do you want?" said Corky.

"The storm," I said, unsure about broaching the subject with such an abrasive little man. "There's a terrible storm outside."

"You're quite the observant one, aren't you?" he replied.

"Are we safe?" I asked.

"That all depends," said Corky. "Were you thinking about going for a swim?" I wanted to tell him he probably shouldn't be so flippant, as being a wooden man in an electrical storm put him at a distinct disadvantage.

"Shouldn't we get out of the boat and onto land?" I said.

"I'll tell you what," said Corky. "I'll stay here, you go stand under those nice trees and we'll see which of us gets electrocuted first. And here, take this nice steel-tipped brolly so you have a head start."

"What would Mr Beard do in the circumstances?"

"It looks like he would sleep." He gestured towards Mr Beard, lifeless beneath the covers. "Pleasant dreams."

I withdrew from the cabin and made a mental note that, should LaFlamme ever master the art of telepathic combustion, Corky would make excellent kindling.

11.
DRY LAND IS JUST
A FIGURE OF SPEECH

I managed a few more hours sleep than expected due to the exhaustion of coping with Corky and other freakish elements of the Wester evening. I was far from rested when I awoke. Mercifully the rain had stopped, but the air was heavy with moisture and the thin sheet I used for a blanket was cool and clammy.

LaFlamme was writing. LaFlamme was always writing. She said somebody had to write something she'd want to read and, as no one else seemed to be up to the task, she'd have to do it herself.

Her unique take on the self-help genre had brought her a certain celebrity. *Help Yourself To Drink* and its follow-up *Help Yourself Two: Drink* were both publishing successes, although they say success in publishing is a limited form of success. Her guide for office drones, *365 Days of Mediocrity*, had also been warmly received by the worker ants for whom it was intended, with the *Times Literary Review* calling it a 'must-have for office stooges everywhere'.

Unfortunately none of this had translated into proper, grown-up money, as her publishers Vague, Vague and Steadfast claimed the 'paper tax' had eaten into a good deal of the profits. When challenged on this they said the 'ink tax' had also risen and that had LaFlamme used a smaller font, her royalties might have been more substantial.

As a consequence, LaFlamme still found it necessary to take on free-lance work. She wasn't particularly upset about this. When I suggested it was demeaning for somebody with her kind of talent, that she could do hack work in her sleep, she said sleep was a particularly boring time for her and it gave her something to do during the night.

This morning she was writing by hand in what looked like a diary or journal. I assumed she had finally begun her astrology assignment for *Toady* magazine – which was good, as work was likely to limit her desire to be difficult. But when I asked how the writing was going, she said "what writing?" then closed the journal and tucked it below her seat.

"The horoscopes," I said.

"Oh that," she replied, producing a second journal and handing it to me. This was interesting. She was working on two journals *concurrently*. "You tell me," she said.

I opened the journal and read the first set of forecasts.

Capricorn: Today you should think about your responsibilities and plan your day around how best to avoid them.

Aquarius: You will receive mixed messages – one from your boss telling you how things should be, another from your brain telling you he's an idiot.

Pisces: Don't just do what is being asked of you. If you give it one hundred and ten percent, your resentment will be all the more complete.

Aries: Your suggestions may not be going down well at work, but a Jack Daniels dispenser was always going to be problematic.

Taurus: Today your imagination will hold the key to your success. Best sit this one out.

Gemini: You must choose between your creative vision and reality. Unfortunately the reality is that your creative vision sucks.

"Are you sure this is what they want?" I asked her.

"Since when do I care what they want?" she replied.

She had a point. She wouldn't be LaFlamme if she cared what anybody wanted. If she cared what *I* wanted, we might be rolling around in bed discovering new and exotic sexual positions and giving them silly names. I would finally get the whole champagne navel thing going and only take enough time out of the bedroom to admit there was a God and to thank him profusely.

Right now I'd have settled for finding out what was in her other journal, as I suspected it might give me some insight and help me open the door to her heart. There was always the possibility that it was a secret diary revealing all her most intimate feelings, or a dream diary full of erotic encounters and intense sexual fantasies. But what if I discovered something I didn't want to know? What if she had a lover or had her sights set on someone other than me? What if she'd taken a shine to Corky? I did not need competition for LaFlamme's affections from a smooth-talking urbanite, even if he was made of wood.

My musing was drawn to an abrupt end when Corky called, "Up your bum, maties!"

"Good morning to you too," I said. I was careful not to let Mr Beard know there was friction between his associate and I, but there was one point I wanted to clear up.

"Would a boat be in any particular danger during an electrical storm?" I asked.

"Danger?" said Mr Beard. "No no no. Narrowboat has a big wooden hull. Acts as an earth."

"So that's why you were happy to sleep through it," I said.

"Through what?" he replied.

I wondered if I had imagined the whole thing. If Mr Beard didn't witness the storm, maybe it didn't happen. Maybe this was all an elaborate illusion dreamt up by some obsessive movie geek with too much money and a Marlon Brando fetish.

I began to question my state of mind. I didn't really think I was losing definition as such, but Mr Beard had taught me some basic boating terms (such as 'stern' – that's the back of the boat – and 'bow', pronounced as in 'wow' – that's the front) and I was proud of my newly acquired nautical jargon. This was surely a sign of an impending mental and physical breakdown.

Whilst everyone was otherwise occupied, I took the opportunity for a moment's calm reflection in our little verandah at the bow. I was shoeless, soaked in perspiration, and stroking my borderline beard when another narrowboat approached on our 'port' side. (That's left to you civilians, and obviously the correct procedure for passing. We stick to the right on waterways at all times.)

We'd seen many such narrowboats pass during the course of our journey and this one was only unusual in that the face of its skipper looked familiar. He was lightly bearded, a chin status similar to my own, and wore Indiana Jones khakis – with a tie. He looked shiftily around at first, pretending he hadn't seen me. Eventually he cast a half-hearted wave, then stopped the boat and reversed until he was just a stone's throw away. It was Suave Gav.

"Heading to Wester?" said Suave Gav.

"Yes," I replied.

"Any particular reason?"

"Fashion," I said, scratching my beard and watching various indeterminate items fall from it. "I've heard it's gloriously unkempt down there. Thought I would see if there was any truth in the rumour that after a week without washing it's impossible to accumulate any more dirt." If I was going to have a mental and physical breakdown, I might as well enjoy it.

"Good for you," said Suave Gav. "I like a man who pushes the envelope. Join me for elevenses after the next lock?" He revved his engine and began to move off.

It struck me that this breakdown might be liberating. I mean, I wasn't feeling remotely constrained by social etiquette or the niceties of conversational interaction. I was in fact being deliberately obtuse and obscure and still getting invited for drinks. Maybe if I were all-out obnoxious it would extend to dinner. This might be similar to what LeSnide had experienced, although I hadn't yet felt any inclination to commandeer a tribe of indigenous people.

To celebrate being freed from the shackles of social etiquette, I thought I would hop onto the rooftop and take a nap whilst The Little Hitler took us further into the wilds. The sun was still in the process of burning off the morning haze, far from its blazing mid-afternoon peak, and the extra shut-eye would be welcome. I would embrace my ill-definition, be as difficult as I pleased and let everybody else work around me.

This was fine in theory but when I woke up over an hour later, I was soaking wet and Corky was barking at me across the rooftop.

"You there," he said. "Have you even a modicum of intelligence? What the devil are you playing at?"

"Now Corky," said Mr Beard.

"I was asleep," I said. "Do you mind?"

"*Do you mind?*" he parroted in a whiny little voice that was meant to resemble my own. I hoped to hell I didn't actually sound like that, because if so I would have to enrol immediately in the Lee Marvin school of elocution. "Do you mind getting your arse onto the towpath and working the lock before we stagnate any further in this rancid cesspool?"

Was it time we stopped leaving tokens for the hobgoblins and set them free? The little one, although knowledgeable and a fine raconteur, had begun to turn nasty. I didn't see why he had to flaunt his intelligence and be so utterly disagreeable all the time. Perhaps it went with the territory. Maybe David Starkey is also from around here.

My concern was that keeping them onboard like this might have domesticated them. If such was the case, turning them loose at this stage could be cruel – they may have lost their survival skills outwith The Little Hitler. This was something the BBC must have had to grapple with over Starkey, but I imagine after setting him free they were satisfied they'd made the right decision.

Hopping down from my makeshift bunk, I realised the front of my clothes were wet and there was a perfectly dry impression of my splayed-out body on the rooftop. Clearly it had rained whilst I was out for the count, but my ill-definition offered me the luxury of being philosophical. I felt inclined to suggest that the impression might be my past. This Boaks-shaped rain-free strip could be considered the physical manifestation of everything that had happened to me in the last hour, and may even contain dreams. But given that my future involved climbing up a ladder and probably falling in the canal, I thought I'd had enough philosophy.

"What's up?" said LaFlamme, scribbling as I made my way through the cabin.

"It's time for the boat to go uphill," I said.

"Like in that movie?" said LaFlamme.

"I'm hoping it'll be a bit easier than *Fitzcarraldo*, but we'll see. Care to join me?"

"Do I look like someone who climbs ladders?" she said.

As I was leaving, I told her I'd seen Suave Gav and that he did his best to ignore me. "Are you sure it was him?" said LaFlamme.

"Yes," I replied. "He was chewing a twig."

"Why would he ignore you?"

"Well, I was dangling my feet out of the boat at the time. Maybe I looked common."

"Was he holding his nose?"

"He was holding his toupée."

Mr Beard drove us into the shallow side of the great lock. I'd read the back cover of *Three Men In A Boat* earlier and looked at the illustrations, so I knew there was huge comic potential in operating one of these masterpieces of Victorian engineering. I would have to climb out of the lock using a rickety metal ladder attached to the canal wall, close the shallow end gates behind us, open the paddles so the shallow end filled with water and raised the boat a good eight or nine feet, then open the opposite gates before jumping back onboard. It would mean crossing the canal at least twice over narrow slippery gates. This less than thrilling process would take around twenty minutes to complete due mostly to the time it takes to fill a lock with water. If you can imagine Lilliputians running a bath for Gulliver you'll get the idea, and in my case the bath analogy was likely to be fitting.

But surprisingly, twenty minutes later Mr Beard sailed The Little Hitler out the other side of the lock, I jumped back on board, and we continued our journey without incident. "What was so funny about that?" asked LaFlamme when I rejoined her. I said I wasn't there purely for her amusement and that it was likely to take several more novels before I felt ready to take on Jerome K Jerome.

Eyeing Suave Gav on the towpath ahead, I asked Mr Beard to moor behind his boat, The Inebriate, and shortly LaFlamme and I stepped out to join him. Corky leered at LaFlamme as she crossed the threshold. "Mind how you go, gorgeous," he said, checking her tight little skirt from behind. I gave him a filthy look and asked him if he'd seen enough.

"I've seen enough of you," he said and called me a dullard, which was entirely unnecessary.

"Aha!" called Suave Gav as we stepped onto the towpath. "Welcome, my fellow phlobophenics. Armstrong, Gavin." He was holding a stem glass and waving an olive on a cocktail stick. "Dry land is purely a figure of speech, you know."

"Glad to hear it," said LaFlamme. Suave Gav stepped daintily back onto the stern of The Inebriate, produced two more chilled glasses from a cabinet and filled them from a cocktail shaker, taking great care whilst adding olives.

"It's not the ideal medicine cabinet," he said, passing the glasses across the threshold, "but any old port in a storm, as they say."

The Inebriate and The Little Hitler may have been similar in overall design, but from what I could make out the interior of the former was markedly different from the latter. The kitchen had an extended, very well-stocked bar and floor to ceiling shelved larder, its contents on the verge of bursting through its glass front casing. Clearly Suave Gav had no intention of gastronomically roughing it.

The living room looked less like an area for relaxation and more like a chemistry lab had collided with a garden centre. On the starboard side an elongated worktop was decked with vials, test tubes, microscopes and other scientific apparatus. At its far end a Bunsen burner carried a low flame and above it a large carafe bubbled with a dark molasses-like liquid within. Beneath the countertops were roughly cut logs, branches and twigs, as if fuel for a wood burning stove. The port side resembled an allotment with raised beds of earth and a wide variety of plants, most of which I assumed were edible judging from the herbal aroma. I pictured Suave Gav tending his crops whilst strolling through the channel between these two adapted spaces, at times fastidious, at others weaving wildly.

"Food science?" I said.

"I might have called it that," he replied, "had the term not been so utterly debased by the antics of celebrity chefs. I mean, just because you look like a Tefal man doesn't mean you invented the kettle."

"Sandwich makers," said LaFlamme dismissively.

"I could wear glasses and shave my head too. In fact I have done. It was high summer at the time and I had taken to wearing a bright orange dress shirt. Unfortunately a group of Hare Krishna devotees mistook me for one of their own and I was shipped off to Nepal. I protested but the Krishnas can be very persuasive. Eventually I began to find dancing at airports hugely fulfilling. It was only when my wife intervened that they realised their error and sent me home. I try to avoid bright colours now. Still – *gouranga!*"

"*Gouranga?*" I said.

"Be happy."

He had taken his abduction very well, which made me think he had studied and practised one of the fundamentals of Krishna's teaching: acceptance. If I'd been snatched by the robed ones I doubt I'd be so tolerant, flapping around like a diddy, handing out flowers and saying 'be happy' to anyone who would listen. It's more likely I'd be saying 'allow me to enlighten you with the flat side of this Tefal iron, and let me just plug it in first'. I'd translate it into Nepalese though, and practise acceptance in that I would accept they were in pain.

"Then there's the *River Cottage* chap," said Suave Gav, continuing his critique. "Whenever he appears, something has to die. It's like clockwork. I know the man likes his meat but what kind of karma can he enjoy if every meal involves slaughter?"

"Meat is murder," I said, because I remembered someone else saying it. I could just as easily have said 'the queen is dead' but that might have been unusual in this context.

"And he always insists on stuffing one beast within another. Good lord, as if it wasn't appalling enough to be reared as food, you then have the indignity of being rammed inside another poor critter just to satisfy the twisted cravings of some decadent waster toff." I thought it was probably best to divert him from the topic before he took on Jamie Oliver, as it would take more than a couple of exchanges to summarise one who was more irritant than man.

"So what brings you to Wester?" I said. His eyes shifted sideways in order to avoid contact with ours.

"Ingredients?" he said, once again testing the extent of our gullibility.

"What are you working on?" asked LaFlamme.

"Working on?" he replied, as if the contents of The Inebriate were standard fittings for narrowboats. Once he realised we were referring to the incredible array of gardening and chemical paraphernalia in the cabin, he said finally, "Punch."

"Punch?" we chimed.

"Ingredients for punch are plentiful in this part of the world." Now he looked downright *nefarious*.

"It's a bit elaborate for punch," said LaFlamme.

"It's a bit of an elaborate punch," he replied. "Did you know by the way that punch originated in 17th century India? Naturally there are many international variants but it stems from the Hindi word 'panch.'"

"How about that," said LaFlamme. She may have been unimpressed but this little history lesson gave me a renewed respect for the Hindu faith. I always wondered who discovered how to get trashed at student parties in three seconds flat. Apparently the original drink was made with alcohol, lemon, tea and spices. Now of course it's only ever made with vodka and whatever was festering in the fruit bowl in the first place.

But I suspected what Suave Gav was calling punch was a variant of what The Admiral and I called Project X. It seemed strange that having once conferred over a possible hangover cure, he now felt the need to deny he was developing one. It aroused my competitive instinct, something which had lain dormant since I first discovered the connection between losing and failure. Now I wanted to rise to the challenge, take the bull by the horns and tell The Admiral to get back to work.

I began fantasising about the moment the Nobel Institute recognised Project X and awarded us the coveted prize for science. "You have saved us all," declares the committee chairman, "from a life of needless moderation." A weeping Suave Gav is seated amongst the invited guests, inconsolable.

"It may take some time to perfect," said the gastrophile of his alleged punch. "Rome was not built in a day. And just as Signor Buonarotti devoted much of his life to perching atop a scaffold before unveiling his Charles Atlas vision of The Bible, I too must suffer for what will surely be my life's greatest work." This was something of a giveaway. Even the creator of the world's finest punch was unlikely to describe it as his life's greatest work. It was positively *duplicitous*.

We took over a nearby picnic bench, a refugee from one of the inns where beards lunched peacefully. Either the bench had been shunned by the others or had tried to escape, possibly intimidated by the abundance of Hibernators in the area.

"I see you're having the same bother," said Suave Gav, eyeing the random tufts of down on my chin. He drew my attention to his own facial growth, which I would have said was about a week's worth. "It's the damnedest thing. Would you believe I shaved not three hours ago? Must be the salty air. The follicles sense a drought and start making exploratory searches. I've a mind to seal up the pores the next time I shave."

"But who knows where the hairs might spring from then," said LaFlamme.

"Count your blessings." I said.

"Well indeed," said Suave Gav. "It's just that I'm a city man through and through, and ordinarily one would never dream of leaving the house in such a state. But I suppose it's a small price to pay for getting away from it all, don't you think? The tranquillity, the air quality, dare I say even the wildlife. The other day I had moored and was just settling down to a predinner martini on the deck when I was approached by a savage looking beast with a red headdress."

"Cherokee?" said LaFlamme.

"Chicken," replied Suave Gav. "A little one with huge reptilian feet. Let me tell you, city life does not prepare one for such encounters. The closest we urban cave dwellers come to fowl is at the cold cuts counter, where of course they've been suitably tamed. I confess my first thought was 'should I be afraid?' and my second, 'will it bite?' Before I could think of a third the little demon had climbed aboard and was making for my herbavorium.

"My initial efforts to shoo her from the premises were met with undisguised contempt. I thought standing in the way might discourage her but she easily body swerved me and continued regardless. Well, I thought, if it's a question of protecting my precious herbs it's time for a showdown."

"What did you do?" I asked.

"I made a lunge and secured the beast in my hands."

"Brave," said LaFlamme. "I wouldn't mess with anything that pecks."

"The thing is," said Suave Gav, "the sensation of holding this creature between my palms was quite extraordinary. It was warm and soft to the touch, and I felt its pulsing life force in my hands. It made no effort to struggle free or, heaven forbid, harass me with its beak – I might have fainted if it had. Instead I was able to step onto the towpath and set her down without much fuss. She looked at me then and I felt that we had a moment. There was something bordering on empathy.

"She seemed disinclined to attempt a reboarding, so I picked off some marjoram and sage leaves and left them for her on the towpath. She pecked at these with delight. It was clear they were a rare treat that she could likely smell some way off. Naturally my organic herbs are exquisite so I can hardly blame her."

"It's a lovely story," I said, as you would if someone just told you they'd bonded with a chicken.

"You may scoff," said Suave Gav, "but the point is if more *urbanos* experienced a chicken in this manner, which is to say another sentient being that's rather beautiful in its own odd little way, rather than an abstract piece of food prepared for their table, they might not be so quick to devour them."

"I know what they should do," said LaFlamme. "Instead of those nice pictures of roasts with vegetables and gravy on the packaging, they should use pinups of the chickens while they were still running around – poultry publicity shots. They could even name the individual on the package and add a few biographical notes so you got to know a little about who you were going to eat."

"That's disgusting," I said.

Suave Gav guffawed loudly. "You're both right!" he said. "But this is precisely the problem. What you see in *le supermarché* is so divorced from reality that all sense of what a chicken really is has been removed. It's not food, it's a little being that likes herbs as much as I do."

"Is grass a herb?" I asked, a tad distracted. "It's just that I once saw a chicken tear up a whole lawn."

"I have to say though," said Suave Gav, paying little attention, "I'm surprised the chooks would need to trouble my little herbavorium. In this neck of the woods most species can be found growing wild. The soil is rich, you see. Nature's larder was never more abundant."

Suave Gav said all this talk of herbs was making him rather hungry and asked if we had eaten. He took us to The Hairy Hamlet, a nearby inn he recommended for its fine vegetarian cuisine. It would be a break from our usual diet of fish pie and gin but I thought one day off wouldn't do us any harm.

We dined heartily and consumed a great deal of white wine, which Suave Gav selected with the eye of one who selects regularly. I had something called 'roasted squash with sage and pecorino'. I had no idea what it was, as 'roasted' was the only word I recognised. But it was a triumph. By the time I was finished I'd nearly forgotten there was no meat in it.

I took the opportunity to ask after Suave Gav's wife Ethel and his stylish friends Dick and Jane. Hadn't they any interest in joining him on his trip to Wester?

"Not for the faint of heart, Mr Boaks," he replied. "The ladies were appalled at the mere mention of shared facilities and that was before I told Ethel the only sunken bath was the canal itself. It's certainly not advisable to get in there with your Imperial Leather. And Dick of course refuses to be seen in the evening outside of a dinner suit. When I explained to him that his suit was likely to dissolve in the mouths of a million gnats before we'd even begun our entrées, he didn't need to think twice about the matter."

"Surely he could have donned casuals for the occasion?" said LaFlamme.

"Dick does not have the sartorial flexibility that you or I might," said Suave Gav. "He refuses to admit that khaki is even a word. And as for a collarless shirt, well he'd be more willing to don an Elizabethan ruffle than embarrass himself with something that has no means of affixing a tie."

Come to think of it, Suave Gav aside, I hadn't seen a single tie the entire trip. I suppose with beards being the order of the day, ties had little chance of making their presence known. The Westerians might *all* be wearing ties without us knowing. There would have to be some serious foraging amongst the straw before we found out, but I doubted anyone was that brave.

"It's very unfortunate," said Suave Gav, "because I know for a fact they would simply adore the Westerchestershire countryside." He pronounced this impeccably. He must have been practising for days.

Suave Gav surveyed the landscape through The Hairy Hamlet's large bay window. It sloped down to the water, which was partially obscured by dense bushes and a line of trees. "It's very Monetesque, wouldn't you agree?" he said.

"Oh yes, very," I said. "What does that mean?"

"Impressionist master. Regular at the *Salon des Refusés*. Beardy."

"They were all beardy," said LaFlamme. "Nothing but beards lining the Seine."

"Judging from their self-portraits, I'd have to agree. I suppose they could have grown them specially for the occasion but that seems unlikely. Can't imagine old Claude noting in his diary, 'self-portrait three weeks on Tuesday. Cease all shaving from tomorrow'. But you never know with those artists. They're a contrary lot. I suppose had the Impressionists been native to Wester rather than Paris, they'd have had no need to mark their diaries. They could shave in the morning, work on their landscapes, then tackle the self-portraits after lunch when the confounded whiskers had made their way south.

"Of course," continued Suave Gav, "their composer counterparts could provide us with the ideal soundtrack for this little idyll. I can almost hear 'La Mer' as we speak, and 'Daphnis and Chloe' have never been too far from my mind. Now there was a clean-shaven man."

"Daphnis?" said LaFlamme. "Or Chloe?"

"Ravel," he replied. "Neat little chap noted for his good hygiene. Most rare amongst composers. Needless to say he was barking mad, which would probably explain his meticulousness."

"Didn't he write that skating song?" I said.

"Indeed," said Suave Gav. "And despite what those prancing nincompoops did to 'Bolero' it remains a fine example of his oeuvre. But it is also a fine example of his madness."

"Nice tune," said LaFlamme. "Bit long."

"It does have a nice tune – repeated nine times in the same key at the same tempo over the course of fifteen minutes. Doesn't that strike you as unusual?"

"You should hear the Velvet Underground," I said.

"By the time the piece reaches its closing bars, the conductor generally has to snap his fingers in order to bring the audience out of the hypnosis caused by the composer's monomaniacal neuropathy. The reason it receives such ecstatic reception after its climactic finale is that listeners are relieved something has finally happened."

"I kind of like it," said LaFlamme.

"There's much to like. Of course the reason it works is that, as well as being a master of hypnosis, the clean little man was also a colourist of note. The infernal theme may not develop, but its delivery does. He called it 'a piece for orchestra without music.'"

This description reinforced the similarities I was seeing between Ravel and the Velvet Underground. There was no doubt that 'Sister Ray', a twenty-minute freeform barrage, was a 'piece for band without music'. I felt sure that its flailing violist John Cale would approve of this, my very first lofty musical notion. In fact I felt a sudden urge to deconstruct 'Sister Ray' in Suave Gav fashion but hastily recalled the words of Dr Seward as he clapped his pincers around my head – I should resist the urge to expound my newly acquired intellectual opinions. Suave Gav was lucky. He didn't know how close he came to hearing my thoughts about one of indie rock's loudest songs. He was even luckier he didn't have to hear the song.

"Of course, I prefer my art slightly more cerebral," said Suave Gav. "Marcel Duchamp for instance."

"Not keen on mime," said LaFlamme.

"*Duchamp*," replied Suave Gav, as if repeating the name with emphasis would prompt us to recall a full and comprehensive knowledge of Western culture. I vowed there and then to at least skim the mighty art tome back at The Little Hitler.

"Great Dadaist. Drew a moustache on the Mona Lisa and titled it 'L-H-O-O-Q'. Doesn't mean anything in English, but if you pronounce it in French you get '*elle a chaud au cul*'." LaFlamme raised her eyebrows, but being in Piafese I had to ask for a translation. "She has a hot ass," replied Suave Gav. For a sophisticated urbanite he was not incapable of coarseness.

"Duchamp eventually gave up art and went on to devote his life to chess."

"He wasted his time thinking up stupid puzzles then moved on to an even bigger waste of time?" said LaFlamme.

"How bored would you have to be?" I said.

"Presumably it was after that he started dressing like a clown and pretending to be stuck in a glass case?" said LaFlamme. Suave Gav must have realised then that we were interested in Dada only as much as an average two-year-old might be, but he took this in good grace and laughed it off.

As the afternoon was wearing on he suggested we think about setting off again. LaFlamme pretended to be stuck in a glass case and said she couldn't because she was trapped.

On the way back to our mooring point Suave Gav produced a pair of mini secateurs, bent down and clipped a low branch from a spindly looking bush. He placed the clipped end in his mouth and began to chew it.

"So come on chaps," he said, "I heard your little jest about the Wester fashions. What really brings you here?"

"We're on a mission to track down The Advocate for Self-Importance," I replied. "He's going to bestow me with riches and grant the power of telepathic combustion to my shipmate."

"Is he now?" said Suave Gav with the utmost gravity. "He must be a very powerful wizard."

"Alchemist," said LaFlamme.

"Alchemist you say? In that case I think I should very much like to meet him myself. You don't mind me tagging along, do you?" After such a fortifying meal I wouldn't have minded the devil himself tagging along, never mind his gastronomic embodiment.

Back at The Little Hitler, Mr Beard started the engine and we set off to try and grab a few more miles in the few hours left before curfew. "About effing time," Corky said to me before smiling ingratiatingly at LaFlamme.

I was so tired that part of my brain had already wandered into that otherworldly land between waking and sleep. I probably could have remained compos mentis for a while with a pep talk, telling myself that if this mission was to be a success it would require monumental determination, unwavering commitment, the courage of ten men and their combined beard powers. But I made the mistake of lying back on the kitchen table, my legs draped over the end. With the droning sound of the engine in the background it was inevitable that I'd soon fade.

The next thing I was aware of was Corky's voice – a sweet and gentle voice in marked contrast to its host's personality. It was another of his 1920s ballads. These haunting renditions of old songs were increasingly creeping me out and helping to ensure my nighttime sleep remained completely unattainable.

> Did you ever see a dream walking
> Well I did
> Did you ever hear a dream talking
> Well I did

I sat up abruptly, sweat having glued the map of Wester to the side of my face. This was undignified in the presence of the crew but by now they had seen far worse. More concerning were the words that first registered after peeling the map from my face. Far from the tight clusters of symbols concentrated on the winding canal was an area labelled 'potentilla fields'. Suave Gav's real intention was suddenly confirmed. This was no punch he was working on. He meant to refine the mental torment plant into a workable morning-after cure, patent it and claim the Nobel Prize for himself.

> Did you ever find heaven right in your arms
> saying I love you, I do
> Well the dream that was walking
> and the dream that was talking
> and the heaven in my arms was you

With this, mercifully, Mr Beard and Corky retired. "See you at dawn's crack," said Corky as they made their way to bed.

Last thing at night is rarely a convenient time to discuss revelations, and I decided the potentilla fields could keep till the morning. But having slept soundly through the entire evening in an alcoholic fug, my body again seemed reluctant to let me nod off once the lights were out. It wasn't helped by the combined decibel levels of the crew and the owls. LaFlamme's snoring was particularly loud and I wondered if the kitchen glassware would survive the night.

I sat up in my bunk, located my jeans and fumbled in the pockets for my watch. It was midnight. I was in for a long night.

LaFlamme awoke with a snort and said, "What's that noise?"

"What noise?" I replied.

"Ticking."

"My watch?" I said, waving it before her.

"Loud," said LaFlamme. "Can you turn it down?"

"It doesn't have a volume control. It's clockwork. You wind it up and listen to the seconds of your life disappear into the mist. Then you realise you're still struggling and wonder how long you have left before you meet a guy dressed in black carrying a scythe."

"What's a scythe?"

"It's something Death carries around."

"Can you leave it outside?"

"The scythe?"

"The watch."

"I could do but wouldn't the colossal vibrations it would produce against the towpath also disturb your precious sleep?"

I stuffed the watch back into my pocket and switched on one of the tiffany lamps. It was quiet now. I realised that all I had to do in order to minimise the racket and get a good night's sleep was to keep LaFlamme awake. "Would you like some strong coffee?" I said. "Red Bull? Amphetamine perhaps?"

"Do you ever think about death?" said LaFlamme, resting her head on her elbow.

"Right now I can't think of anything else," I replied.

"I mean, not like the act of dying or the method or anything, but the fact that it's the end of everything."

"I'm thinking I'll be sent to some limbo underworld with narrow-boats and talking wooden men."

"Everything you knew, everything you learned, all that money you made. It's all gone. You're nothing again."

"What money?" I said.

"Some people never think about death. They spend all their time wondering how to make money. They worry that if they don't make more and more money they'll be unhappy at some point in the future. But that point in the future doesn't exist. They get older and the point in the future is always just somewhere in the distance. And you know why?

"Why?"

"Because they never think about death. That's what *makes* them unhappy. So they try and buy off their unhappiness by making more money."

"It doesn't sound so bad."

"But they don't know what to do with the money because all they've ever done with their life is pursue it. They've bought all the personalised licence plates they could dream of and got a kick out of that for a while. But that's not real happiness. And before they reach that point in the future, the one they were worried about, guess what happens?"

"What?"

"They die."

LaFlamme was remarkably coherent for someone who had just woken from a drunken slumber at midnight, but I was struggling to keep up. I think she might have lost me around about 'the end of everything'.

"What do you think about first thing in the morning?" she continued.

"Breakfast."

"Before that."

"There's something before breakfast?"

"The minute you wake up."

"I don't know."

"You know what I think?"

"What?"

"I'm alive. This is my life. I might not feel so good but at least I'm not dead. If those people who spend all their time worrying about money spent more time thinking about death, they'd lighten up."

"They'd lighten up thinking about death?" I said.

"Of course. Only then would they feel what it's like to be alive."

LaFlamme may have been right but by now I didn't much care about those people and their money. I figured if they had enough of it they could hire someone to explain death to them. At night the hiree could tuck them in, reassure them they were going to die then have Corky sing one of his melancholic songs. That was bound to cheer anyone up.

I was hitting a sleepy pocket and couldn't afford to pass it up. I switched off the tiffany lamp. Within seconds LaFlamme had piped down and the snoring resumed in earnest.

12.
PARALEGAL ACTIVITY

I woke up and thought about breakfast. Mr Beard had been taking care of the cooking and generally fried anything he laid his hands on; bacon, sausage, potatoes, beans, bread, tomatoes, mushrooms, eggs, black and white puddings. This had been an essential part of the diet Dr Seward prescribed for the journey, along with other staples such as fish pie, gin and vigorous dark ale. And we'd managed to adhere to it more or less, apart from occasional lapses when Suave Gav led us astray. We couldn't afford to let healthy food impede our progress up the Kenneth & Keith.

As Mr Beard began preparing, LaFlamme headed for the shower and I was left alone in the cabin. I desperately wanted to know what she had been writing in her second journal. I knew exactly where it had been left and it would be easy enough to take a swift glance while she was indisposed. Of course I faced a certain moral dilemma here. But that didn't trouble me nearly so much as the fact that she might emerge from the shower any minute. I would have to be quick.

I eased the journal out from under her bunk and opened it. I was immediately struck by its sloppiness; the handwriting was unkempt and ignored all the printed grid lines on the page. It was one hundred per cent wraparound shades LaFlamme, as were its contents. And it wasn't quite what I was expecting.

Publishers bothering me again. That's what I get for brightening their dreary lives. They suggested memoirs. I said they surely didn't expect me to write somebody's life story but they said no, my memoirs. Who has time for this stuff? I said okay but only if I could get the most expensive ghostwriter in the world. They said they could get the dweeb who wrote Blair's book. I said if I wanted it to be that dull I could ask Junior the mute minion to do it. Then I thought getting Junior to do it wasn't such a bad idea. I'd make sure she got some of the money, of course. Up her allowance, but not too much. She's a terrible soak.

Tony refusing to shave, along with the rest of the locals. Nothing but Brillo pads as far as the eye can see. Like being at a ZZ Top gig without the laughs. Even looking at them makes me want to scratch. Says he's forgotten his razor but it's more like a dirty protest. It may be time for drastic action.

New piece in the LaFlambé puzzle. Seems the body they recovered from the ruins of the theatre, the one they identified as LaFlambé and buried, wasn't him at all. Turned out to be his stand-in who was dressed the same. LaFlambé's remains were never found. What does this mean? I don't know. Imagine his stand-in wasn't too happy though.

I heard the turning of the lock mechanism on the inside of the bathroom door and immediately returned the journal to its hiding place. (I had slightly more time than I thought because LaFlamme had difficulty with locks. Although brilliant, her grasp of basic mechanics was slight. She called my bike 'the thing with the wheels'.)

When she finally appeared, I was fully dressed and pretending to study the map. Tracing a line across it with my finger, I caught sight of something unfamiliar in the corner of my eye, a dark shadow hovering below my nose. I thought a caterpillar might have fallen on my chin and tried brushing it away. It was certainly soft like a caterpillar but despite repeated brushing, it refused to budge. LaFlamme asked if I was having a seizure. Only then did I appreciate the extent of my facial growth, which seemed to have accelerated during the night.

"Never mind," said LaFlamme. "I have a solution." She stepped into the bathroom and returned with a substantial wad of toilet paper, then started wrapping it around the lower half of my face and neck.

"If you're trying to mummify me," I said whilst I could still be heard, "you're a little early."

"I'm not so sure," said LaFlamme. "It looks like you're on the way out."

"Breakfast," called Mr Beard from the kitchen.

"I need to eat, you know," I said.

"That's okay, I can fix you up," said LaFlamme. She parted several layers of paper in the general area of my mouth and thrust several fingers into it to make enough room for food to pass through. This had the effect of making me look like Santa Claus, although I didn't realise this until LaFlamme sat on my knee and started telling me what she wanted for Christmas.

When the others joined us, Mr Beard suggested I may prefer milk and cookies before I returned to my sleigh and Corky said I would make a fine Kris Kringle because I was a bit 'roly-poly'. I suffered all of this in silence. It was too early to negotiate with hobgoblins. Besides, a plate of fried food had just been placed in front of me and I was setting about it eagerly when Captain Pantling called to give me his daily update on LeSnide.

"The line's rather crackly," he said.

"I'm sorry," I replied. "I've been partially mummified. Just a minute." I pulled away the layers from my face and in doing so discovered a piece of fried bread that had fallen there earlier. I didn't want to appear common in front of Corky so I turned away from him before stuffing it into my mouth. This didn't make me any more intelligible to Pantling but fried bread is fried bread.

"Is everything all right there?" said Pantling tentatively.

"Oh yes," I said through breakfast remnants and streams of soggy paper. "Except last night some other boat had the *temerity* to be sailing after 8:00pm. It was probably closer to 9:00. Made quite a noise and substantial waves for those of us who'd been moored for over an hour. I had half a mind to report them to the authorities."

Pantling was silent for a moment.

"Are you *sure* you're all right?" he said finally. "We may be counting on you to fulfil this mission but should you for any reason feel that you're not equipped to reach Wester and make the necessary rendezvous, it may be better to turn back now."

"No no, it's fine," I said. "Beard's driving." Again, Pantling was silent.

"The *beard's driving*?"

"Yes. He knows the area well and I have every faith in his navigational skills."

"*He?*" said Captain Pantling. "The beard has navigational skills?"

"Absolutely," I said, finding more fried bread in the folds of paper and filling my face with it. "Better than mine anyway. He also has a little goblin friend who advises him. A difficult character but he's company for Beard."

"Well I'm glad '*beard*' has company. We wouldn't want '*beard*' to get lonesome, would we?" I wasn't sure why Pantling had adopted the tone of a mental health nurse but I reminded myself that he was the Advocates' Clerk and had been around lawyers for a long time. "I'm wondering," he continued, "if Dr Seward was thorough enough with you in his examination."

"It's fine," I said. "We're making good progress and there's still plenty of gin."

Pantling sighed. "Well, by my reckoning you should have passed the Crowley lock by now and most likely the Blavatsky lock too."

"The locks have names?"

"At least the locks I like."

"At least the locks you like?" I said. "Are you standing in for Dr Seuss today?"

"Soon you should arrive at Lock 13," he continued.

"Is that a lock you like?" I asked.

"No."

"Why not? Does it leak? Does it lack? Does it lurk by a lake?"

"It's bad luck," he said.

I had to remind myself that there was money at the end of this journey. All I had to do was bundle LeSnide into the boat, get his signature and return to my drab little existence, which from this distance was starting to look quite appealing.

"Lock 13," said Captain Pantling, "was where the Broughton sisters practised witchcraft. It's said that the water is riddled with the bones of their sacrifices and that the lock keeper is the devil himself."

"I see," I said. "What's not to like?"

"I would advise you to pass through it with minimum delay. Now regarding another matter," he continued, "I have some bad news."

"Other than the fact that we may be about to cross paths with the dark lord?"

"I'm afraid we've lost LeSnide."

"He's dead?"

"Not him," said Pantling. "The tracking device battery. I told Seward to use Duracell but he wouldn't listen."

"So how am I meant to find him?"

"We must resort to more traditional methods of tracking. We have an approximate location for his last base camp, close to an area known as The Cludge. You're still some distance away. I suggest you continue to this location then do some tracking of your own. Despite what I said earlier about turning back, we'd all be deeply disappointed should you fail."

If Pantling expected me to be able to find one man, even a man with a very large chin, in an area as dense as Wester he was losing his definition. I began to wonder if LeSnide had handed the baton of madness to his clerk after he fled the advocates' stable. But it sounded like he was also ready to have me taken into care, so we had probably reached a stalemate. I could return to picking pieces of fried bread from my paper beard without fear of a dart gun.

We had just set off when The Little Hitler became unsettled by the wake of an overtaking boat. It was a flagrant breach of *The Waterways Code* to overtake another narrowboat unless it was safely moored but the offending vessel was also travelling wildly beyond the speed limit, easily six miles per hour. I stepped through to the bow of the boat and leaned out port side in order to voice my outrage. Steaming ahead of us was none other than Suave Gav, tiller in one hand, camcorder in the other. He was filming the landscape around him, his hair rippling in the wind as only his hair could.

I returned hastily to the stern and addressed Mr Beard.

"Follow that boat," I said.

Mr Beard put The Little Hitler into full throttle and we chased The Inebriate over a considerable stretch. We encountered much hostility en route as moored boats and overtaken boats alike were dealt seismic waves caused by our lightning six MPH. Strolling beards complained bitterly about noise and the abuse of *The Waterways Code*. Normally I would have respected other users of the canal but I was incensed.

Soon we were nose to tail with The Inebriate but were forced to a standstill by a checkpoint where many other boats had formed a queue. If Captain Pantling were to be believed, this was the notorious 'Lock 13'. It didn't look any more sinister than the other locks, which tended to all look like they might be inhabited by demonic sprites, if not the prince of darkness himself. But I'd take Pantling's advice and pass through it with minimum delay. That is, I would were it not for the ten boats in front of us and a similar number on the other side of the lock travelling in the opposite direction. It looked like 'delay' might be today's most frequently used word. After 'balls'.

"What's the holdup?" said LaFlamme.

"There's a queue," I replied.

"Can't we just head to the front?" This was an understandable question coming from LaFlamme, as it was her general modus oper-andi. I tried to explain what was wrong with that approach in these circumstances.

"It would make us unpopular," I said at first. This didn't faze LaFlamme so I continued. "At the front of the queue we'd have to wait for the water level to fall before we could sail into the lock."

"Yes," she said, "but then we could make a quick getaway."

"No," I replied, "then we'd be trapped in the lock waiting for the water level to rise again. All in all our quick getaway could take around forty minutes and we'd have travelled about thirty feet."

"We could *Fitzcarraldo* it in that time," said LaFlamme.

I asked Mr Beard what would be the best plan of action. "Busy time of day," he said. "Best moor here for a time until the congestion eases."

"But isn't this the devil's lock?" I said. "I was specifically told not to dilly-dally around this area."

"Oh my," said Corky. "I do believe the stupid one is afraid of the devil."

"Perhaps we could fashion you a crucifix, Mr Tony," said Mr Beard, trying to suppress his laughter.

"I thought I detected a whiff of sulphur earlier," said Corky. "But then I do have the most appalling wind." He made a rasping sound with his little wooden tongue.

LaFlamme rose with determination. "Pub o'clock then," she said. I agreed. It would be a good opportunity to confront Suave Gav, who had moored directly in front of us and would no doubt have come to the same conclusion.

We headed for Satan's Onions, a gastropub with a fine collection of devil themed etchings on the walls. As LaFlamme claimed a picnic table in the beer garden, I ordered fish pie and gin and looked for the special ale of the week, groaning to myself when I clocked it.

"I brought you gin," I said on my return.

"Am I or am I not still on holiday?" said LaFlamme.

"I refuse to order these ridiculously named beers."

"Again?" she said. "What a delicate little flower you are. It's not haemorrhoid cream we're talking about, it's beer. Which tap is it?"

"It has a picture of a skyscraper."

"What can possibly be embarrassing about that?" she scolded. "Just get a couple of pints and think about The Admiral's face when you tell him you scoffed a different vigorous dark ale every day of your trip."

I sighed heavily, returned to the bar and ordered two pints of Steel Erection.

Suave Gav stepped briskly from the towpath and joined us at our table.

"Video diary," he said, explaining the camcorder with which he'd been too preoccupied to notice his poor waterway etiquette. LaFlamme took the device and began toying with it.

"You cut us up back there," I said. "Don't you know it's bad form to overtake another non-stationary vessel?"

"Overtake?" said Suave Gav. "Did I really? I say, I do apologise. I hope a Steel Erection will go some ways to make amends. Cheers." We clinked glasses and the tension I felt earlier began to dissolve. "In my haste I often overlook waterway etiquette. It's a failing."

"What's the rush?" asked LaFlamme. "You know you're going to hit one of these bottlenecks eventually then you have to either chill out or go Herzog."

"Herzog?" said Suave Gav.

"It's not important," I said.

"You're absolutely right, of course. I have been guilty of a certain overzealousness in my quest. But between you and me there is an urgency about my plight that spurs me on."

"What plight?" I said. "And what exactly is your quest?"

"Oh come come," he replied, "there is surely no need for games at this stage."

"Okay," I said. "I happen to know there are potentilla fields nearby."

"Potentilla *erecta*," said LaFlamme, now apparently filming the proceedings.

"And they could be harvested to produce enough Bavarian liqueur to see out your days."

"Well done, Mr Boaks," said Suave Gav. "It is indeed true that the region has the highest concentration of wild tormentil anywhere in the world. And its gifts are so little understood that we have yet to encounter any poppy-style warring over its harvest. But there is a limit to how many Bavarian summers or Alpine winters one man could want purely in the interests of imbibement. I think we all know the real reason we have been drawn to the area."

"Nightlife?" said LaFlamme, concentrating her lens on Suave Gav's toupée.

"Lord knows," continued Gav, "it's not for the social intercourse. Without your fine selves I should have cut a very isolated figure, alone on my narrowboat every night with only a flimsy hairpiece to keep me company. I'm almost ready to give the blessed thing a name." LaFlamme began trying to entice the toupée with a piece of bread.

"Look," I said, "I know you're searching for a morning-after cure and we suggested you need the mental torment plant for that. But to be honest I'm kind of sorry I mentioned it, because it may well be a myth."

"I do have considerable interest in such an elixir, should it exist," said Suave Gav. "And it may transpire that it is indeed mythical. But I am willing to devote myself to finding out one way or the other and I've fitted The Inebriate with sufficient laboratory apparatus for experimentation with anything that we may discover along the way. You have to understand old boy, I believe my need to be substantially greater than yours."

"You might be a bigger lush," I said. "But I can't see how that makes your need any greater."

"I suspect at this stage you're unaware of the more profound usage of the potentilla – and I'm not talking about raising a thumper downstairs." I was glad he wasn't talking about 'raising a thumper' as it's not something I was keen to discuss with another man, least of all one with a toupée companion. But I still had no idea what he meant. Wasn't the mental torment plant gifted enough, being capable of producing a sixty per cent proof drink and a possibly mythical other beverage that could deal with the consequences of such a drink? Was Suave Gav suggesting there was yet another use?

He wouldn't be drawn further. He changed the subject and we whiled away a couple of hours getting tipsy and making fun of various beards as they came and went from Satan's Onions. LaFlamme would wander off with the camera from time to time, utterly taken with her new toy. At one point she returned with a saucer of milk and placed it at the foot of the picnic table – in case the toupée (which she was now calling 'Verdi') got thirsty.

By the time we left the beer garden it was late afternoon and we were sufficiently fortified with Steel Erections. The queue of boats had thinned a little but it was clear it would still be some time before we could get through Lock 13. Suave Gav said since we were in the area, he could take us to a nearby potentilla field. I couldn't see any reason why not; since Pantling told me he had no idea where he was sending us I felt resigned to the fates. I was as likely to find LeSnide in a potentilla field as anywhere else. Besides, it was a glorious day and I felt a distinct post-Erection need to stretch my legs. I reminded Suave Gav that we had to get through the lock and find a suitable place to moor before curfew. He waved in the general direction of the walkway across the lock.

"By the time we return," he said, "this queue will have evaporated and we shall be free to sail through at our leisure."

LaFlamme continued to film the proceedings and appeared to be narrating as we progressed (I heard her David Attenborough impression and a brief monologue on the mating habits of toupées). A few moments later she had fallen behind and I became concerned about the consequences should she encounter any of the natives. That is, I was concerned for the natives.

"We'll be there in two shakes of the devil's tail," said Suave Gav, which prompted me to ask him about the notorious Lock 13. Was there any truth in the stories about devil worship in the area?

"If there is any form of necromancy," said Suave Gav, "it would not surprise me to hear it. You have to remember we are in an area with a high concentration of solicitors, and therefore local beliefs tend to be quite primitive.

"Try to put yourself in the mind of one of these savage legal practitioners. The internet for example is an instrument of science fiction for most. Email is something to be printed and left on their desks – sometimes it must even be folded into an envelope before they can understand it's a form of communication. And then there is the oath."

"The oath?"

"The solicitorial equivalent of the Hippocratic Oath. It's more of a pact really, and I think you can guess who else is a party to that pact. It would be very difficult to be an effective legal professional without it."

"For an area with a high concentration of lawyers," I said, "I'm not sure I've seen any."

"Does that upset you?"

"No."

"Well then," said Suave Gav, his arms open as if to ask what more I could want. "Outwith their chambers they're generally nocturnal and keep to their own. You won't find much cross-pollination of the professions in Wester – local people are all too wary of the outcome."

This somewhat obscure response raised more questions than it answered (a common occurrence for me and the reason I was never overly keen to ask questions). But by now we had reached a clearing in the woods and after my eyes had adjusted to the light, a jolt of recognition registered in my mind. Stretching out before us was a field containing what must have been a couple of thousand examples of the unprepossessing mental torment plant. Stout, straggly and scratchy to the touch, the potentilla erecta may have been gifted, but it certainly was ugly.

"Try some?" said Suave Gav, producing his mini secateurs. Against my better judgement, which had bailed out on me when I first decided to venture into this godforsaken beardy wilderness, I accepted a clipping. It tasted exactly as I thought it would – like a twig clipped at random from a short ugly bush. Perhaps Captain Pantling had been right to be concerned about my mental health. I'd only been here a few days and was already eating twigs.

"On the hard stuff?" said LaFlamme when she caught up. (She continued to film as if gathering material for some magnum opus, although it was an unlikely magnum opus that would feature two men chewing sticks.)

"It's only mildly habit-forming," said Suave Gav.

"Habit-forming?" I said. "You mean this is some kind of drug?"

"It's a light stimulant," he replied.

I wondered what Suave Gav meant as I continued to chew on the rough cutting. Perhaps it was like tobacco, a pointless drug that doesn't do anything except to those who are already hopelessly addicted to it, and even then just brings them back to something resembling normal. The rest of us might as well smoke something from the garden centre – that won't get you high either and you won't be giving ninety per cent of the packet price to the government.

In my art college days, like most teens who showed little enthusiasm for the university's Conservative & Unionist Debating Society, I had a rather heightened interest in getting off my face as often and in as many different ways as possible. When it was rumoured that banana rinds were effective ("what do you think 'Mellow Yellow' is about?" said The Admiral at the time), we put any food money we had left after beer into bananas, then saved the rinds – the delicate strips between the peel and the flesh – and hung them to dry. After some experimentation I was able to confirm that banana rinds are about as useful as tobacco. Nowadays of course, smoking banana rinds is more socially acceptable than tobacco.

Although unsure the twig was doing much for me, I was certainly relaxed. Suave Gav and I sat at the root of a great oak enjoying the late afternoon sun as LaFlamme circled with the camera and occasionally poked it in my face.

"Does being trapped inside a man's body present you with any special difficulties?" she said suddenly from behind the lens. I had to suppress a sudden urge to sink my teeth into her thigh, which may or may not have been an effect of the light stimulant.

"I've been trying to preserve it in gin to make the experience a little more bearable," I replied.

"And when the doctors said you had to lose ten stone immediately did you wonder how you would live without lard?"

"Yes," I said. "Lard is so much a part of my life."

"And it's so much a part of *you*," said LaFlamme.

"Are you saying I'm getting heavy?" I said, patting my stomach and wondering how a strict diet of fish pie, fried breakfast and vigorous dark ale could ever result in weight gain.

"Only around the body area," she replied. LaFlamme put the camera down, yawned and sat next to me, laying her head on my shoulder. I immediately tensed up. Not that I was in any way uncomfortable – on the contrary, I began to feel tingles in places I had forgotten existed and knew that remaining perfectly still was the way to prolong the moment for as long as possible. After a few moments I was so tense my muscles began to ache. But I was willing to suffer for LaFlamme's touch.

Suave Gav too appeared to have fallen into some peculiar reverie. He was glassy-eyed and swaying slightly, his teeth blackened by the twig fixed between them.

"Are you all right, Mr Armstrong?" I asked him. His demeanour changed immediately.

"Of course I'm all right," he said with some hostility. "Are you mad?"

"Um," I said. "I just wondered."

"You just wondered," he said dismissively.

It was a surprising and uncharacteristic outburst. Despite generally consuming a great deal of alcohol in our company and having a number of opportunities for bad behaviour, Suave Gav had always been the perfect gentleman. But given a stumpy teeth-blackening twig to chew on, a change occurred – a sudden change, like the flick of a switch. And this was a switch you're best keeping in the off position at all times.

I too had been on the mental torment but I had no sudden aggressive or hostile urges. I had no urges at all other than the strong desire to sink my blackened teeth into LaFlamme's thighs. I'd have been content to doze off with her at the foot of the great oak, be savaged by gnats and still be there when a whole new generation of them came to savage us the following day. Whatever chemicals were active in this strange plant, they had no adverse or other effect on me. It was becoming clear however that the same could not be said of Suave Gav.

He stood abruptly but somewhat shakily.

"Listen Boaks," he said, "you're on a sticky wicket. You think I don't know why you're here in Wessershessershersher, but nobody comes to Wessershesh... Wester without a plan."

"My plan was to get paid."

"I told you my need was greater than yours. Can't you just accept that and back off?" He pointed a threatening finger at me and looked set to utter some bizarre accusation or curse. Instead he turned and ran back into the dense undergrowth.

I looked down at LaFlamme whilst trying to remain motionless. "I'm getting sleepy," she said casually, as if she hadn't just witnessed an arboreally intoxicated middle-aged man with black teeth stropping off into the afternoon shade.

Was this the face of addiction? I wasn't sure. I had no real frame of reference for it. LaFlamme and I, although enthusiastic drinkers, only appeared to be physically compelled to get trashed at weekends. I suppose that would be enough for those who have sworn off it to call us 'borderline', but some people think anyone who has more than a single sherry is borderline. It's what happens if you replace drink with God. God hates anyone who has fun.

No disrespect intended towards anyone struggling with the condition or the groups who advise them to put their faith in a higher power, as they say this doesn't necessarily mean God. If I am ever obliged to join their thirsty ranks I plan to put my faith in that god amongst rodents, the grey squirrel.

Impervious to man's continuous attempts at eradication, the grey squirrel laughs in the face of those who try to prevent them eating their birdseed. Their only real predator was Elvis Presley (who liked them deep-fried with parsley), and since the king's demise they've pretty much had a free reign. They don't even need to hibernate anymore. They're indestructible.

Of course you might say, 'But God created the grey squirrel'. To which I would reply, 'I'll have a pint of lager'.

The blissful sensation of LaFlamme napping on my shoulder had to come to an end eventually. When she snorted awake and raised her head I said, "I suppose we should probably be getting back." But had she slipped back into sleep I wouldn't have put up a fight.

By the time we returned to The Little Hitler the queue of boats at Lock 13 had dispersed, just as Suave Gav predicted. However, Mr Beard and Corky had also dispersed and I realised their glasses were empty. Although I was secretly pleased, it meant we would have to drive the boat ourselves and I wasn't sure I wanted another dip in the canal.

"My minions," said LaFlamme. "I demand to see my minions."

She filled a glass with gin and struck the rim with the side of a knife. Then she held the base of the knife to the table top where it resonated in what I imagined might be the key of C. I have no real way of knowing but LaFlamme assured me she has perfect pitch when it comes to gin. Sensing it was slightly off, she drank a little and struck it once more. Again holding the base of the knife to the table top, this time it produced a purer and slightly higher note that was more pleasing to the ear. LaFlamme declared with confidence that the drink was now in tune.

Within a minute I heard a familiar muttering on the towpath and sure enough Mr Beard stepped aboard with Corky, took a drink and began checking the gauges.

"Good of you to return, dumbo," said Corky, addressing me directly. "I'd have organised a search party had it been anyone worth finding." He looked down at LaFlamme below deck. "Always delighted to see *you* back, my dear."

LaFlamme wasn't listening. She had connected Suave Gav's camera to the television and was replaying her video footage, making notes as she wound it back and forwards. It was clear she was taking her role as documentarist seriously. I asked her if she was working for Channel 5 or if she was going to make something good instead. With hindsight, I don't know why I singled out any one broadcaster.

I tried to imagine the sort of documentary that would truly have the networks salivating. A bottomless man for example would make the perfect subject.

"When exactly did your buttocks fall off, Mr Thompson?" asks the nosey filmmaker, moving his beady little geek lens in for a close-up.

"I just woke up one day and realised they were gone," says the man.

"And did you ever manage to track them down?"

"Yes, they're in the next room."

The camera follows the man, focussing on the completely flat upper leg area where his cheeks used to be. In an adjoining room, sympathy cards line the table. 'Sorry for your loss', says one. 'All good things come to an end', says another. And there resting on a metal platter, as if ready to be presented as a main course, are two large buttocks. The camera zooms in.

The documentarist decides to take a multi-faceted approach to this film in order to fully engage the audience and create a warm feeling about our common humanity. He wants to hear the buttocks' side of the story and asks if he can speak to them directly. In so doing, it is revealed that the buttocks didn't just fall off, they left of their own accord. These cheeks have attitude and are in the midst of some odd rebellion; twin James Deans of the arse world. Probing further, the filmmaker asks if they left because they were a little behind in their work. And so on. What the hell, I don't really watch much TV.

I'd like to see David Attenborough make a documentary about a bottomless man. But he's from an era when they used to spend money on documentaries, and spending money isn't really something commissioning editors do anymore. It might be worth mummifying Attenborough or covering him in Cryofreeze to preserve him and his budgets. Just a thought.

Mr Beard said we were all set and that we should get through Lock 13 and moor in order to avoid another bottleneck situation in the morning. I said after all this time I didn't see why, as it seemed like a fine place to see out the rest of my days. But I was quietly relieved.

I was preparing to go and work the lock gates when LaFlamme said, "Just a minute. Look at this." She was studying a clip of Suave Gav taken over lunch at Satan's Onions. LaFlamme had been circling Suave Gav, the camera focussed on the back of his head. She was playing a five second snippet on a loop, winding it back to the same point over and over.

"See that?" she said.

"What?" I replied.

"Look closely." I stepped closer to the screen and squinted my eyes.

"What am I looking for, split ends?"

"Watch the top of his head." She put her finger to a point on the screen that seemed to show where Suave Gav's toupée ended and the rest of his hair began.

"The man wears a hairpiece," I said. "It's not exactly news."

"Hello?" said LaFlamme, rapping the top of my head with her knuckle. "Look again." I scrutinised the screen once more and this time I saw it. Slowly but very assuredly the toupée moved. It wasn't simply that it shifted slightly – it rose up on his head by at least an inch and resettled, as if making itself more comfortable.

"Verdi's stretching his legs," said LaFlamme.

I knew I was starting to reach weirdness capacity when all I could say in response was, "You might make it onto Channel 5 after all."

"Hoi, stupidworks!" called Corky. "If we don't get through the devil's lock tonight there'll be hell to pay." He laughed.

This made me sit up. I was more than a little concerned about the time and the fading light. Although narrowboats are fitted with a headlight, these are meant for use in the winter months and should not, I repeat not, be an excuse for post-curfew manoeuvres. And of course there was no way I wanted to be moored overnight by Lock 13, whether there was any truth in the rumours or not. The area looked welcoming enough in the daytime, but who ever gets concerned about Satan worshippers in the daytime?

I stepped onto the towpath and walked towards the lock, passing The Inebriate. It was terribly bad form to be skipping the queue in this manner but as there was no sign of Suave Gav (I suspected he'd gone native), I didn't think we had much choice. The water in the lock was already at our level so I only had to open the lock gates and let Mr Beard guide The Little Hitler in before opening the paddles at the other side. Unfortunately once the boat had manoeuvred into the lock and I closed the gates behind it, I had some difficulty opening the paddles.

"What's the trouble up there?" cried Mr Beard from the stern.

"Devil got a hold of you?" said Corky.

"They're stuck," I said. "I can't get either side to shift."

"They're not the gates of hell, you know," called Corky.

"Can I help?" said Suave Gav, appearing out of the bushes on the opposite side of the canal. He seemed perfectly subdued and acted as if I hadn't just seen him behaving like a total fruitcake.

"I'm not sure," I said, concerned I might say something else to flick his mental switch and trigger another freak-out.

"Actually," said Suave Gav, "before you open the paddles, let me bring The Inebriate in alongside you. It's big enough for two and means I won't have to wait for the water to empty again. Then we can tackle the paddles together." I didn't particularly want The Inebriate sidling up to The Little Hitler but I was feeling guilty about having jumped the queue – *The Waterways Code* is quite clear about disrespectful behaviour. So I agreed to reopen the first set of gates whilst Suave Gav prepared to cast off The Inebriate.

Once inside the lock, the two boats sat tightly together with barely a foot between them and just a little more on either side of its high walls. Being on the low water side it felt dark and distinctly claustrophobic. But once it filled with water the boats would rise up and we'd be free to tank ahead to find a suitable place to moor, hopefully somewhere not inhabited by devil worshippers.

"They're stuck all right," said Suave Gav when he joined me at the lock paddles. He made no further effort, much to my annoyance, and even when he saw me struggling with the steel winch he seemed disinclined to assist.

"If we could both grasp the winch at once I think we could force it open," I said.

"I doubt it," said Suave Gav.

"You don't think our combined strength is capable of opening a paddle?"

He pointed to a heavy gauge padlock on the far side of the gates. "Not when it's locked," he said.

"The lock's locked?" I said in disbelief. "How could that happen? Who would want to lock it?"

"Presumably the lock keeper. Some of these older locks do still have keepers and I'm afraid some of these chaps are quite strict."

"What are we going to do?" I said.

"Nothing much we can do. Just wait it out, get a fresh start in the morning."

"Surely we can't spend the night in a lock, least of all the devil's lock. We should go back and moor somewhere suitable."

"Alas, that would mean queuing again in the morning. There's no doubt that for the purpose of getting to the other side, we are in the very best possible place."

Excellent, I thought. I'm going to be stuck overnight in the devil's lock with hobgoblins, a budding documentarist, and an all-round weirdo with possible addiction issues. Maybe if we invited the AA round it would be even more fun.

Reluctantly I climbed down the stepladder into the lock, clambered aboard The Little Hitler and explained the situation to the crew. I was hoping for some practical suggestions.

"*Fitzcarraldo*," said LaFlamme.

"Pulling the boat out of a lock would be even harder than pulling it up a hill," I said. "But nice thought."

"Ah well," said Mr Beard. "It's a sure way to get an early start. Would you like some toast?" He handed me a basket with half a loaf's worth.

"No, I don't want any toast," I said, taking two slices and tackling them with gusto. "Is there any cheese?"

"Cheese will give you nightmares," said Corky. "You surely don't want nightmares tonight, do you?"

I was distinctly unhappy about this situation. If we planned on squatting overnight in the devil's lock there was a possibility that the landlord might appear, and who knows what he might expect in the way of rent. Despite working in the design industry I still felt I had a soul of sorts and was eager to try and retain it for as long as possible. But I had to admit the others were right – mooring outside the lock risked a repeat of today's events and one day like today was enough for anyone.

As LaFlamme busied herself with video footage and Mr Beard and Corky took up a game of cards, I tried to settle into some reading. But I was finding the *Collins Concise* a little *anhydrous*. By the time darkness had fallen I was distinctly *dolorous*, also a bit *querulous*, and thought I needed to get some air.

Up on the deck I could hear Suave Gav singing 'That's Amore'. And something smelled delicious. Onions and garlic stewing in red wine, I guessed. Tomatoes, herbs, maybe some peppers. I smiled to myself. He might have had problems but cooking was not one of them.

I climbed the lock ladder and set out into the night. I didn't know what I was going to do but it was a warm night and I figured I could spend some of it beneath the stars, out of Beelzebub's reach. I followed the nearside towpath towards Satan's Onions and thought perhaps a nightcap might be a good start. But the Satan was closed, unusually early. In fact, save for the sound of crickets, the whole area was deathly silent. It was extraordinary how this boating hub by day, home to a thriving community of beards, could become a ghost town post-sunset. Even the interminable jungle drums had ceased and, sure enough, somewhere in the distance were the strains of a particularly tedious bass solo.

Just as I thought I recognised a Weather Report riff, I rounded a corner and caught sight of firelight. It seemed there might be life here after all. A dozen or so men with long rather greasy looking hair and cheap ill-fitting suits stood around a campfire, chatting and drinking beer. Although a little pale and wizened, as if having spent too much time indoors, they were refreshingly free of whiskers and didn't look like they were about to sacrifice anything. Emboldened by an afternoon's drinking, I decided to join them.

"Warm night," I said to nobody in particular.

"27 degrees Celsius," said one.

"80 degrees Fahrenheit," said another.

"80.7 actually," said a third.

"Nearer 81 then," said another.

"I merely rounded it down," said the first.

"Is there any call for rounding it down? I think you'll find if you follow the exact equation, $F = (1.8 \times C) + 32$, you will arrive at 80.6 Fahrenheit. Respectfully suggest the interlocutor refrain from making sweeping generalisations and 'rounding numbers down' in future."

"Duly noted. However, in the context of this discussion I would put it to you that there are reasonable grounds for doing so."

This was no ordinary gathering of boaters. For one thing they seemed quite bright. And there was a competitive nature to their banter that was *incongruous* given that they were essentially a group of suited crusties getting drunk around a bonfire.

"I put it to you that you are basing your figure on the assumption that it is *precisely* 27 degrees Celsius. Were you to produce evidence that it was in fact *precisely 80 degrees Fahrenheit* to begin with, your figure of 27 degrees Celsius would be quite inaccurate. In which case one would employ the reverse equation C = (F - 32) ÷ 1.8, arriving at 26.6 degrees Celsius – some way short of your quoted 27."

It was remarkable. In just over a minute they had managed to lower the temperature by nearly half a degree – 0.4 of a degree, to be exact. It didn't feel any cooler but I *was* standing next to a fire. Perhaps if they kept this up they could lower it further and give us all an excuse for lighting midsummer fires in the first place.

"As for rounding the figure down," the gentleman continued, "I would suggest to my learned colleague that a figure of 80.7 is more likely to be rounded up."

"Well," I said, addressing the gathering with confidence, "that all depends." Silence gripped the overeducated group. I stroked my beard in order to add weight to what I was saying.

"If you worked in a bank you would only round up a number like 80.7 if it were in the bank's interests. For instance if it were bank charges levied on a customer, you'd certainly want to make it 81. If it were in the customer's interests, say for example if it were 80.7 in interest credit, you would more likely round it down to 80." This was a moderately intelligent observation for me, and all the more notable given that I'd consumed enough alcohol to round down an elephant.

There was a general hubbub of agreement amongst the group and I heard somebody whisper, "One of us." I felt honoured to be included in this way at first, but when two or three others used the phrase in unison I began to feel unsettled. That's when it hit me. This was no ordinary group of drinkers. They were lawyers.

I had no idea what to expect. It's not every day you stumble upon a gathering of LLB KnoBs having a night out. If it went well, I could be handed an honorary degree. If it didn't, I might be looking at a custodial sentence. If any of them started complaining about the legal aid system or how nobody liked them, I could be marooned there indefinitely.

When the low chanting of "one of us" rose to become more of a sustained lawyerly frenzy, I decided it probably wasn't a safe place for civilians and left, offering the excuse that I had to return to feed my goblins. I made a mental note that it was probably unwise to be wandering in this area after hours.

I didn't particularly want to return to The Little Hitler just yet, berthed as it was in hell lock, but between the lawyers and the devil worshippers I didn't feel I had much choice. Approaching the sunken vessel, I became aware of a general hilarity rising from below. I thought at first the gates of hell may have opened up, but it wasn't *that* far below. Suave Gav had joined the crew and together this quartet of oddballs were seated in the cabin dining area, quaffing an iced drink from tumblers and discussing, of all things, schooldays. As it turned out, Suave Gav and Corky had both attended the highly exclusive Chapterhouse school and were reminiscing about some past scrapes.

"Do you remember that peculiar old duffer," said Corky. "Maths master, appalling halitosis, used to beat the chalkboard with his fist?"

"Bramble," said Suave Gav.

"Bramble," said Corky. "One day he raised a cloud of dust so great, I lost sight of the old bugger. Took the opportunity to slip out and have a fag. I did once round the courtyard at quite a clip and when I returned I thought I'd proven part of Einstein's theory of relativity – the faster you travel, the more time slows for the traveller."

"What made you think that?" said Suave Gav.

"Every blighter in the room had grey hair," said Corky.

"Old bugger," said Suave Gav.

"Old bugger," said Corky. "When the beak arrived, Bramble tried to pass it off as volcanic ash and closed all the windows, thereby depriving us of any remnants of oxygen. Said there'd been an eruption at the local version of Vesuvius, which was implausible as it was all of three hundred feet. Flat as a badger's arse, that neck of the woods."

"Badger's arse," said Suave Gav.

"Badger's arse," said Corky. "Bramble was so caked in chalk dust that everywhere he went he left a cloud in his wake. They'd often raise the alarm after he did his rounds in case anybody got lost. It was all very well having a school bell but what we really needed was a foghorn."

"Wonder what happened to him," said Suave Gav.

"I imagine he was calcified by the stuff," said Corky. "Turned into a pillar of dust, like a limestone Job."

"Good lord," said Suave Gav, suddenly noticing me and revealing his blackened teeth. "This man doesn't have a drink."

"Actually," I said, "I'm quite tired. I thought I might turn in soon."

"Don't be ridiculous," said Suave Gav. "It's Bavarian summertime. And as your neighbour, I should like to welcome you to the area with Armstrong's finest on ice."

"You're in purgatory now," said LaFlamme, revealing *her* blackened teeth. "Might as well make the most of it."

"As I'm currently moored on your starboard side, let me mix you a little something from my medicine chest."

"Port," I said.

"I'm afraid I'm all out of port," said Suave Gav, "but can I suggest a little iced Blutwurz?"

"*Port*," I said, pointing to the left side of the boat. "You're moored on our *port* side."

"What a ninny," said Corky.

"Ah," said Suave Gav, chuckling. "And how many years have you been at sea? I'm quite the landlubber in this company."

"I don't want anything, thanks," I said.

"Well look at the time," said Mr Beard. "What are you going to sing tonight, Corky?"

Now I wanted to drink. Heavily. If I had to get through another of Corky's maudlin, gin soaked renditions of creaky old numbers, it was the only way. I picked up LaFlamme's glass and took a swig of Suave Gav's foul bloodroot beverage.

"'With a Song in my Heart,'" said Corky. "Though I suspect I may have forgotten some of the words." He winked at LaFlamme.

"Just do your best then," said Mr Beard. Corky launched into the following number, which from the outset I knew was beset with problems.

With a thong in my parts
And a hand up my shirt at the base
It's an ignoble start
It's an interesting sort of embrace
When the curtain falls
Where's your other hand?
Wish you wouldn't stand so near, and…
If I had but a choice
I'd report you to local police
I would surely rejoice
When they catch you in nightie of fleece
Yes you're awfully weird
You're that pervert Beard
With a thong in my parts for you

"Now Corky," said Mr Beard, "you know fine that was quite unnecessary."

"Up yours, sea dogs!" said Corky, bidding us goodnight.

Suave Gav applauded and said, "Marvellous." Then he stood, bowed slightly and announced, "With that, I too will bid you adieu." He drained his glass and set out for the narrowboat next door. It was so close I could feel it colliding gently with The Little Hitler as he clambered aboard, repeating Corky's twisted refrain, 'with a thong in my parts for you'.

I began to make up our bunks and LaFlamme returned to her edit. She was in danger of becoming engrossed in her newfound pastime so I reminded her that not only was it late, but that television hadn't been an art form since *Sergeant Bilko*.

"Actually," she said, "this might be more of a movie. Like the one we saw with the lawyer and the ghost."

"Which one?" I asked.

"*Paralegal Activity*," she replied.

"You're not going to set up cameras all over the boat, are you?"

"I only have one," she said, "but it's a small boat." She stood up and attached the camera's strap to a hook in the topmost corner of the room so that it rested above my bunk pointing towards the kitchen.

"Why does it have to go above my bed?" I said.

"I could put it above mine but I think the microphone's quite sensitive."

I reached into the bathroom for my toothbrush and paste. I was still thoroughly uneasy about being moored in the so-called devil's lock, and told LaFlamme so.

"There's really nothing to be afraid of," she replied. "The camera will catch everything."

"Is that meant to comfort me?" I said between brushes. "I don't remember ever hearing that the presence of a camera prevented bizarre ritualistic deaths or demonic possession."

"But we'd have it on *film*," emphasised LaFlamme, as if she had just played a trump card. It was this total disregard for the safety and well-being of others that told me she had exactly what it took to be a brilliant documentary filmmaker.

"Okay," I said, beginning to wonder why the toothpaste tasted peculiar. "Bud ifff I shood die shomesime shuring sa nite, I promish I won't be washing yoor shtoopid shfilm."

"You're drooling, Boaks," said LaFlamme. "You've hit a new low."

I rinsed and picked up the toothpaste to check if it was a new formula or something. Unfortunately it was Cryofreeze. Very soon I began to lose all feeling in my face.

"I say," said Suave Gav, reappearing suddenly at the helm and stepping below. "Do you mind if I borrow a cup of sugar?"

"Helf yourshelf," I said, now frothing heavily and contorting my jaw in an effort to locate my chin.

"Good show," said Suave Gav, heading for the kitchen. "Mind how you go with that novocaine."

"Ish nod nawvacan," I said, grimacing. "Ish Cyofeege."

"It's what?"

"Cyofeege!"

"Well I'll be," said Suave Gav. "Any left?" I didn't have to respond. I was foaming at the mouth and grimacing wildly so I believe he got the message. "Just sugar," he said, retreating with the bowl.

"So," said LaFlamme, "you can't feel anything?" She squeezed below my cheekbones with her thumb and forefingers, making my lips protrude in a particularly unattractive manner. "Can you feel that?"

"Naw," I said.

"How about this?" LaFlamme jiggled one cheek so that it made a horrible squelching sound.

"Naw," I said.

"How about this?" LaFlamme placed her two hands on the sides of my face then slapped them together.

"Naw," I said. "Bud id shounded shore." It was probably lucky my beard was reasonably advanced, as it cushioned the blow.

"You're not meant to enjoy it," said LaFlamme. "This is an examination."

"Shorry," I said. "And it'sh nod thad I'm ungratevul. It'sh the mosht attenshin I've had in weeksh." As if this wasn't undignified enough, every 'S' sound I made was accompanied by whistling. "What'sh your diagnoshish?"

"Hmm," said LaFlamme. "Drooling, frothing, incoherent speech, numbness of the head. Are you from Dundee?"

"It'sh nod funny," I said.

"It's *quite* funny," said LaFlamme.

"I say," said Suave Gav, boarding once more. "I've just run out of balsamic. Do you happen to have any?" I waved him towards the kitchen rather than try to engage in a conversation that I felt sure would irritate me further.

"Good show," he said and began rummaging. "Glad to see you're still partying." I was about to explain that this was not my idea of a party and that only a twisted degenerate such as himself would consider it so. But I realised how many 'S' sounds this would entail and decided against it.

Once LaFlamme had finished plying my face into various distorted patterns in the name of a medical diagnosis, she stepped back and weighed up the options. "Mr Boaks, it's clear to me that you're intoxicated."

"I'm nod intokshicaded."

"Not only that, you're a stranger to bathing and a small family appears to have taken up residence in your beard."

"Whad are we going da do?"

"I suggest we amputate."

"The beard?"

"The head," said LaFlamme. "Make a clean sweep of it. It's for the best."

"How long doesh it lasht?" I asked.

"I'm afraid it's permanent."

"Not the ambudation," I said, dribbling heavily. "The Cyofeege." LaFlamme stepped into the bathroom and examined the tube.

"Apply to the affected area every three hours," she said. "So take your next dose around 2:00am." I groaned. I was used to heading to bed under a degree of sedation, but it was most unusual for the sedation to be localised in this way. Had it been a party as Suave Gav suggested, it would have been two separate events – one for my face and one for the rest of my body.

"I say," said Suave Gav, appearing yet again at the boat's entrance. "I have some nitrous oxide. How about a trade?" I wondered how I might find a way to demonstrate in mime that for once and for all, this was not a party. Nothing came to mind but I found chasing the reprobate back to his own lodgings with a tube of Cryofreeze and closing the hatch behind me quite effective.

After waiting a sufficient amount of time to ensure Suave Gav was not going to reappear, LaFlamme and I settled into our bunks and I mentally prepared for a long night of what might be described as 'adverse conditions'. Normally when a boat faces adverse conditions you might expect strong currents, high winds and lashing rain. We had none of these; in fact it was a perfectly still, warm summer night. But I was bunking ten feet below the surface of the ground in a haunted lock with a crew who made me nervous and a substance abusing food alchemist with dubious intentions a couple of metres away. I could only guess how the night would unfold.

Whatever happened, we could be sure LaFlamme's documentary lens was set to record it.

Play. LaFlamme activates the record button and stands down from the bunk. "There's really nothing to be afraid of," she says through the tinny speaker. "The camera will catch everything." From its hook on the topmost corner of the room, the wide-angle lens takes in both bunks, the passageway between them and the kitchen beyond.

11:03. Suave Gav appears. I begin gesticulating. I have my back to the camera so it is unable to fully capture the frothing.

Fast forward. Suave Gav makes further appearances. I am now facing the camera and every grimace is recorded. LaFlamme moulds my frozen mug. Fast, fast forward. This is not pretty.

We settle into our bunks. The tiffany lamps are switched off and the camera lens opens to compensate for the lack of light. A glass of water by LaFlamme's bunk rattles due to her seismic snoring.

Three hours pass. From time to time the two sleeping figures turn. In unison. I start to watch the burnt-in timecode as it is more interesting than anything onscreen. I imagine wading through rushes for a living and struggle to think of anything worse, other than watching the finished programme.

Stop. It is 3:16am. At the bottom of the screen, something stirs between our bunks. It is a little man. He steps slowly and deliberately through the passageway and on into the kitchen before opening the latch door and clambering outside.

Thirty minutes pass. The shadowy figure returns, leaving the latch door open and stopping at the foot of our beds. Here the camera's autofocus kicks in. It is Corky. He stands motionless, as if in a trance. After several minutes he wends his way silently between the bunks and exits bottom right of screen. It is unclear whether he has retired or whether he is just out of shot.

Fast forward. Stop. 3:44. Corky reappears. He climbs onto my bunk and looks directly into the camera's lens. He smiles wickedly and says under his breath, "It's a lovely night for romancing." I feel like I might pass out.

LaFlamme revives me by tugging at my beard. We continue. Fast forward. We see how far the moon travels as it shines through the open latch on to the steps leading to the kitchen floor below. Soon the moonlight fades and the sun begins to rise.

Stop. Rewind. Something is shuffling above deck in the early morning light – a small cat or rodent. It edges down the stairs and stops where LaFlamme left a saucer of milk. It begins drinking from the saucer. It looks like a toupée.

13.
SMOKE ON THE WATER

LaFlamme finally agreed I was having a nervous breakdown. I'd been telling her for days but she wouldn't listen. I think the screaming clinched it. Pretty sure it's cabin fever, which is caused by being enclosed in a tight space with little to do for an extended period of time. Having a walking ventriloquist doll next door probably won't help. Cabin fever is not unusual amongst seafarers due to the difficulties involved in just popping out to the shops for a paper. It's less common amongst narrowboaters. Symptoms include restlessness, irritability, paranoia, irrational frustration and general mistrust of those around. I've had it loads of times on dry land.

My teeth have begun to feel soft. And I've lost all track of time. I've been relying on the movement of the sun for the hour of day since my watch began deliberately misleading me. As the sun is almost directly overhead, it is clearly not five o'clock either AM or PM, you twisted little automaton. You have delusions of grandeur. You're a Casio, not a Hal. LaFlamme asked why I was talking to my watch.

Yesterday around lunchtime, I took a rough guess and set the wayward timepiece to 1:00pm. Since then it's been moving in reverse. I don't think this means we're travelling back in time or anything, just that it's broken. If we were travelling back in time I think everything would sound backwards.

The Admiral once showed me how to play heavy metal records backwards in order to hear hidden satanic messages. The records didn't sound any worse that way, and some of them were much improved. At school there wasn't a record player handy so he'd run the sharp point of a pair of scissors through the grooves and you could hear the contents quite distinctly. He had to buy all his own records though, as no one would lend records to someone who liked running scissors over them.

If I had scissors now I'd take them to my demented Casio. Unfortunately as was painfully clear, scissors were in short supply in Wester. If you happened upon a pair you were likely to have a better use for them than trying to discipline a rogue Casio or playing records backwards, regardless of how much fun it might be.

I stroked my fulsome beard and stared at the ceiling above my bunk. What was I doing here? Day after day we sailed these murky waters, tried and failed to take refuge from the overbearing heat and all the while edged further into the realm of ill-definition. Night after night we drank heavily, suffered abuse at the hands of the insufferable hobgoblin Corky, often in the form of song, and slept fitfully whenever possible. It was probably lucky that the unusual events taking place during the night were occurring during the periods of fitful sleep.

I had to take frequent naps throughout the day in order to compensate for the nocturnal goings-on, and these were made considerably more urgent by the monotonous drone of the engine. Most of my waking hours were spent in semi-stupor, which was considerably more than the quarter-stupor I experienced normally.

Just how vital was it that I be remunerated for my work with The Advocate For Self-Importance? Vital enough to risk losing my admittedly feeble mind in ninety-degree heat whilst being tormented by forces outwith my control? In the chaos that had taken over my life, not to mention my chin, it was easy to forget that remuneration was the primary purpose of this journey. That and the retrieval of Guy LeSnide, but if truth be told I had very little interest in that particular outcome. LeSnide can be a god in Wester if he wants to. It's only being a god in my vicinity that's a problem.

The secondary *ulterior* purpose was of course to try and bring LaFlamme and I closer together. Well, we may have been physically closer but I was no nearer my goal of sipping champagne from her navel. Between writing in her two journals and working on a documentary film, her time was all but taken up. She had figured out how to edit within the camera she had recently appropriated from Suave Gav, and was utterly engrossed in creating some kind of reality show based on our travels. I could think of better things to do with our time but I had to agree there was no way Channel 5 wouldn't love a film about a walking toupée.

In fact our being physically closer had not even been an altogether good thing, as nothing will test a union quite like sleep *apnoea*. Love may not tear us apart but snoring might. However much I may have fantasised about 'sleeping with LaFlamme', nothing could have prepared me for the brief lapses of consciousness that barely passed for slumber whilst LaFlamme shook the boat with her colossal respiratory system. Her heavy breathing had topped my desires list for years, but now that I had it all night every night I had to admit it wasn't quite what I imagined.

LaFlamme too expressed reservations about our proximity. I found out through reading her journal, something I could only do when she was in the shower. I had mixed feelings about this prying. On the one hand, it felt sneaky and not befitting a man of my moral standing. On the other, I didn't really bother about such things.

I waited till I heard the distinctive sound of the shower curtain rattling closed.

> Amusing little man by the name of Cocky, or something. Sings. Has a good line in abuse. Like his style. Pleasant distraction from the tedium and Tony being nuts. Worse than usual today. Preoccupied with some misery or other. May need the dart gun sooner than expected.
>
> Have decided to call the memoirs *Inflammable*. Makes sense. Junior's going to start as soon as we get back. I better let her know.

Junior was not a child, but LaFlamme's mute and hearty-imbibing assistant. She had been a terrific asset in the past on account of her divining skills, which could locate the nearest bar in any given setting.

Channel 5 liked my film idea, *Two and a Half Men and a Little Lady on a Boat*, which goes to show how far they've sunk. I was only kidding! But since I had their attention, I hit them with *Beardy Goes Ape*. Then they really sat up. What a bunch of losers. So we're going all out for that one unless I think of something even worse.

Called Junior and gave her the memoirs skit. She doesn't speak but has an array of sounds at her disposal in order to make herself understood. I said if she had any objections to tell me there and then. I heard a cork pop.

On another matter it seems my great uncle was quite a card. Some suggestion of a scandal. Mostly rumours. Haven't seen any 'Great LaFlambé locked up' headlines yet. Apparently at the end he was deeply in debt and had made some powerful enemies. Showed signs of drug dependency. There was an incident with a rival. Somebody died. They knew how to have fun in those days.

The lock on the bathroom door was being worked feverishly from within. I returned LaFlamme's journal to the corner where I found it, just in time for her to emerge. It was lucky she was such a klutz with locks or this time I could have been rumbled.

"All right Boaks," said LaFlamme, "I know what you're up to."

"I didn't see anything," I said defensively.

"You're planning on growing that beard until there's no room on board for the rest of us. It'll just go on expanding like a liberal dose of quality soap suds, then we'll be forced out by the sheer mass of it."

"Well," I said, "if you can think of a way of removing it I probably wouldn't object. It itches like a demon." I scratched furiously.

"You might have mice," she suggested. Only then did it occur to me that scratching a heavy beard might not be helping my chances with the unrequited love of my life. Something had to be done to crank this relationship up a notch. I needed to impress or enchant her in a manner that would make me irresistible; come up with something that would make her swoon – maybe a sophisticated joke or entertaining anecdote.

"I don't think it's as big as a mouse," I said. Bugger.

LaFlamme could tell it was time to get me off the boat. She ordered Mr Beard to find somewhere to moor and mentioned a dart gun.

Mr Beard had made such an early start that my Cryofreeze was only just wearing off. The lock keeper (who although swarthy, bore little resemblance to the prince of darkness) finally released us, and Suave Gav, revving madly before the lock gates opened, wasted no time in making a break for it. His hairpiece reinstated, he sped on ahead at a cracking pace and flicked V signs at us with his fingers. The politically incorrect word 'mad' once again came to mind, but as I believed I had just seen a toupée drinking milk I decided to keep it to myself.

We were several miles from Lock 13 when Mr Beard said there was a filling station in the area. That would be the ideal place to stop, fill up both the petrol and water tanks and give LaFlamme a chance to do her mental nurse routine with me, something I found simultaneously erotic and irritating.

"We can get some exercise," said LaFlamme. "Have a scout around, maybe do a little research."

"On beards?"

"We're experts on beards," said LaFlamme. "We could write books. No my furry friend, we're here to track down an alchemist. Remember?"

"Advocate," I said.

"Right," said LaFlamme. "Well look where we are." She pointed to an area on the map with a cluster of buildings and a 'public library' symbol circled within.

"You're not going to make me read another book, are you?" I said.

"Look at the name." She took the scruff of my neck and pushed me closer to the map. We had reached the vicinity of The Cludge. This was the last known sanctuary of The Advocate for Self-Importance, Guy LeSnide, and the point at which Captain Pantling said we should do some tracking of our own. I suppose a public library was as good a place as any to find out how to go about it.

"Here's what I had in mind," said LaFlamme. With one hand she traced an as-the-crow-flies route to The Cludge starting from the filling station, and with the other she followed the route of the canal, which diverted eastwards as if to avoid the area before turning sharply west again. "We can get out and walk, the muppets can take the boat and we'll meet up here." Her two index fingers converged on a point where the canal returned to its northerly inclination. It centred on a canalside pub by the name of The Stiff Upper Lip. "Ask them how long it'll take."

I walked through the kitchen and poked my head up to the deck. 'The muppets' were in the midst of some tortuous exchange.

"I still say it's the silliest stage name I ever heard," said Corky.

"I don't see anything wrong with it," said Mr Beard. "A S Proby was well liked in his day."

"Why would anyone who trod the boards want to be known as A S Proby? It was inevitable I'd want to call him Ass Proby, and that's a little close to the bone in our line of work."

"Now Corky," said Mr Beard, "you know very well that Arnold Seward Proby only used the abbreviation to save time."

"You'd have to be in an almighty hurry to want Ass Proby for a moniker," said Corky. "Surname, Proby. First name, Ass. What a peculiar fellow."

"Excuse me," I said.

"It's the divot," said Corky.

"How much longer before we reach The Cludge?"

"Man wants The Cludge," said Corky.

"We'll be through Throgmorton's Pass in a hand spank," said Mr Beard in his unfathomable Wester accent. This meant little to me and I was ready to return below deck empty-handed when an almost clean-shaven young man approached the boat. Mr Beard cut the engine in order to speak.

"Hello Mr Beard," said the young man. "Everything shipshape?" This was evidently a favourite saying of Westerers, but I couldn't see why. There was nothing particularly ship shaped about a narrowboat.

"Oh yes Master Kevin," replied Beard. Nodding in my direction, he said, "We're carrying strange cargo but it's good to be back on the high seas."

"I'm glad to hear it," said Kevin. His face looked so fresh and appealing that I had an urge to stroke his chin. It had been some time since I'd seen anyone without heavy growth, other than Corky, and stroking Corky was not advisable.

Even LaFlamme, although stubble-free, had reported a rogue hair growing at an alarming pace on the outside of her upper arm. I asked why she couldn't just pluck it. She said she was reluctant to do that in case it was something trying to escape – a painful childhood memory perhaps – in which case, doing anything drastic might prove traumatic to its host. She said she preferred to interrogate it but it was moving too fast to be quizzed. I suggested a dose of Cryofreeze to slow it down and surprisingly this did in fact stop the hair abruptly in its tracks. Even better, rather than have to pluck it, it fell out of its own accord. No questions necessary.

It took LaFlamme a mere nanosecond to make the connection between her single rogue hair and my beard, and before I had the chance to object, she'd smeared a wad of Cryofreeze over my chin. Sure enough, soon my whiskers began to crisp up and turn an icy blue until I resembled an eighty-year-old. In turn, this made my head begin to crisp up and turn an icy blue. I believe then that I was in danger of succumbing to a kind of localised hypothermia of the head, and in an effort at resuscitation I slapped the side of my own face. Incredibly this caused the entire beard to fall away and hit the ground with a heavy metallic clunk, leaving me with the cleanest shave I'd ever had. Naturally I was unable to feel it due to the numb-ing effect of the freezing agent, and by the time it was wearing off I had five o'clock shadow once more. However, LaFlamme insisted my near cryogenesis of the cranium was a small price to pay in order to remove the unsightly growth that had been cluttering her horizon. She suggested twice daily applications.

Maybe the youthful Kevin had been experimenting with Cryofreeze, or maybe he was just lucky. He was no child; he was a grown man, per-haps in his early twenties. Children seemed to be scarce in Wester – I couldn't recall having seen a single one the entire journey. Corky was child size, but he was a hobgoblin and although many children can be mistaken for hobgoblins, very few of them actually are.

I wanted to ask Kevin how he kept his complexion so smooth and clear, but Corky was watching him intently and whistling a tune I vaguely recognised, an old Fred Astaire number. I thought this may have been his way of flirting, so I thought asking a personal question would be inappropriate.

"How's your grandfather?" asked Mr Beard.

"He's up ahead," said Kevin. "Working on Little Cinders."

"Is he now?" said Mr Beard.

"Engine trouble," he continued. "Story of his life, I'm afraid. It's either too little fire or too much."

"I should certainly say so," said Mr Beard. They both laughed and Mr Beard re-engaged the engine. I slipped below deck and began drawing ship shapes on our waterways map. After half a dozen they began to look more like pears, which was probably quite appropriate.

A few minutes later Mr Beard began veering the great lunking vessel towards the starboard verge, then cut the engine and announced that we had reached The Cludge. Ahead of us was a ramshackle vessel, somewhat shorter than a narrowboat but substantially wider. It was a dark creosoted tone overall but much of its surface was charcoaled, as if having been struck by lightning. Several cats lounged on its rooftop and a heavily lined old man sat by the tiller, whittling with a pocket knife. Written on the hull below were the words 'Little Cinders', accompanied by an artistic rendition of what might have been Cinderella – it was difficult to make out because much of the paintwork appeared to have been scorched.

LaFlamme stepped off the boat and Corky, although mercifully silent, leered at her in his typical fashion. "Meet us at The Stiff Upper Lip," said LaFlamme.

"Are you sure, miss?" said Mr Beard.

"Do I look like someone who isn't sure?" said LaFlamme.

"I don't rightly know what you're looking for, miss," said Mr Beard. "But you see that gentleman up ahead? That's Mr Covey, one of the oldest men in Wester. A wiser old bird you'll never meet. He might be able to help."

"Good," said LaFlamme. "Show him where the dishes are."

The filling station formed a gateway to the quaint little village that was The Cludge – a sleepy hamlet built around a single pedestrian thoroughfare lined with coffee shops and other small businesses. LaFlamme and I strolled cautiously amongst the beards, trying to blend in as well as we could. This was obviously helped by my having what appeared to be a few weeks' whiskerage.

"Why do they call it an ironmonger?" I said, reading the shop signs.

"Monger is originally from the Latin word 'mango', meaning trader," said LaFlamme. "But that got confusing, what with the stone fruit, and the chutney people weren't happy either, so in Old English it became 'mangere'. If you worked with iron you were an iron mangere, if you traded in fish you were a fish mangere, and so on. It has no connection with the French verb 'to eat', by the way. I mean, 'fish manger' might almost make some weird etymological sense, but 'iron manger' definitely would not."

"Pretty sure you made that up," I said.

"Maybe some of it," she said. "Good though, right? Better than the real answer."

"Which is?"

"I don't know."

We stepped into a sunny tearoom and LaFlamme ordered a pot of decaffeinated coffee. She felt that my stimulant intake had peaked and it was time I went cold turkey. I didn't fancy turkey so I asked for a chocolate truffle. She said sugar was also off the menu. I said if that were the case, I'd be having a double espresso. Finally she agreed that a chocolate truffle was likely to cause the least damage, except where my thighs were concerned.

We sat rather stiffly awaiting our order. I could easily have made small talk (nobody generally expects me to say anything very profound), but there was an elephant in the tearoom and I wasn't sure how to bring it up. In my fragile state, I didn't feel fit to analyse what LaFlamme had captured on tape during the night, but equally I wasn't convinced that it would just go away if neither of us mentioned it. We'd have to get this ball rolling somehow and I thought I could start by simply stating the facts.

"So," I said. "Last night a little wooden man walked through the boat."

"Mm," said LaFlamme.

"How do you explain that?"

"Magic," she replied.

I gazed vacantly across the airy shop.

"Something that looked like a toupée crept into the boat and drank from a saucer of milk," I said.

"Mm," said LaFlamme.

"How do you explain that?"

"Magic," she replied.

Once again I looked across the tearoom and defocused slightly. When I looked back at the table, my chocolate truffle had gone.

"A minute ago I had a chocolate truffle. How do you…"

"Magic," said LaFlamme, licking her lips.

After several decaffeinated and therefore pointless cups of coffee, we located The Cludge Central Library and LaFlamme wasted no time asking one of the librarians for a local telephone directory. She opened it at the letter L and began scouring the names.

"LeSnade, LeSneed, LeSnod," said LaFlamme. "Is he ex-directory?"

"He's ill-defined," I said. "Probably doesn't have a phone now."

"What are we going to do?"

"We could look at some books," I said without enthusiasm, as I always got depressed around books.

I honed in on a row of the hideous fun suppressants. They each appeared to be devoted to the subject of hair, with an emphasis on the facial kind. There was *The Language of the Beard, Beard Styles for the Bon Vivant, An Adjunct to Beard Typology, Rococo Beard Design 1790–1800.* The entire gallery was devoted to the subject; we'd hit the beard mother lode. There was an entire section devoted to the upkeep of the Hibernator – clearly a god amongst beards – and subsections dealt with ornamental wigs, capillamenta and merkins. It was a vast reservoir of knowledge but I wasn't sure how it was going to help us identify LeSnide, unless he had a part in a BBC costume drama.

Luckily the librarian, sporting a pointed flaming red beard, sensed our bewilderment and approached.

"You look as if you could use some assistance," he said, pointing the thing straight at me. I shifted uncomfortably to one side.

"We're looking for somebody," I said. "Has there been any talk of a man by the name of LeSnide?"

"The alchemist?" he replied.

"He's not an alchemist," I said. "He's an advocate."

"They say he's a very powerful one."

"Where can we find him?"

"I believe the LeSniddians have taken up residence in the Balding

Hills, several miles north of here. But I wouldn't approach without first having a reading."

"That's why we're in the library," I said. "To do some a-reading."

"You misunderstand," said the librarian. "What I meant was..."

"Look Conan," said LaFlamme, "I don't know how you Amish do things around here, but we need to find this wizard character before my associate completely loses his marbles."

"Sensitively put," I said. "And he's not a wizard, he's an advocate."

The librarian handed us a calling card with the name 'Dr Simmer' on it. "Can I suggest you begin here?"

"You can suggest it," said LaFlamme, taking the card, "but we might not pay any attention."

"Or we might suggest something different," I said. He retracted his fiery beard and returned to his duties, whatever they were.

LaFlamme collapsed into one of the mezzanine floor's armchairs and rested her feet on a study table. "What's all this about?" she said, studying the card.

"Well," I said, patting my beard and hoping it made me look like a wise prophet, though a confused lumberjack was probably closer. "You remember that story about the odyssey? There's a guy called Odysseus in it. Him and his mates, you know, they go on an odyssey kind of thing? It's all about an odyssey."

"*Jason and the Argonauts*?"

"That's the one. Before they set out, they consult Sybil the Soothsayer to find out if the fates are on their side."

"Gibberish, Boaks. Have you got heatstroke?"

"I think that's what this guy Simmer does. If we cross his palm with silver, he'll study the patterns of my beard and advise us."

"If he studies your beard, the only thing he's likely to advise is washing."

We returned to the librarian.

"Am I correct in thinking this is somebody who makes it his business to read beards?" I said, admittedly an unusual first volley to a librarian.

"Indeed," he replied. "Dr Simmer is just one of many here in Wester. You'll find that pogonomic practitioners in this area are as common as your barbershops." This was good news to me, although not as good news as there being a barbershop.

"First though," said the librarian, "can I give you a word of warning?"

"You can but we might not take it," said LaFlamme.

"Or we might warn you back," I said.

"It is as well for me to mention it, as I believe you are visitors here." He lowered his voice and brought his flaming red beard closer. "Lives have been known to change as a result of consultations. Always be aware that what the augur tells you may not chime with what you want to hear." I said as long as he doesn't tell me LeSnide is broke, we'd be fine.

The librarian pointed us towards an area called 'Chinnatown', a nearby section of the hamlet centre dedicated to chinwear. "Perhaps here you can familiarise yourselves with some of the local fashions and customs. Now is there anything else I can help you with?"

"Do you have any Jeffrey Archer?" said LaFlamme.

The main focus of Chinnatown was a cobbled stone street called Chinnery Row, a bohemian spot lined with boutiques and curiosity shops. There was Chin Chin and Chin Up, both specialists in beard accessories, and a few grooming salons such as Chinobyl and Hairy Krishna, where oiling and braiding were practised. At the end of the street I saw Pog Hall, evidently an assembly room of sorts. Finally I spotted a sign that read 'Augur: Proprietor Dr A Simmer' and although this seemed promising, I thought I should ask LaFlamme what an augur was before I inevitably found out to my misfortune.

"You just told me, Boaks," she replied. "He interprets the will of the gods, like Sybil."

"Right," I said. I wasn't sure the will of the gods would necessarily reside in my beard, but I decided now was not the time for scepticism.

LaFlamme noticed a mall across the street called The Capillamenta Centa. "You go on into the surgery," she said. "I might check out the cappies first."

I was less than thrilled about the idea of entering one of these emporiums alone but figured it probably wasn't any worse than a doctor's surgery, and I'd been going to the doctor alone for years. In fact he'd told me to stop bothering him.

"Afternoon sir," said the proprietor, tending to a customer. "Do you have an appointment?"

"Um no," I said, optimistic at the possibility of a reason to turn around.

"Not to worry," he replied, checking an appointment book. "Take a seat for now and I'll be right with you."

It was the kind of place that might have seemed high tech in the early part of the 20th century. The fittings and furnishings were distinctly Art Deco and everything was made of Bakelite. There were Bakelite countertops, ornaments, a Bakelite cuckoo clock on the wall, even a Bakelite air conditioner which I assumed was a dehumidifier – it was likely to be a controlled environment in order to maximise beard receptivity.

The customer was strapped into a barbershop chair, a lead apron covering his chest and tucked under his beard. On the counter before him was an array of scientific instruments which could have been lifted from the set of *Frankenstein*. The doctor moved between these and a hefty ledger where he was documenting his findings with a quill pen. I tried not to stare at the augur and his customer, but unfortunately when I try not to do something I usually end up doing it even more. Inevitably the doctor caught my eye and at that point I looked for something to read.

I picked up *Hair Today*, a local newspaper with a front page headline that read 'Another victim for the Wester Ripper'. According to this lurid report, a vicious razor killer was loose in the Wester area and had already claimed three lives, all men of an 'indeterminate' age. The story raised certain questions in my mind. For one thing, where the hell did he find the razor? Couldn't he have utilised his skill with the instrument and opened a barbershop instead? Maybe he *was* a barber, an unemployed one, bitter about not being able to find work and taking it out on the beardies. Maybe he shaved them *first*.

Whatever the killer's motivation, it was clear Wester had its fair share of problems. Anyone thinking of settling here ought to study the news closely, and *Hair Today* was the oracle. Not that I was thinking of settling here. In fact I couldn't wait to get home. I was decidedly restless, so after a quick scan I flipped towards the back thinking there might be a comic strip or horoscope. I found a problem page written by a strange agony aunt by the name of Mr Andy. His take on dealing with the problems of local people was most unusual.

Dear Mr Andy,
On Monday I took the day off work and thought I would drop in to Chin Chin for a spot of braiding. Unfortunately the shop was closed and I returned home prematurely. To my horror, I found the next door neighbour in bed with my wife. Apparently this arrangement has been going on for several years and they are very much in love. Now it seems my wife is leaving me and moving in with the neighbour. I am distraught. What should I do?
Albert Hall, East Wester

Dear Albert,
I'm very sorry to hear about your misfortune. I can certainly imagine your pain and frustration. However, it is not unusual for styling boutiques to close on a Monday – most open on Saturday and take Monday as the second half of their weekend. I would always recommend making appointments in advance with any boutique, as this is the only way of avoiding such problems in future.

This was the kind of local knowledge we needed. I would never have known Mondays were potentially a no-go for beard maintenance.

Dear Mr Andy,
Last week I was settling down to *Fat Fatter & Fattest* on Channel 5. I fired up my pipe and was having a good laugh at the fatties when a lit piece of tobacco escaped the pipe chamber and burned a hole through my beard. It fell on to the armchair which, as I had removed the 'do not remove under penalty of law' certificate, was no longer fireproof. It took light and within minutes the entire house burned down. Now I am homeless. Where can I turn?
Abel Oliphant, The Cludge

Dear Abel,
This is a most unfortunate state of affairs. I personally don't

know how I would cope if I wasn't able to laugh at fat people on Channel 5. But you can always stream live programmes onto any smartphone, even if the limited screen size can never fully do justice to the lardasses. Additionally I appreciate the embarrassment and humiliation caused by having a hole in your beard. However, there have been tremendous advances in cosmetic beard enhancement. If you visit your nearest Capillamenta Centa, they will be able to advise you on the best solution for your particular growth type.

Dear Mr Andy,
I have been banned from my local swimming pool. Apparently my beard has been causing such a wake that several small people were washed up on the tiles. I'm being sued by one woman whose husband failed to materialise and there have even been outrageous allegations that I am harbouring the gentleman somewhere within the kinks of my Hibernator. Now I am seriously considering ending it all. I need guidance.
James Longfellow, West Wester

Dear James,
This is not an uncommon situation. Many of us have considered removing our beards, or as you put it 'ending it all' in times of crisis. It's important to remember that you are not alone and shaving will not solve anything. The world will not be a better place with one less Hibernator. As for the suggestion of harbouring a small man, perhaps you can come to some arrangement with the lady regarding visitation rights.

The augur was winding up his appointment. He had removed the lead apron and other coverings from the customer and briefly swept the floor as the customer donned his jacket and prepared to settle his bill.

"Thank you sir," said Dr Simmer. "Do come again." I prepared to get into the chair as he swept the seat with a small hand brush.

"What can I do for you today?" he said. This completely floored me, but thankfully he continued. "Just a checkup?"

"Yes please," I replied and sat down. Even the chair was made of Bakelite, but it was leather upholstered and remarkably comfortable. The doctor drew a dark sheet over me and tied it at the back of my neck, first ensuring that it was tucked tightly beneath my beard. I'd have assumed I was going to get a haircut until he laid the lead apron on my chest and moulded it across my shoulders.

"Heavy," I said.

"Oh yes," replied the doctor. "It has to be in order to minimise static voltage in the atmosphere."

"Of course."

"Day off?"

"Sort of," I sighed. "I had a bout of existential angst aboard The Little Hitler and my friend suggested The Cludge. I wasn't in the mood for turkey, didn't see any truffle, had no luck finding Jeffrey Archer, and now I'm here."

I could see him wondering which social services department to call first, but after a minute he said, "Sounds like you need it."

"Are there any good bars around here?" I asked.

"Stiffies," he replied.

"Stiffies?"

"Yes," he said. "Cask ales, good food, fine selection of combs." I realised then he was referring to The Stiff Upper Lip. "You'll probably want a drink by the time I'm through." We both laughed, although mine was more of a nervous schoolboy squeal.

As the augur busied himself with preparations for the reading, the street door swung open and a customer swanned in. It was hardly surprising that the customer sported a beard – a Van Winkle if I wasn't mistaken – but it *was* surprising that they bore a remarkable resemblance to LaFlamme.

"Afternoon sir," said the augur.

"Afternoon," said LaFlamme, taking a seat in the waiting area and picking up *Hair Today*.

"Do you have an appointment?"

"Actually," said LaFlamme, rising with the newspaper, "I'm with the patient." She pulled up a chair next to me and scrutinised the doctor's movements. The doctor set to work and began by running a light brush through my beard before asking if I had any holidays lined up.

"Yes actually," said LaFlamme before I had time to respond. "My cousin owns Scotland and he's invited us to stay. It's a small country but there's a spare room with bunk beds."

"Scotland, eh?" said the doctor. "Very exotic." It was an unusual description of our homeland and I wondered if the doctor had ever been out of Wester. "My wife and I once spent two weeks in Easter," he said. "Bit of a culture shock to be honest."

Dr Simmer placed his hands on the underside of my beard and gently rubbed his thumbs through my moustache. "It's an unusual barb," he said. "Very kinky."

"It's crumply like the rest of his head," said LaFlamme. "Could you talk us through this process, Doc?"

"Well," he said, "having noted the beard density, I'm now gauging surface texture and coating prior to employing the instruments. I'm seeing some impurities."

"I think that's toast," said LaFlamme, studying with a magnifying glass.

The doctor pointed to an area directly below my chin. "And some slight contamination."

"More toast," said LaFlamme. On this basis it was hard to see what kind of predictions the augur could make, other than that tomorrow I'd be having toast.

He activated one of a bank of Bakelite monitors and squeezed some lubricant onto a handheld scanning device. Both were connected to an electrical control panel similar to a compact mixing desk. As he passed the scanner over my beard and tweaked several settings on the panel, detailed images of my beard's every fibre appeared on the monitor.

"Look," he said, examining a tight cluster of filaments in the centre of the screen. "There's its heart."

"It's really more of a knot," said LaFlamme. The augur made some notes in his mammoth ledger. "When do we get into actually interpreting the will of the gods?"

"First," he replied, "we must calculate the beard's odylic force, which is essentially its divinatory receptivity to occult insight – it's important to undergo this phase thoroughly to ascertain whether the beard is capable of giving a true reading. Yours is in reasonable condition but appears rather weak. Has it suffered any trauma recently?"

"Yes," I said. "It fell off in an ice related incident."

"Nasty," said the augur.

"It didn't work out too badly," said LaFlamme. "We put it to work chilling a bottle of wine. By the time it was drinkable, he'd started a new one." The augur was rather shocked at our nonchalance regarding the icing episode and warned that freezing can result in permanent loss of beard. He said this as if it was a bad thing but I knew immediately that LaFlamme was thinking about stockpiling Cryofreeze.

Satisfied that my beard was going to be sufficiently responsive, Dr Simmer produced an instrument that looked for all the world like a waffle iron, clamped my whiskers within it and connected it to the control panel. He then hooked up a second set of wires to the panel and attached the opposite ends, via sticky felt pads like band-aids, to his temples. This part of the examination, he explained, would be the most intense. He asked us to concentrate – he was about to interrogate the beard.

Sparks shot out of the waffle iron the moment it burst into life, accompanied by the unmistakeable smell of toast. Dr Simmer closed his eyes and after a prolonged pause and several deep breaths, spoke in a high-pitched fey little voice.

"I see bars," he said.

"Excellent," said LaFlamme. "Nearly drink o'clock."

"Bars all around," he continued. "Steel bars. A cage or prison."

"Prison?" I said.

"Probably LeSnide," said LaFlamme. "After we slip him the old dart gun we'll be boxing him up like *Mighty Joe Young* and shipping him home." Leaving aside her confusion with *King Kong*, I was inclined to go along with this interpretation. I had a very rational and understandable fear of prisons due to the whole being locked up thing. If I thought the augur might see *incarceration* in my future, I'd have given him someone else's beard to interrogate. But LeSnide might well need a cage of some sort. If he was as barkingly ill-defined as everyone suggested we'd need something to stop him mounting the Empire State Building, or the advocates' equivalent, Saint Giles Cathedral.

"What else do you see, Doc?" said LaFlamme.

"Smoke," he replied, "on the water." LaFlamme assumed this was a William Shatner-style reading of the Deep Purple song and continued in dramatic fashion:

"Fire... in the sky." The Bakelite cuckoo clock chimed three.

"I see a man... who appears to be sick," said the augur.

"He's just hungover," said LaFlamme.

"And another man... with medicine."

"Am I the one who's sick?" I asked. "Or the one with the medicine?"

"It's not clear," he said. "But I see an award."

"Nobel," I suggested.

"Darwin," said LaFlamme.

"Who is Kevin?"

"He's the guy in the song," said LaFlamme. "'Feels Like Kevin.'"

"I see a quest," he said. "A long and arduous journey."

"It's an odyssey," I said.

"A man of great importance."

"Do you know where he is?" asked LaFlamme.

"Does he have any money?" I asked.

"I see a clearing in the jungle, high in the hills. A temple. Graven images. A stone effigy. And... I see plants... incredibly ugly plants."

"Potentilla," I said.

"*Erecta*," said LaFlamme.

"Revellers. They have gathered to worship the sun. It is a festival of fire, the summer solstice. But I see detractors. They are saying so much madness on a small hilltop is geologically unstable and they must disperse."

"Spread the madness out a little," said LaFlamme.

"I see... I see..." Veins bulged in Dr Simmer's temples as he battled to put voice to his vision.

"I see lawyers!"

He collapsed under the strain, the leads from the waffle iron falling to the floor. Smoke rose from my beard and I had to resist the opportunity to offer an alternative lyric for the Deep Purple song. Unclamping the device, I shook myself free and watched an array of charred crumbs scatter.

"Do me, Doc," said LaFlamme, disconnecting her capillamentum and handing it to the augur. "No need to do the checkup bit, just stick this in your toaster."

"It would be most unusual," said the augur.

"I promise we'll leave you alone if you do." This proved too tempting an offer for the augur and he agreed, composing himself before placing the detached barb in the waffle iron, lowering his eyelids and concentrating.

"I see more smoke," he said.

"I think your glasses have steamed up," said LaFlamme. The combination of high humidity and the heat from the iron had brought a fog to the augur's lenses. He wiped them with a handkerchief before continuing.

"I still see smoke," he said, "and a figure rising from ashes."

"Phoenix," said LaFlamme.

"Deep Purple reforming," I said.

"A magician," he said. I'd have preferred Deep Purple reforming, but reminded myself that magic circle types used to be fun and weren't always the weird little guys with no friends we see nowadays.

"I see old people," said the augur. "Very old."

LaFlamme looked puzzled. "Like forty?"

"They are from another time. They are young on the outside but old on the inside."

"Do they work in a bank?" I asked.

"Who is McCorkadale?" said the augur. "Who is the singer?"

"Pearl's the singer," said LaFlamme.

"Who is the man with the razor?" he said with a growing sense of alarm.

"If I knew that," I replied, "he'd be my best mate."

The augur stood abruptly and screamed at the top of his voice.

"Red rum! Red rum!"

Sensing we had exhausted the poor man and that we could all indeed use a drink, LaFlamme and I settled our bill and left him to his toaster.

Outside Stiffies we caught up with The Little Hitler as agreed. It had been a most relaxing few hours on dry land – this time it really was dry – and I felt much better for it. It was just possible that LaFlamme had my best interests at heart after all. I spent the remainder of the day drifting in and out of sleep as Mr Beard took us further into deepest Wester. Beard, Corky and LaFlamme were all oddly subdued. I wondered if my state of mind was skewing perception of events or whether they were genuinely quiet. Either way I wasn't hearing anything.

I had *Music Hall Luminaries* by my side and picked it up from time to time between sporadic zeds. I found the fabled A S Proby and one or two others who interested me. Then I discovered a vocal group called The Osborne Trio, contemporaries of The Great LaFlambé who shared billing from time to time.

Originally a duo, the Osbornes were a vocal harmony group from Oxford who found some stage success. Brothers David and George Osborne came from an affluent background, were privately educated and given constant training and encouragement from their mother, Margaret. Margaret Osborne had herself once trod the boards as a Cilla Black impersonator long before Cilla Black was famous.

But with an exhausting touring schedule, which meant travelling the length and breadth of the country forty weeks a year – eighty if it was around the Wester area – the Osbornes soon grew tired of their limited vocal repertoire and developed other sidelines to their act. David Osborne made an acceptable tap dancer whilst younger brother George became a rather poor hypnotist. George often tried to convince entire audiences that what he was doing was brilliant and that they were extremely fortunate to have him as their entertainer. Unfortunately he was usually the only one to fall under, and this self-confidence, which bordered on mania, kept him afloat in his own self-worth for many years.

The brothers teamed up with Thomas McCorkadale, a childhood friend with a singing voice that outshone his cohorts, and a wicked sense of humour that often saw him roasting the brothers and ultimately tormenting them on stage. When the Osbornes became unhappy with their reduced roles in the act, McCorkadale developed a sideline in ventriloquism and this gave him a dummy to abuse in their place.

Whilst McCorkadale's stage persona was that of a dashing and debonair man about town, his dummy 'Timothy' was a scruffy carefree sort with a slow wit and a homegrown charm that audiences found agreeable. The easy banter that followed between the two ensured the act was a crowd favourite.

In real life however, McCorkadale was an abrasive character capable of bullying and humiliating anyone who displeased him. Even given a dummy, the Osborne brothers continued to be his onstage targets. One night at a sell-out show in the London Palladium he repeatedly referred to them as 'the Bullingdon bumboys' and had the act banned from the venue. (In those days the word 'Bullingdon' was strictly taboo.) Soon his abusive and erratic performances with sidekick Timothy began to consist of nothing but insults hurled at the brothers, who had by now taken to cowering backstage.

Finally the Osbornes revealed to a stunned audience that McCorkadale had been involved in a riding accident which resulted in him being unable to perform. They reverted to a duo and continued for a short spell as The Bellingham Bonbons, but by now audiences knew them better as the Bullingdon bumboys and the act soon fizzled out. (Even today the word Bullingdon is considered offensive to most.)

It's unknown how McCorkadale lived out his remaining days. Rumours abounded that he had been the victim of ritual magic and that his incapacity was revenge for years of ill treatment doled out on the slow-witted. There is no way of knowing for sure, but the end of his brief career was one of the great tragedies in all of music hall history.

Music Hall Luminaries was an interesting read, in as much as any book can ever be called interesting. I must have been quite engrossed because the hours flew past and I barely noticed when Mr Beard asked Corky what the evening's closing song would be.

"'Cheek to Cheek,'" said Corky. "Though it's been such a long time, I may have forgotten some of the words." He leered at LaFlamme.

"Just do your best then," said Mr Beard.

Corky launched into the song he'd been whistling earlier, but experienced the same lyrical difficulties he'd encountered the previous night.

> Kevin, I'm with Kevin
> And I've drunk so much that I can hardly speak
> And I seem to find the manly love I seek
> When we're out together mooning cheek to cheek
> Kevin, I'm with Kevin
> And my heart beats so that I can hardly speak
> And I know I've found the manly love I seek
> When I'm spanking Kevin's cheeky little cheeks

"Oh good god," I said.

Corky cut it short and chortled. "Bonne nuit, bitches!" he declared at considerable volume.

Play. 12:15. LaFlamme and I settle into our bunks and the camera lens adapts to the reduced light. Three hours pass without any distinguishable movement. It reminds me of working from home.

Stop. Rewind. At 3:37, a blaze of light in the top left of the screen causes the lens to overexpose. Once it has adjusted, we see the contents of an ornamental bowl on a wooden shelf at the foot of my bunk are alight. The flames rise six or seven inches at first, then extinguish naturally within the space of a minute. A light fog of smoke fills the cabin but shortly this too dissipates.

Fast forward. At 4:56, our eyes are trained on the wooden shelf. LaFlamme spots the subtlest of movements next to the extinguished ashes and rewinds slightly. A spider plant is sending out a child stalk from within the midst of its green shoots – tentatively, as if in search of water. The stalk grows in an upward trajectory, thickening at the base until its weight forces it to the floor. Once at the foot of my bunk we lose sight of its roving tip. Shortly there is movement beneath the covers. The probing stalk is travelling up the length of the bed, inches behind where I lie. I feel like I might pass out.

LaFlamme revives me by tugging at my beard. Fast forward. It is ten minutes before the stalk begins a slow retreat, winding its way down the bed, back up to the shelf and returning to within its ceramic enclosure.

14.
SIX DEGREES OF STUPIDITY

LaFlamme asked if I've had any trouble sitting down this morning. I told her it wasn't remotely amusing and that although physically unharmed, I was feeling emotionally confused. She said I was obviously popular and that I should embrace this new plant love, which singularly failed to console me.

Next to the innocuous looking spider plant I found the bowl with charred remnants of what were either leaves or papers. I raised the dish to my nose. Somewhere just beneath the smoky scent was a distinct rose fragrance. "Potpourri?" said LaFlamme in her ridiculously authentic French accent.

It was altogether too peculiar and upsetting to contemplate further. I needed a distraction and was unusually grateful when The Admiral called, saying he'd made some progress with Project X.

"I tried a new batch after an excess of Old Crowther's Fine And Dandy," he said. "Next day I felt fine."

"And dandy?" I asked.

"Not really."

I explained to The Admiral that Suave Gav was in the area and that we may have some competition on our hands for our morning-after cure.

"Hell's bells," he said. "Best keep the Cryofreeze handy. How are things panning out?" I said that in terms of plant life the area was certainly lively, especially at night, and that if we were looking for a source of the mental torment plant we'd hit the jackpot. But otherwise I might have stepped into the seventh circle of hell and I'd probably know for sure as the day progressed.

"Day?" he said. "What time do you think it is?"

"Well I've just had breakfast," I replied. "Ten? Eleven?"

"Try midnight."

"Midnight? Are we in a different time zone?"

"It may be Wester Mean Time."

"What?"

"Not a time zone as such," said The Admiral. "Physics anomaly. In Wester, everything takes twice as long as it does everywhere else. Einstein discussed it. Part of the effect of travelling at high speed."

"We've been doing four miles an hour."

"Very fast in Wester terms," he replied. Certainly I had to agree that life in Wester had been playing out at a snail's pace – probably the fastest thing I'd seen in the area was Suave Gav's toupée. If Einstein were familiar with the area it would explain the physicist's wayward hair.

"Give it a while and see if it settles down," said The Admiral. "You've only been gone three days."

"I've seen seven sunsets," I replied.

"The faster you travel, the more time slows."

I didn't like the sound of this at all. I might end up being ninety by the time I got home and that wouldn't help my chances with LaFlamme. Admittedly she would be eighty-eight but I still didn't like the odds. With this in mind, I thought I should keep an eye on just how many of Corky's mournful songs I was enduring and perhaps start a journal of my own. It might be that my record of our epic quest turned out to be an important document and considered the work of a master of letters – a diarist, say, of equal stature to Samuel Pepys. As yet there was no sign of any plague or great fires but these were details.

I had every reason to feel confident of my writing ability, after all. One time I wrote a short story and sent it to an online writing symposium for their opinion. The resulting assessment concluded that my mini masterpiece (about a magic roll of Sellotape that's also a part time crime fighter) was 'engaging in a somewhat pointless fashion', a glowing review if ever I've read one. I knew then that I had the makings of a scribe of distinction and might soon join the author of *The Maltese Falcon* (Dan Brown, I think it was) in the pantheon of literary greats – drunk, refusing to wash and asking the others what pantheon means.

I showed the review to The Admiral. He said I was 'damned with faint praise', and I agreed they must have really liked it. The Admiral also harbours a desire to be an author and has often said he wishes to write 'a classic of 20th century literature'. Despite my misgivings about the timing of this effort, he remains undeterred and continues to pound away at his keyboard regularly, if only in frustration.

He even showed me a sample of his writing. It appeared to be in CSS. I didn't want to discourage him because many classics of 20th century literature are also written in code. *Ulysses* for example, which is as much fun as *The Book of the Dead* and five times as long, requires an even bigger tome on hand for deciphering. I told The Admiral if it were his intention to compose something equally obscure, Ms-Dos might be closer to the correct time period.

Anyway, I believe there's only room for one great author in any social circle and my Sellotape adventure (possibly one of an extensive series of titles in the magic office accessory/part time crime fighter genre) put me some way ahead of the fold. But then I had a sobering thought. What if history decided LaFlamme was the true master of letters in our group? Although far from dedicated to the art of writing, she was surprisingly prolific in the rare moments she found the inclination to commit thoughts to paper. And as *Ulysses* demonstrates, it's sheer volume of wordage that counts.

Her secret journal lay tantalisingly close. As she was safely in the shower and my only task for the morning was to remove debris from my beard, something that grew more difficult as its density increased, I once again fought the temptation to pry. But then I remembered the saying 'you should choose your battles' and decided this wouldn't be one of them.

Tony's chin has taken a turn for the worse. It was already pretty bad but now there's so much in the way of toast crumbs that birds have started going for him. Not sure if it's the crumbs they're after or just good nest material. Made a joke about him not usually having to fight off birds and he laughed for a bit until he discovered something had hatched.

Made a start on *Inflammable* but having some motivational issues. It's easy enough to see why someone might want to read about my life but who can be bothered writing it? This is where Junior's meant to come in. She texted to ask when we'd be back. I said she'd know because I'd open a bottle of something strong. She's unstoppable once she gets the scent in her nostrils.

Looked up LaFlambé on Wikipedia. (I wasn't too fussed about factual accuracy, reliability of sources or any of that stuff.) Nothing much there so I looked up Houdini. Escapologist, master magician, born 1874 in Hungary. Took the name Houdini because he admired the Scottish contortionist Hugh Deany and couldn't spell. Blah blah blah. Jeez for a master showman it made dull reading. He should've spent less time getting out of handcuffs and more time thinking about his Wiki legacy. Still, it linked to another site with a bit about the great uncle. A couple of interesting points:

1) LaFlambé fathered a child, a daughter by the name of Mari (pronounced 'marry' to rhyme with Harry after his Hungarian friend). Not much known about Mari except that she got hitched to an entrepreneur, the inventor of the potato peeler. He was also an escapologist of sorts, in that he managed to evade the clutches of the Inland Revenue for years. They had a son called Kevin. With a magician and an entrepreneur for parents, I imagine the son just wanted a nice office job where he could make more money than both.

2) After LaFlambé died a performer by the name of Pierre Covey – 'The Burning Sensation' – began touring with an unusually similar act. It included all of the relative's set pieces, most notably *The Combustor*, and hence there was talk of plagiarism. In his defence Covey said it was 'a LaFlambé tribute act'. The act was short-lived anyway because the pyrotechnic style of theatre was falling out of favour both with theatre owners, whose annual

insurance premiums had gone through the roof, and with audiences, who were tired of being singed.

I'd like to have known what else LaFlamme learned about her mysterious relative and indeed how she felt about the whole chin situation, but my prying was interrupted suddenly when a woman's scream punctured the air. The journal fell clean through my hands and a rush of adrenalin made my heart race. It's not that I was alarmed by the woman screaming. I just worried it might hasten LaFlamme from the shower.

I squirrelled the book back to its hiding place and headed to the back of the boat to investigate the cause of the commotion. A fair-haired woman of academic appearance rushed past and despite Mr Beard expressing concern for her well-being, would not stop to explain. Beard and I stepped out onto the towpath, our eyes following the woman until she rounded a corner and was gone. Turning to face the direction from which she had come, I could see only the canal snaking towards a dense and impenetrable morass. It wasn't pretty but it wasn't worth screaming about either.

We untied the mooring ropes and set off at an amble, apprehensive of what might lie ahead. Mr Beard donned waterproofs and navigated with more than usual caution. Corky, also in waterproofs, sat motionless by his side – apart from his eyes, which swivelled occasionally. Dark clouds made it feel like twilight, although I'd just finished shaking breakfast from my beard. The air was heavy with moisture and steam rose from the canal. It didn't seem to matter how much it rained, there was never any let up in the oppressive humidity. I tugged at the top of my t-shirt trying to create a breath of air but the effort required to cause a breeze made me sweat even more. I gave up, resigned to being a mess for the foreseeable future.

I switched on the lights in the cabin below and ventured into a storage cupboard thinking I might find tools or weapons in case we needed to flee the boat. Instead I found an old cassette player (which was better, but not particularly useful in a fleeing-type scenario) and a box of tapes. There was a limited selection; mostly Wester folk singers with predictable beard difficulties – as if folk music didn't already have an image problem. Mercifully I found The Doors. 'This is the end, beautiful friend', went the song. It was particularly dirgey, which was fine by me as happy music tends to make me uncomfortable.

"Gin rummy?" said LaFlamme when she appeared from the shower.

"It's a little early," I said, before realising she meant cards. It was a little early for cards too, but this was probably not the point to be seated at the front of the boat enjoying the view.

"Is this a funeral?" said LaFlamme, removing the Doors tape and dropping it from the open window into the canal. "Do you have any Stranglers?" I wanted to explain the irony of this to LaFlamme – that without The Doors, The Stranglers would not have known what to do with musical instruments and would most likely have remained in the teaching profession where they could have corrupted a whole genera-tion in a far more subtle and *insidious* manner. But LaFlamme wasn't somebody who appreciated lessons in pop music history, and anyway there were no Stranglers tapes. Now there were no Doors tapes either.

"Where do you suppose we are?" I said. I consulted the map, though why I thought that would help I don't know. Canal maps are confusing to say the least. Unlike ordinary maps there are very few place names, because there are very few identifiable places. The map is loaded with symbols, tiny circles with obscure markings within, and the canal path is traversed with lines representing locks and bridges. There's a key that helps you identify the symbols, so you end up shifting your gaze from map to key regularly. Once you've figured out what a symbol means, you've generally lost your place and have to start again. In order to really establish your location, you have to separate the things you've seen from the things you haven't seen. The point between the last thing you've seen and the first thing you haven't seen is where you are. It's not really an exact science.

"Let me have a look," said LaFlamme, joining me. She began tracing a route from The Cludge with her finger. "We left here about an hour ago. There's the swing bridge with the metal railings and then there was that little narrow bit where we held up the traffic."

"I don't see any angry face symbols," I said.

"Meh," said LaFlamme. She continued to follow the weaving line of the canal until reaching a green circle with a boat symbol within.

"What's that?" I asked. LaFlamme consulted the key.

"Boat hire," she said. "Must have been that little jetty with all the canoes." Further on she reached an orange circle with an 'i' symbol within.

"What's that?" I asked. She consulted the key.

"Information," she replied. "Must have been that little supply store with the duelling banjo guys outside." Further still, she reached a larger orange circle with an indistinct shape within.

"What's that?" I asked. LaFlamme looked a little closer then wiped it from the map.

"Marmalade," she said, licking her finger.

"I don't remember seeing that."

"I've just erased it from your mind," she replied. I asked if she could erase any of the forthcoming locks from my mind, as dealing with them was starting to wear me down. They may be a remarkable feat of Victorian engineering but it's surprising how little you care for such things after you've been through fifty of them, each one adding twenty minutes to your journey.

"Butter stain," said LaFlamme, continuing to follow the route. "Tomato sauce. Chutney. Unspecified grime." She reached a blue circle with a tap symbol within. "Water."

"Lots of water," I said. "Nothing but water. Water, water, water."

"Tap water," said LaFlamme. "I don't remember seeing any taps." Next to the tap symbol was a red circle with a star symbol within.

"Vietcong?" I asked.

"Place of interest," she replied. "We definitely haven't passed that. A duller stretch I've never seen."

Mr Beard popped his head into the cabin. "Need to make a stop shortly," he said. "Fill up the water tank." I said I wasn't sure it was strictly necessary as I'd given up on washing some time ago. But this at least confirmed our exact location on the map. It could best be summed up as on the northwestern verge of the butter stain.

We pulled up behind a similar sized narrowboat where an exotically attired white man with an alarming Afro hairstyle was using a hose to fill his vessel's water tank. He wore a beige suit, which was surely a bad choice for the ninety-degree swamp conditions we were enduring.

"Ahoy!" he called, extending his free hand in a wave. It was Suave Gav. The alarming Afro might account for the screaming.

"What happened to your... um... hair?" I asked, as LaFlamme and I joined him on the towpath.

"Oddest thing," he said. "I was irrigating a particularly thirsty bonsai and left the plant food by the shower. Later I mistook it for shampoo and applied a liberal dose to the old melon. Next thing I knew, I looked like Phil Spector."

"He'd have been envious," said LaFlamme.

"It's marvellous to have discovered a cure for baldness of course, and I did consider the commercial possibilities. But unfortunately there are very few Caucasians who suit a kinky Afro. Anyway I believe it would only work in Wester, so even if one were content to look like a major goon, it would be prone to shrinkage outwith the area. I'd be facing lawsuits from irate baldies and as I'm sure you'd agree, Wester is not a place to take on the law." He was right. I'd met Wester lawyers and it wasn't pleasant. Not that meeting lawyers elsewhere was a joy, but in Wester it seemed dangerous.

Satisfied that his boat's tank was now full, Suave Gav turned off the water tap and disconnected the hose. Mr Beard duly approached with The Little Hitler's water *accoutrements* and began the filling-up process.

"Took me an hour," said Suave Gav.

"The hair?" said LaFlamme.

"The tank," he replied. "You might want to amuse yourselves for a bit."

"Well apparently there's a 'place of interest' here," said LaFlamme. She used her fingers to denote inverted commas, although I remember her once telling me that people who did that were, in inverted commas, 'twats'.

"Is there really?" said Suave Gav. "That I'd like to see. Been nothing but places of sheer tedium for the last few miles. I wonder what it is."

"That'll be The Old Barnett," said Mr Beard. "Theatre museum. This area was once quite the thriving metropolis."

"I'm not sure we should stray too far," I said. "It's a jungle out there."

"It's true, the theatre is a difficult career path," said Suave Gav. I rolled my eyes.

"I mean it's overgrown and possibly hazardous."

Mr Beard looked pensive. "Way back in the day," he said solemnly, "this area was a hive of activity for the variety stars. There was The Barnett, The Philament, The Vibrissa, The Tendril, The Mane. Then of course there was The Fringe. Some of the acts never left. They could go from theatre to theatre, one engagement at a time, make their money over half the year then lie low the other half."

"But it's a wilderness now," I said. "What happened?"

"Fertile land, Mr Tony. Only takes a short while for them vines to get a hold. They grew over the theatres and sucked them in. The Barnett's still here but who knows how long they'll be able to hold onto it."

This was beginning to make me nervous. Knowing how quickly a beard could take hold, I was concerned that I too could be taken over if I didn't keep on the move. I said if we wanted to see The Old Barnett we should do it post-haste, before anything else rooted. Mr Beard having indicated a path for us across a vine coated footbridge, LaFlamme and I, Suave Gav and the alarming Afro set out. I was glad the hobgoblins would have to remain as I didn't need to hear Corky's museum commentary.

On the other side of the bridge I very soon lost site of the canal, the combination of lack of light and heavy undergrowth making visibility difficult. I became aware of the rustling of plant life ahead and the sound of a man's voice, strained as if struggling with something unwieldy.

"Get back," said the voice. "Get back, I tell you."

As the man came into view, Suave Gav was first to address him. "Excuse me," he said, a protective arm strewn across the top of his massive do. "Are you talking to us?"

"Heavens no," said a squat little gardener setting down his rake, his face so blackened with sweat and soil that all I could make out were the whites of his eyes. "Go right in."

"In?" said Suave Gav.

"You want The Old Barnett?" said the gardener. He extended an arm to his side and only then was I able to discern the shadowy form of a building so well camouflaged by vine that I could easily have walked into it. I reached out to touch the wall and felt my way along it before finding an alcove. Judging where the doorknob might be, I clutched at a mossy substance. This turned out to be Suave Gav's head.

"Steady on, old man," said Suave Gav, who had fallen to his knees also trying to locate the doorknob. We stumbled into the museum together, LaFlamme bringing up the rear. (LaFlamme's hair didn't appear to have dried since her shower, such was the moisture content of the air. "I always wondered what a Turkish bath would be like," she said.)

The Old Barnett was a cavernous and dimly lit Victorian theatre with two vast chandeliers hanging from the ceiling. It was remarkably cool inside and had a stale vegetal aroma. It made me think I should probably eat more greens.

We were greeted by an earnest bespectacled attendant with a soft-spoken voice. "We don't get many visitors any more," he said.

"I can't imagine why not," said LaFlamme. "It's such a lovely day out for all the family."

"Are you local?" he asked.

"Oh yes," said LaFlamme. "We've been here for years."

I wasn't sure what to expect in a theatre museum and asked the attendant if there was an audio guide. "I'm afraid not," he said, "but I can give you some pointers." He sprang eagerly from behind his desk and I immediately regretted the question.

"Unlike other areas with theatrical traditions," he began, "Wester has no early theatre. Not for us the religious drama from the time of Henry VIII. Not Shakespearean drama, nor restoration drama. Theatre in Wester begins in the 19th century and is entirely music hall." I was glad to hear this as it meant there'd be fewer Simon Callow types popping up.

We wandered through the vast building, the air filling with the echo of Suave Gav's brogues clicking against the hard stone floor. There were frequent interjections from the attendant, who did indeed speak like one who was unaccustomed to visitors. The exhibits were plentiful but a little decayed and neglected. I cast an eye over some etchings of early theatre performances. In one image, waiters moved between aisles carrying bottles chained to trays. This seemed obscure until I spotted another image with actors performing behind a wire grille. It took me a minute to connect the bottles to the grille, but I doubt whether early Wester theatregoers had any such difficulty.

The engravings told the story of a wide and eclectic range of per-formers who had graced the stages of old Wester. It wasn't just singers, dancers and comedians – magicians, acrobats, animal artistes and puppeteers were all legitimate forms of live entertainment, and in fact it seemed that anybody who could endure a live audience might find themselves a star of the stage. When I mentioned this to LaFlamme, she said the clue was in the title.

"Museum?" I said.

"Variety, dumbo."

"He called it 'music hall'. What's a magician doing in a music hall?"

"Magicians are everywhere," said LaFlamme in a way that made me want to check if there was one behind me. When I did, there was a huge Afro peering over my shoulder.

"Quite educational, wouldn't you say?" said Suave Gav.

"If I'd known it was going to be educational," I said, "I wouldn't have come."

Despite my misgivings, the exhibits were engaging. It was interesting for example to see renderings of The Old Barnett in its prime. An exterior view showed the remarkable architecture of the building (now obscured by plant life); how it was fronted with long Doric columns and topped with ornate arches and Ottoman spires, as if the architect was unsure which empire he was trying to ape. The overall effect was oddly pleasing.

The building was at the centre of this odd little cultural microcosm and had been a popular spot. Pictures showed couples strolling along the theatre promenade in their finery, past water fountains and gas streetlamps. The Balding Hills loomed in the background shrouded in mist, and in the foreground was an indication of what was to come: a group of malignant low-lying shrubs. An early photograph of the theatre, taken from the same angle but obviously at a much later date, notably showed fewer people and considerably more shrubs.

The interior appeared to have changed very little. The mezzanine floor that acted as a balcony still extended across three sides of the hall and the stage remained intact. It even had curtains in place, although I suspected if anyone tried to close them they would turn to dust. The only noticeable difference was the wall between the foyer and the hall. It had been removed, allowing a ghostly light to filter through the arched stained glass windows high above the main doorway.

"Would need an awfully big ladder to clean," I said to nobody in particular.

"Never mind that," said LaFlamme, studying a selection of theatre programmes. "Look at this. 'Adults over the age of 21 must be suitably barbed.'"

"You had to be beardy to get in?" I said.

"Not just beardy, but *suitably* beardy. Yours probably wouldn't have cut it."

"There's nothing wrong with my beard," I said, not yet ready to admit that itching was getting to be a problem. As I tugged at it and watched assorted debris fall to the floor, LaFlamme looked at me with distaste and moved swiftly on to the next exhibit.

There were dozens of playbills – posters advertising the acts that were due to grace the Barnett stage. Each performer's name was laid out in bold lettering and accompanied below by a tagline description of the act, their unique selling point: Bettina Richman – In daring and thrilling Dances. Pauline Crothers – and her Incredible Violin. The Hearnes – Keeping things Lively. The Osborne Trio – Never a Dull Moment. Pierre Covey – The Burning Sensation. I was struck by their quaintness, their peculiar designs and of course their mould – the frames were virtually alive with the stuff. I thought it was green cotton wool at first and made a mental note that this would be a fine place if you needed antibiotics.

There were numerous studio portraits, which was surprising given that photography was still in its infancy when The Old Barnett reached its heyday. Although monochromatic and generally faded, there was no doubting the full Technicolor glory of the performers captured in the images – I hadn't seen an odder assortment of weirdos and misfits since art college.

A few short lines of biographical detail accompanied each photograph, and it was clear from these that often very little were known about the performers. Most were sketchy on dates and frequently resorted to (?) when facts were scarce. For example, one image showed a clean-cut man with dark slicked back hair and an upturned moustache. He wore a white barber's jacket and was bowed slightly towards the camera, a cheesy ingratiating grin playing across his face.

Buster Shaver
Born 1862(?) Milan – Died 1912(?) Wester
Buster Shaver was an amazingly talented(?) novelty performer, much loved for the unusually named 'Buster Shaver and his Tiny Razor', a shaving based act completely at odds with the light touch exfoliating habits in Wester. Shaver would ask for a volunteer and completely denude them of hair in a matter of minutes – this included the pubic region, much to the surprise of volunteers, who were quite oblivious to his presence in the area. Ironically he died when a paper cut wound turned septic. His last words were: 'Those who live by the sword must die by the sword.'

Sketchy biographical details or not, one thing that never appeared vague was the place of death. It was remarkable how many of these entertainers met their demise here in Wester. It must have been the go-to place for showbiz termination, the Las Vegas of its day.

I wondered what kind of lives these people must have led. Constantly travelling, combating loneliness and difficult audiences who drank, smoked, heckled and stank their way through every performance. They probably only ever associated with other theatre types, regarding the rest of society as 'civilians'. Civilians had different values, different moral codes. They dressed differently, had families and responsible jobs. I imagine this is what keeps performers youthful, as all that stuff is horribly ageing.

I wondered if it was the same for performers today – were they still outsiders, rebelling against the tedium of straight life? I could only imagine, but I suspect theatre in Victorian Wester was very different from the one Andrew Lloyd Webber filled with his horrible songs.

I was about to join LaFlamme when I was struck by a photograph of a man almost entirely engulfed by flames, but apparently unfazed by fire. The caption read 'Born 1865 Bordeaux – Died(?) Wester.' (I quite liked the 'died – question mark'. When I die I will insist on similar wording on my tombstone just to keep everybody on their toes.) It was of course The Great LaFlambé. Several live shots captured the pyrotechnician in his prime, mostly with some degree of conflagration and surrounding clouds of smoke. But there was nothing in the biographical informa-tion that I hadn't heard before – until I reached the final image in the series, which showed him removing makeup in front of a stage mirror. I assumed it was makeup but it may well have been soot.

Later Years
LaFlambé's last days were tainted by controversy. A nursing home, which housed an elderly theatre star who claimed LaFlambé had stolen his act, burned down, killing the performer. LaFlambé said he was delighted the old man had died as he owed him money, but he was in no way responsible and had an alibi in that he was washing his hair that night. Not surprisingly, the man credited with the gift of telepathic combustion had some difficulty persuading authorities that he was washing his hair and not perfecting some nursing home-based part of his rep-ertoire. He was about to be formally charged when, performing in The Old Barnett, a trick that went wrong(?) reduced the interior to ashes leaving only the shell of the building intact. LaFlambé was said to have died at the scene but this has since been questioned, as his assistant Henri appears to have been the one buried.

The unfortunate assistant Henri was pictured with a small dog.

Henri Cheval
LaFlambé's assistant became known as 'the most unfortunate man in show business', a reputation which may have arisen after naming his dog 'Macbeth'. Cheval often acted as body double for LaFlambé, and was frequently mistaken for his master. When LaFlambé had apparently fallen down a flight of stairs into a theatre basement breaking a leg, audiences were shocked and upset. When later they discovered it was Cheval, their pain turned to delight. On another occasion they were relieved to discover it was not The Great LaFlambé who had fallen into an orchestra pit, lodging his head so firmly within a euphonium that he was forced to wear it for several days. It was only Cheval.

This suggested that an image of LaFlambé's funeral, showing a cortège passing through a cemetery with four horses pulling an open-sided carriage, coffin on top, might actually have been Cheval's funeral – although smoke wafted from within the coffin. A crowd had gathered and elaborate floral tributes lay by the graveside. One such was shaped like theatre curtains with bright carnations representing flames.

Funeral of The Great LaFlambé
LaFlambé's funeral was so well attended that special crowd control police had to be drafted in to deal with it. Written tributes by the graveside were numerous. 'You lit up our lives.' 'I shall never forget your radiance.' 'How am I going to make toast now?' Fans were united in their grief. LaFlambé had touched many people's lives and scorched countless others.

In a grainy and indistinct photograph showing the aftermath of LaFlambé's ultimate performance, the unfortunate one that reduced The Old Barnett to ashes, the sun cast beams through the smoke-filled air as a group of rescue workers combed the burnt out shell of the theatre.

The Old Barnett 1912(?)
The fire gutted both the theatre and its owners, but especially its owners. After painstaking reconstruction it reopened in 1913, but its second flourishing was short-lived. After just two seasons it was razed again and this time the word 'gutted' hardly does it justice. The owners were livid. Convinced that The Great LaFlambé was either still alive and had not yet perfected his craft or that he harboured some deep-seated grudge towards them from beyond the grave, they were determined not to be beaten by his antics. They rebuilt the theatre once more and this time burnt it down themselves before LaFlambé could wreak further havoc.

The exhibition concluded with a compendium of latter-day performers and those they said had been influenced by The Great LaFlambé. I gathered that few performers could follow him technically, most preferring to capture the spirit and showmanship of the man. But one who it was argued had taken the act to new heights was fellow Frenchman Pierre Covey. Covey was pictured wearing a headscarf and a mask which obscured the top half of his face like a gypsy Lone Ranger. His arms were extended and between his hands hovered a magnesium flare, as if he had captured light itself.

Pierre Covey 1915

The 'burning sensation' that was Pierre Covey probably came closest to emulating The Great LaFlambé's success, at least in terms of charring. But it was usually said that his act lacked the subtlety of LaFlambé. Where LaFlambé 'had been sprinkled with fiery stardust', Covey they said 'had been touched by the blowtorch of God'. Of his May 1916 performance in The Old Barnett, one critic said, 'Covey used a sledgehammer to crack a walnut, and within minutes both were headed for the ashcan.'

As I continued to read, I became aware that the Barnett gardener was still struggling valiantly outside. I didn't envy his job but nevertheless felt he was making heavy weather of it, heaving and grunting, cursing all the while. I wondered if he might prefer a quiet office job, maybe in insurance or advertising. He could even take up graphic design as long as he didn't mind a pay cut.

However, when his heaving and grunting combined with pronounced scraping and scoring from one of the stained glass windows some thirty or so feet above, it occurred to me that there may be more to his struggle than just trying to deal with an obstinate shrub. The earnest attendant, showing a level of concern that seemed out of proportion for a gardening misadventure, rose from his station and grabbed a long tentpole. I couldn't imagine what he was going to do with it other than maybe pole vault his way up to investigate.

"Please," said the attendant. "You should think about leaving."

"Leaving?" said Suave Gav. "We haven't visited the gift shop."

He made it clear that it wasn't safe and he was worried about legal liability should anything untoward occur. I told him I'd suffered museums when I was young and didn't remember anything untoward *ever* happening, or anything toward for that matter. If it had, it might have given me a reason to keep going. LaFlamme added helpfully that nobody asked for my life story, and the attendant was in no mood for debate anyway. "It's closing time," he said. The scraping became more of a creaking, and now it sounded as if something was bursting at the seams.

As he urged us towards the exit one of the stained glass panels split and shattered, sending broken shards crashing to the moss-trimmed stone floor below. The sound was painful to the ear, brittle echoes filling the air and bouncing off the museum walls.

"Holy hell," said Suave Gav, turning his head skyward and pointing. Torn rubbery leaves had breached the window and flopped into The Old Barnett's eaves, unfolding from a solid green stalk as thick as Popeye's forearm. Smaller shoots and tendrils followed, inching their way through the window frame.

"Once again," said the attendant, understandably concerned about the possibility of having to speak to lawyers, "I must ask you to go." He edged us towards the exit with his tentpole.

"Can I buy postcards?" I said.

"Get out!" he screamed. Admittedly it was a long shot.

Once outside, the rustling of plant life intensified but oddly the gardener's voice became more muted. With the limited daylight it was difficult to make out exactly what was happening but it appeared that a grotesque and malevolent plant stalk had wrapped itself around his neck and covered his mouth. "Shouldn't we help?" I called, but LaFlamme, Suave Gav and the alarming Afro had moved on. As I followed in their steps I remembered the words of Orson Welles: 'The theatre is built on sand.' It was unfortunate that he only meant metaphorically because had this particular theatre literally been built on sand and not on *rapacious* greenery, it might have had a better chance of surviving.

For all the museum's problems (customer service was obviously not a high priority, and I would have suggested they offer inhalers as I had begun to feel vaguely asthmatic), it was easily five degrees cooler than anywhere else in Wester and that alone had made the visit worthwhile.

"I could use a drink," said LaFlamme when I caught up. I agreed the tropical conditions were thirst-inducing and that we should probably be working on a plan for approaching the Balding Hills, where the librarian suggested Guy LeSnide may be stationed. I could think of no better place to solve both problems than a bar.

I don't know what I'd do without bars. Imagine a world without them. Or just take a nineteen-hour flight to Brunei and see how upset you get when you realise you can't get a drink. I've spent a lot of time in bars. Dusty little town dives, upmarket city bars, rural hideaways, hotel bars, theatre bars, I've never been too fussy. Maybe I've spent too much time in bars. It doesn't seem that much when you consider we spend a third of our lives asleep. That's a vast waste of time compared to the mere eighth or so I've spent in bars.

If anyone offered to give me back the time I've spent in bars, I'd have to politely decline. Because I'd probably spend it sleeping and then that wasteful third would creep up to a half – who wants to spend half of their life unconscious? On the other hand, I'd gladly take back the time I've spent sleeping. I'm always aware that beyond those glorious initial zeds lies a world of pain. I've no sooner let some airport doorstopper slip from my fingers than I'm wondering why I don't understand exam questions, can't remember lines, am being chased by Morlocks and, throughout, not wearing pants.

Time spent in bars is time well spent. And time spent in bars with LaFlamme is even better.

By the time we emerged from the undergrowth and spotted The Furball, Suave Gav was nowhere to be seen. Most likely he had fallen behind, distracted by some barky intoxicant. I wasn't overly concerned. I felt sure his instincts would eventually lead him to The Furball, a friendly little local where all of the beards seemed to know each other. It wasn't busy but the combined chinwear helped fill the place up. LaFlamme and I sat at a corner table where she checked her mobile phone.

"Still in touch with the outside world?" I asked.

"Publisher," she replied. "Hardly counts."

"What do they want?"

"I don't know. I told them to stop bothering me."

"Isn't that biting the hand that feeds you?"

"You think publishing leads to food?" LaFlamme went on to warn me never to lend money to a publisher because they would invariably give it to Jeremy Clarkson. I said there must be some who had creative drive and had built up publishing houses based on quality material choices and sound investments. She said publishers were really just people who had done everything else they wanted and had leftover life to fritter away.

"Are they still going to publish your horoscopes?" I asked her.

"Oh yeah."

"How are they coming along?"

"Piece of cake," she said. "It's like falling off a bike."

"Shouldn't that be falling off a log?"

"Who falls off a log? The point is I'm on target. As long as I crack a week's worth every day, I get paid."

"What's mine then?"

"What's your what?"

"My horoscope."

"You're going to start drinking heavily with the most beautiful woman in the world. Try not to ask any stupid questions." It was remarkable. I can't imagine how she could have predicted this with such accuracy.

LaFlamme tipped the base of her empty tumbler of gin towards me. "Have you seen the bottom of my glass?"

"What about it?"

"Can you read the inscription?" I leaned in and peered at the base.

"Just about," I said.

"Well fill it up till you can't." It was far too easy for LaFlamme to simply say 'it's your round' but sometimes her alternative methods were too subtle for me. "And get a couple of pints of the guest ale." My heart sank. I wondered what embarrassingly named cask ales were on tap, and sure enough the guest ale didn't disappoint. It was from South America and the tap badge showed a buxom girl with two magnums of beer set against a backdrop of rolling hills.

A stout blonde woman stood behind the bar, flicking through TV channels with a remote control. I rattled some change in order to attract her attention. That didn't work so I clinked our empty glasses together on the bar. That didn't work so I cleared my throat. That didn't work so I said 'excuse me'. I wondered if it was only my spirit that was walking the earth, if my physical being had bailed out on me. Just when I was ready to begin rattling my Jacob Marley chains, a loud voice behind me called out, "My, you're a big one, aren't you?" The barmaid turned to face me with a look of ferocious intent.

"That wasn't me," I said, but as there was no one else at the bar or even remotely near me, I don't think it washed.

"What can I get you?" she said, setting the remote below the bar.

"Mount Titty Kaka," said the voice from behind.

"Pint?" she asked.

"Um yes," I said. "Two please." At least I was saved the embarrassment of ordering it myself. "And two large gins."

I turned to establish the source of the impertinent comments. Two beards were playing pool nearby but neither looked as if they would have the brazen upper class tones of the heckler. Beyond them were mostly empty tables followed by a row of benches with a few stools casually strewn around. There were a few lightly inebriated faces. A few enjoying fish pie.

And Corky.

The barmaid turned to pour gin from an optic. "What a handful," called Corky, his voice carrying remarkably well.

"I'll mind you to keep a civil tongue in your head," said the barmaid.

"That wasn't me," I replied. "It was that guy over there." I pointed to the far side of the bar.

"Shame on you," she said, taking my ten pound note and heading towards the till.

"Big girls are best," called Corky. "I'll bet you go like a steam train." The barmaid swung around and looked set to deck me.

"Keep the change," I said. It was going to be difficult to talk my way out of that one.

Mr Beard raised a glass in greeting. LaFlamme had joined them and it looked as though we would be their guests whether I liked it or not. Corky was chortling away when I reached the bench and pulled up a chair. Beard scolded him for his discourtesy and Corky blew a raspberry, his pink wooden tongue rattling in his head.

"Aha!" said Suave Gav, bursting through the swing doors of The Furball with the alarming Afro. Now my happiness was complete. The captain of The Inebriate appeared dishevelled and was covered with offshoots of vine. He explained that his hair had gotten caught in some branches as we made our way from The Old Barnett. "Damn things took a hold and wouldn't let go. I think they had a mind to claim me for their own and cocoon me had I been a little less alert."

Corky chuckled merrily. "You know, I'm going to miss these people," he said. "Even the dullard." I gave him my most disapproving look but as it was somewhat masked by facial hair, it was operating at less than full potential. "I thought you were quite the nincompoop when you first arrived," he continued. "Not much going on upstairs. But you're not a bad sort and you've started to grow on me."

"Ooh you better watch this one, Mr Tony," said Beard with a wink.

"Admittedly there's more than a degree of the stupid about you," said Corky. "But it's endearing. You're like the simpleton son I never had."

"Thank you," I replied.

"That reminds me of a game," said LaFlamme. "You think of all the people you know and all the people they know, and in less than six steps you find you're connected to somebody stupid."

"That sounds like jolly good fun," said Suave Gav, quaffing a pint of Mount Titty Kaka.

"Surely it wouldn't take six steps to connect to somebody stupid," said Corky. "Present company alone would suffice."

"I think the winner's the one who needs *more* than six steps," said LaFlamme. "But that hardly ever happens."

"You're getting mixed up," I said in an unusual moment of clarity. "It's about degrees of separation. They say any one person can be connected to any other person by just six steps."

"Stupid people?" asked Suave Gav.

"It's not about stupidity," I said, although there seemed to be no shortage of it here today.

"There are degrees of stupidity, naturally," said Corky. "If you take the average stupid person, they may rate a three or four on the stupid scale. But some are guilty of stupidity in the first degree."

"Heavens," said Suave Gav.

"Therefore," continued Corky, "if you take the average stupid person, it's worth bearing in mind that half his sort are even worse."

"I always thought it was six degrees of that actor chap," said Suave Gav.

"Kevin Costner," said LaFlamme.

"It's Kevin Bacon," I corrected.

"It's certainly a stupid name," said Corky, implying that the star of *Footloose* was off to a good start.

"Then there's six degrees of Stephen Fry," said LaFlamme, but I knew the only six degrees of Stephen Fry were the ones the overeducated lump got in Oxbridge.

"Whoever you are on Twitter," she said, "it's been proven you're connected to Stephen Fry in less than six steps. Usually just two. There's no escape."

"How very unpleasant," said Suave Gav.

"You mean to say," said Corky, "that if Bacon was twatting, he'd be Fry'd?" He chuckled heartily at this, although I think you'll agree it's probably the worst joke in the book.

"I think I prefer the original concept," said Suave Gav. "Whatever that was." I sighed and drank up. It was truly a conversation of first-degree stupidity.

After leaving The Furball we ploughed our narrowboats further down the Kenneth & Keith for several hours before curfew. Notably, this time Suave Gav and The Inebriate did not race on ahead and instead followed closely behind The Little Hitler the entire way. It's possible that he remembered our ultimate goal was to track down the wizard and have our wishes granted. Losing sight of us would not be in his interests.

Did I say wizard? I meant advocate.

By nightfall our two boats were moored nose to tail and Suave Gav joined us for drinks. As the evening progressed Corky became more agitated and aggressive, not at all like the gentle soul who said he thought the barmaid might go like a steam train. I was concerned he was on the verge of becoming difficult and wondered what he meant when he said he was going to miss us. Surely if he was going to miss us, that suggested the possibility of him going somewhere? I didn't want to give too much credence to this idea as my hopes had been dashed before.

"Gentlemen, may I ask what your plans are?" I asked as casually as possible. But then I couldn't help myself and blurted out, "Are you going to be leaving us?"

Corky began singing. "*I'm leaving on a jet plane, don't know when I'll wear my pants again.*"

"Well Mr Tony," said Mr Beard, "I rather think it's you that shall be leaving us. Come first light you should be able to begin an approach to the Balding Hills and that's the best place to start looking for your wizard."

"He's not a wizard," I said. "He's an advocate."

"Right you are," said Mr Beard.

"And he owes me money."

"I should think he could conjure it up without too much trouble."

"He's not a wizard," I repeated. "He's something to do with the law. I don't really care what he does, I just want paid."

"Does he have a wand?" said Mr Beard.

"Didn't you hear the man?" said Corky. "He's chasing a debtor, you clod. I must say, were we in the land of the stupids we'd most certainly have the king and prince regent present."

"You mean to say," said Suave Gav, "that you've come all this way to collect an unpaid bill?"

"Now he's starting," said Corky.

Suave Gav continued. "You're not here for the botany, the theatre, the fire festival, even the excuse not to shave?"

"I told you already," I said. "I'm here because I made the mistake of working for a total wacko and didn't get around to invoicing him while his vanity could still be punched out of him. Now he thinks he's a god and is worshipped by a legal subtribe apparently not too far from here. I'd have been happy to go without all the supposedly wonderful things this area has to offer just to work with someone who wasn't completely nuts."

"Not to find a cure?" pressed Suave Gav.

"Hello slow ones," said Corky with impatience. "Can we establish once and for all that the divot is here to pick up checky? Checky!"

"Now Corky," said Mr Beard, "there's no need to be nasty."

"Oh fuck off, drone!" said Corky sharply. We all sat up, a little taken aback by his sudden change of tone. "Your very existence bores me into the earth. Without the little semblance of wit and intelligence I've managed to retain, I'd have simply given up and been found buried in the dust literally bored to death. I've been shackled to your vacant carcass for so long I've forgotten what it means to live. If it weren't for you I could have been headlining in Pigalle right now." He launched into a defiant 'La Vie En Rose' with remarkable gusto.

"I'm very sorry," said Mr Beard. "I thought this might happen tonight. You see, tomorrow is..." He paused, stumbling over the words, "Corky's birthday."

"It is not my birthday," said Corky. "How dare you."

"Anniversary then."

"It is not my anniversary!"

"It's a difficult time of year for Corky." Corky began snarling, his little wooden teeth biting together sharply, his eyes batting frantically. Then he started to sob. Streams of water flowed down his cheeks. "It's time we were saying goodnight, Corky," said Mr Beard. "You've had your song."

"That wasn't my song," said Corky, abruptly ending his tears. "I've prepared something special tonight. Play the tape."

"Now, Corky."

"Play the tape or I'll cut you ear to ear!" He made a slicing gesture across his neck. Mr Beard reached for the cassette recorder and pressed play.

Heavy industrial electronica bellowed out of the primitive device at a volume I wouldn't have thought possible. Corky began weaving from side to side, eyes rolling in the back of his head as he screamed in time to the music:

"Change my pitch up! Smack my bitch up!"

The narrowboat lights began to pulsate with the hypnotic rhythm and Corky's face turned a peculiar shade of orange. (I half expected his hair to turn green like the mohawk sported by the song's late lead singer – a look that only people called Keith find appealing.) Corky knew all the breaks in the track and used each to great effect, howling the simple and repetitive refrain with a violent intensity, pushing himself into a frenzy and getting hoarse with the effort.

"Change my pitch up! Smack my bitch up!"

The gathered individuals responded to this curious exhibition in rather different ways. I was aghast and more than a little frightened. Mr Beard looked uneasy but somewhat resigned. LaFlamme, behind wraparounds, was her usually expressionless self, and Suave Gav was in his element, smiling broadly and clapping along. I can't imagine this was the sort of entertainment they shared in their days together at Chapterhouse, but I really had no idea what went on at boarding schools – only that someone was always fagging for someone else and that I would probably never know what fagging meant.

"CHANGE MY PITCH UP! SMACK MY BITCH UP!"

As the track finally drew to its dramatic close, I feared Corky would be more fired up and abusive than ever. In the subsequent silence we awaited his next move. But none was forthcoming. His body sat quite still and behind his eyes was only a vacant stare that suggested the life had drained out of him. Mr Beard stood, sighed, and without so much as a good night, lifted the little man as if he was an inanimate object and made his way to their quarters.

3:15. Corky appears by my bedside, his back to the camera. He is fidgeting with the front of his trousers. I fear the worst. When he turns, there is something wriggling around his crotch area. He has a hand stuffed down his trousers and his index finger is poking through the zipper. "I've got wood," he says to the camera with delight. He swings his hips and performs a little dance with his finger, making it turn circles, stand to attention and weaving it this way and that. I feel like I might pass out.

LaFlamme revives me by tugging at my beard. We continue. The little man tires of his dancing and ventures out into the night.

4:18. Corky returns. He stands at the foot of my bunk and remains frozen for so long that LaFlamme is obliged to fast forward. We see the quality of light change over the following thirty minutes. Eventually Corky raises his arms slightly and LaFlamme re-engages the play position. His tiny frame rises from the ground and hovers, suspended in mid-air. As if encased in an unseen vehicle, he edges smoothly towards the wall with what looks like a marker pen in his hand.

15.
THE LONGEST DAY

As soon as I opened my eyes I knew something was wrong. It wasn't a sixth sense or anything, it was the fact that every available inch of the interior wall space, including the ceiling, had been covered in graffiti. At first glance it looked like blood, but on closer examination turned out to be deep red lipstick.

The graffiti consisted of crude, childlike drawings – a sequence of stick figures reminiscent of ancient hieroglyphics, like Lowry with OCD. They were tight concentrated scenes, at least tight given the soft waxy medium, and many had cartoon speech bubbles extending from the figures' mouths. (The text was mostly illegible but one line clearly said 'smack my bitch up'.) And it appeared to be a sequence, like a comic strip or storyboard. If I began at the kitchen and made my way in a clockwise direction, continuing on the ceiling after a full circuit, I could tell even from my loafing position that there was an attempt at a story. But what story? Certainly there were recurring characters – a boy and his father perhaps? But then there was what looked like the cast of *La Cage Aux Folles*, and I couldn't see why Einstein was there at all. Clearly I didn't have a monopoly on madness during this trip.

Whatever was being said, it was undeniably compelling. Like a crazy Sistine Chapel by an abstract expressionist with only one paint pot. A burgundy Franz Kline. It easily topped anything by Cy Twombly, but as the right-handed Twombly deliberately worked with his left hand, this was hardly surprising. I generally prefer paintings by people who don't set out to be crap.

I wondered what the Sistine Chapel would have looked like had Michelangelo deliberately used his left hand (a question I'm sure art historians have been asking for centuries). He could have produced something that looked more like Picasso, revolutionised European painting and been four hundred years ahead of his time. This would have made him the father of modern art, though I can't imagine the Pope would have been too happy.

I suppose one crucial difference between the Sistine and this psychotic miniature was that, as LaFlamme had diligently re-engaged the camera before turning in each night, we had a record of its making. This kind of documentation leaves art historians in no doubt as to the work's authorship and can give fascinating insights into the artist's methods. Imagine how invaluable a film of Michelangelo painting the chapel would be. Admittedly, watching a guy lying on his back for ten hours a day over the course of several years might not be great TV but I'd still prefer it to anything on Channel 5.

"Turner Prize?" said LaFlamme, stirring from her bunk. "My four-year-old child could have done this." I reminded her that she didn't have a four-year-old child and we both smiled, relieved that we were the only people in our lives having tantrums and throwing food on the floor.

LaFlamme leaned up on her elbow and put the tip of her index finger to her chin, a sign that she was about to behave as if she had just stepped out of Kenneth Clark's *Civilisation*. "It may be a biography of sorts," she began, "but could also be seen as a comment on the human condition." She fished amongst a pile of clothes by her bedside and produced a pair of black-framed glasses of the Buddy Holly variety. They were heavily magnified and had the effect of making her eyes bulge within the little windows. "It's an intensely personal vision which not only shows a steadfast commitment to enriching our understanding of our fellow man, but also elevates our perception of the artistic impulses which allowed him to give us a view onto nature's mysteries."

"You don't have any idea, do you?" I said.

"No," she replied. "But I sound pretty convincing when I wear glasses, right?"

"Since when do you wear glasses?"

"They're Junior's."

"Won't she be missing them?"

"Trying to wean her off them. Besides, they're of more use to me. When I wear them I'm more likely to be taken seriously by other bug-eyed types."

"Can you see anything?"

"Not really. But if you're speaking to other bug-eyed types, that's usually a blessing."

I asked LaFlamme if she could read any of the writing in the waxy opus and if she thought the artist had used his left hand. LaFlamme peered across the top of her glasses and studied the material.

"It's in French," she said.

"French?" I replied, despondent. "Now I've got no chance of understanding it."

"Well it's hard to make out," said LaFlamme. "But I suppose we could always ask the artist to explain." I wasn't so sure about this because artists' explanations tend to leave me even more bewildered than their paintings. If I have to figure out what emotional topography and modes of address are, I'd sooner take the bewilderment on a purely visual level. "Go on," said LaFlamme, nodding in the direction of the hobgoblins' quarters. "Nothing to lose. Not much, anyway."

I rose from my steamy pit and approached the cabin bedroom, finding the door ajar. I nudged it gently open. The room was empty and the bed did not appear to have been slept in.

"They've gone," I said, returning to my bunk with two empty gin glasses.

"Bad timing," said LaFlamme.

"How?"

"We'll have to fix our own breakfast."

"I can do it as long as you don't mind your food either raw or burnt."

"Never mind," said LaFlamme. "I think it's time we disembarked. It's not that I don't enjoy being surrounded by Jeffrey Dahmer's *This is Your Life*, but once the sun perks up it's likely to get a bit melty in here."

She was right. Unless the artist had used a proper grounding and the correct levels of beeswax and linseed oil with the lipstick, this piece was destined to be *ephemeral*. I imagine Michelangelo was keen to observe the correct preparations before he began work on the Sistine, as having to paint it twice would be a nuisance.

"Do you know where we are?" I asked LaFlamme, picking up the map.

"North of the coffee spill," she replied. I followed the winding path of the canal as it weaved its way beyond the caffeine circle, located the 'place of interest' symbol – The Old Barnett museum – and continued north, looking for anything of note that we may have since passed. The trouble was the further we travelled into Wester, the fewer landmarks there were.

"What are these little V-symbols?" I said. LaFlamme leaned across, but unable to read the map without falling out of her bunk, slipped into mine, nudging me over. This was a fantastic development. Had I known map reading could be so exciting I would have taken up cartography years ago.

"Where?" she said, her body so close to mine I feared sudden cardiac arrest.

"I've lost it now," I said in a deliberate attempt to delay the moment for as long as possible. Unfortunately there were so many Vs straddling the canal that LaFlamme recognised the symbol immediately as a lock. I should have found a really obscure symbol or secretly drawn something unfathomable to keep her guessing for longer.

"So how many locks have we been through since The Old Barnett?" she asked.

"Three? Four?" I said. "Masterpieces of Victorian engineering all look the same to me now."

"I reckon there were five," said LaFlamme. It sounded feasible so I counted five lock symbols from The Old Barnett and came to rest at a tight cluster of Vs, six or seven of them apparently spooning, like a sergeant with double stripes.

"That looks ominous," I said. "What is it?" LaFlamme consulted the key.

"Staircase lock," she replied.

"What's a staircase lock?"

"A bunch of locks stuck together like a staircase." LaFlamme turned to face me. I looked at her. I could feel her breath as it made the not so little hairs on my arm stand on end. Timing is everything in matters of the heart – I learned this through having a brief crush on Carol Vorderman during an early episode of *Countdown*. One minute I thought she was looking good, the next she'd started the clock and I was trying to make something out of the letters E E I L M O S T T. (The Admiral managed 'mistletoe'. I was quite pleased with 'toilets em'.)

It was a great opportunity and, aware I might not get another like it, I leaned in to kiss her. Sadly LaFlamme chose this particular moment to see if there was a staircase lock outside, exiting our newly shared bunk in her t-shirt and shorts, completely oblivious to my advance. I realised then with regret just how dull cartography actually was.

I was consoled by the vision of her milky-white thighs climbing the kitchen steps to the bow of the boat, but I wasn't consoled for long because whatever the rest of her was looking at didn't sound good. "You'd better come and see this," she said.

I slunk out of bed and climbed the first two steps, stopping inches from her legs. I could see every turn, every freckle and tiny imperfection, the smooth texture of her skin. Her legs were so pale it made me think of ice cream and it took all my energy not to take a lick. I'm not sure why I resisted because I'd long since given up on dignity.

"Are you proposing?" she said. "Get up here."

I climbed the remaining steps. It took a moment to adjust to the light and make sense of the sweeping panorama that stretched out before us, but once I did I realised we were in trouble. Straight ahead was a sequence of seven enormous locks, arranged as LaFlamme suggested, like a staircase, each stepping higher into the hills and receding further into the distance. The seventh met the horizon and who knew what lay beyond. Surrounding the locks were what I presumed to be the Balding Hills, and if I was correct this was a serious misnomer. First, there was nothing 'balding' about them; if anything, they were wildly hirsute. And second, even though LaFlamme and I were unlikely to know the difference, I'd have called them mountains. It didn't really matter – both meant climbing.

To top it off, there was another more pressing concern:

We were not alone.

From the foothills down to the banks of the canal, the landscape was teeming with people; silent, straggly-haired people, some with beards, some without. They stood virtually motionless on various levels of the staircase lock and as far back in the opposite direction as we could make out – hundreds of them, studying the incomers. The unbearded ones stared at LaFlamme as if they had never seen a woman before. They were probably lawyers.

It was eerily still. No one spoke and the only sound was the dull roar of one of the most distant locks filling with water.

"What do we do?" I whispered to LaFlamme.

"*Fitzcarraldo*?" she replied.

"I don't think there's much chance of Fitzcarraldoing the boat up the mountain without anyone noticing."

"Not the boat," said LaFlamme. "Me."

Somebody pointed at me in an accusatory manner and said, "That's him." It was the barmaid from Stiffies. Her recollection of me was probably tainted by my apparently having suggested she went like a steam train. This wasn't looking good.

The unbearded amongst them, suspiciously LLB KnoBby and carrying long staffs similar to shepherds, began to advance, striking the staffs against the ground and muttering the word 'assassin'. LaFlamme and I prepared to duck below deck. But just then an excitable fellow in harlequinesque pants with alternating red and white diamonds approached and quelled the advance.

"Back off people," he said to the crowd.

The man introduced himself as Phillips, an American, and said this as if it should be some comfort to us. I didn't want to tell him that meeting Americans in foreign lands hadn't been fun for anyone since Desert Storm, so instead I told him I had a screwdriver named after him.

He welcomed us ashore and as we stepped down from The Little Hitler, he told us he was on our side – which unfortunately just made me think we would all be invading somewhere soon. Nevertheless we were grateful, because at this point his voice seemed a lone one amongst what was potentially a considerable number of vexatious litigants.

"Is this the approach to the Balding Hills?" I asked him.

"Oh man," he said. "It's the approach to the kingdom of heaven."

"We only need hills at this point," said LaFlamme. They still looked like mountains to me.

I nodded towards the cast of *Night of the Living Dead* and said, "What's their problem?"

"Ah," replied Phillips, grinning, "they think you've come for him."

"Who?" I said.

"Who, he says." Phillips laughed maniacally. "The wizard LeSnide."

"He's not a wizard," I said with some impatience. "He's an advocate. But I have come for him. It's payback time." The lawyers reacted to this by lurching in my direction but Phillips raised his arms, stopping them in their tracks. He smiled at me in a placating manner.

"It's probably best if you don't talk so much," he said.

One of the beards emerged from The Little Hitler and announced, "It's a bloodbath in there." There was a collective murmur from the assembled throng.

"No no," I replied. "It's just lipstick."

LaFlamme took a step towards Phillips. "I didn't catch your name," she said, "and that's probably no great loss. Look, I don't want to keep you from your juggling so if you could just tell us where to find LeSnide or unicycle us in the right direction, we'll leave you to it."

"I can't do that," he said.

"Why not?" I asked.

"He's resting."

"We just want to talk to him."

"Man, you don't talk to LeSnide. You listen." He had a point. I'd tried talking to LeSnide before but his royal oddness tended to zone out unless he could hear the sound of his own voice. It was as if his brain filtered out all frequencies except those generated by him. He was one vast soliloquy.

"The man's a poet, an artist, a visionary," said Phillips.

"He's an advocate," I said, now with real irritation.

"We are his children."

"I thought advocates only had edicts," said LaFlamme, not really helping matters.

"Why, just the other day he said to me, 'Phillips you really are a cretin.' And he pronounced it 'cree'. I was humbled that he'd even noticed me."

"Listen Mr Cretin," said LaFlamme, also taking care to pronounce it 'cree', "I don't think I made myself clear." She put on her heavy glasses and gave him the bug-eyed stare. "Take me to your leader."

"It's not that simple," he said, taking us aside. "These people are his protectors, his foot soldiers. They think you want to take him out."

"Take him out?" I said. "I don't even like him."

"They won't let you pass. The only way I can take you to him is by persuading our guards to transport you by litter and have you presented before him." He pointed to several foot soldiers attending sedan chairs, hammocks stretched between the poles instead of cabins. This was timely as it saved me having to look up 'litter'.

"That'll do fine," said LaFlamme, ushering me towards the sedans. "Wake us up when we get there."

"There's just one problem," said Phillips.

"Yes?" I said, already boarding.

"You'd have to consider yourselves under arrest." We paused briefly, weighing up the consequences of arriving at our destination only to be banged up. But then LaFlamme made a snap decision and waved him off.

"Get us up that hill," she said, "and we'll clear up this little misunderstanding." We sunk into our hammocks and eight guards each took a corner of the two litters and prepared to *Fitzcarraldo* us up the hill. As we set off I spotted Suave Gav's boat The Inebriate moored directly behind us. Canvas coverings bound the roof and sides, and the boat was padlocked from the outside. The skipper looked set to be gone for some time. And now so did we.

"Are you sure this is a good idea?" I said to LaFlamme. "Isn't this *tantamount* to a guilty plea?"

"Don't be ridiculous," she replied, clasping her hands behind her head and preparing to settle in for the ride. "We can change our plea whenever we want. I know a bit about the law."

"You do not." LaFlamme put on her heavy glasses. "Okay whatever," I said wearily.

It was a long, arduous trip up the Balding Hills. At least it was for the people carrying us. I was pretty relaxed. After thirty minutes I asked one of them for a back rub. But still there was a gnawing sensation at the back of my mind – the question of why I persisted with this mission. Was it worth being arrested and Fitzcarraldoed up a hill stroke mountain simply to get paid for a stupid job? Was I really going to follow every outstanding invoice, every wayward client, and if so, just how *far* was I prepared to follow them? What insanity drove a man to such lengths? In truth I knew exactly what lay behind my obsession:

Arithmetical equilibrium.

Failure to balance monthly accounts may mean nothing more than nail biting and sexual impotence but if it remains unresolved and spills over into the quarterlies, panic attacks, IBS and hair loss can set in. Should it fail to be resolved by annual return time you might as well don an orange robe and cry *gouranga* because the alternatives are not good. Even if I were a millionaire graphic designer (a contradiction if ever there was one) the imbalance would still cause merry hell. I could put my affairs in the hands of a high-flying firm of accountants, but I'm pretty sure they're no fans of panic attacks, IBS and hair loss either.

For a while I paid The Admiral to do my accounts, which was fine until I realised he wasn't inflating my expenses. The Admiral was quite strict about this and said there was no point arriving at all those numbers if he was then going to replace them with much higher ones pulled out of thin air. I told him that's what accountants were for and to get on with it. We agreed to differ. Now I'm going to jail.

Eventually we arrived at a clearing in the woods. Ahead of us, carved into the face of the mountain, was an uncanny likeness of LeSnide, his square-set jaw prominent, his eyes narrowed in the manner he had when trying to project an image of nobility. Beyond the edifice was a magnificent modernist building that would not have looked out of place in *Architecture Now* – a striking glass and steel-fronted design that might have been a Yamaguchi. One of the Guccis, anyway. I was expecting a sweaty log cabin, but why would LeSnide hole up in a log cabin if he could hire an architectural interfacer and stiff him the way he stiffed me? At least the architect would know where he lived.

"I suppose you'd like a tip?" said LaFlamme to one of her carriers as we disembarked.

"Yes ma'am," he replied.

"Not so fast next time," she said. "Now who do I have to flog for some gin?"

Adjacent to the building was a great wicker cage, about the size of my bedroom but bound together by rope and much tidier. It seemed this would be our temporary accommodation until we straightened things out. As I was being unceremoniously thrown inside, LaFlamme donned her bug-eyed glasses. It looked like she had a plan.

"Pick me up at eight," she said to the guards and walked up to Phillips. "Now listen Pagliacci, where are the counsel chambers? I need to freshen up."

"It's Phillips," he replied.

"What if I call you Pip?"

"You're not thinking of resisting arrest, are you?" he asked.

"Arrest?" said LaFlamme. "I'm the bozo's legal representative. Now stop flapping your gums and show me the shower rooms before I have your badge." This was sufficiently confusing for Phillips – who after all was American – to have one of the guards lead LaFlamme in the direction of the architectural compound.

"I'll try and locate this LeSnide character," said LaFlamme under her breath. "How will I know him?" I pointed to the image chiselled out of the mountainside. "Right," she said. Then she removed something she had tucked down the back of her skirt. "Hang on to this for me while I'm gone, will you?"

I couldn't believe my luck. It was her secret journal.

"It's not meant for your eyes so no peeking, okay?"

"Okay."

"Promise?"

"Promise."

With time on my hands and LaFlamme's secret journal in my safe-keeping, it seemed cruel and unreasonable to be forbidden from combining the two in a productive way. But I'd have to try and honour her wish.

I contemplated my next move. As my next move was limited to fifteen feet, I swiftly decided against any kind of moving at all and tried to think of something, anything, that might take my mind off the journal. I remembered that today was the longest day of the year. The solstice. Normally I try to shorten the longest day by sleeping an extra three hours, waking just in time for breakfast TV – the one o'clock news. But it looked like today really would be the longest ever. Time passes slowly when you're in a wicker cage and with the added effect of Wester Mean Time, I would need a lot of imagination to continually distract myself. So I was pretty screwed.

I probably wouldn't have minded being in a Wester prison high in the Balding Hills awaiting my fate at the hands of a hundred threatening lawyers, if only fate hadn't also thrown LaFlamme's journal into the mix. What did she mean it wasn't for my eyes? It couldn't possibly be because of her disparaging comments about my beard – she made those to my face anyway. Maybe there was newer hotter material that involved me. Maybe our cartography moments were getting under her skin and she was finally coming round to the Boaks charm, even though recently the Boaks charm had mostly just been screaming and passing out.

How did she define peeking? If I were to open it in plain view and casually scan the pages, surely that would be more like glancing. Were it to accidentally fall into Phillips' hands and I asked him to read select passages aloud, that would be listening. Well I suppose it was all academic because I'd given my word that I would respect her wishes. I was a man of honour, of integrity.

Maybe just a little look.

Tony really losing it. Gone all fey and wispy, like his beard. He's more beard than man right now. It's a pity because I was starting to think he was quite cute. I don't know, I can't decide. He's sweet when he's like this but I'd probably prefer it if he wasn't having a nervous breakdown.

Junior's being difficult. I told her she could write *Inflammable* but now that she knows Channel 5 are hanging around, she wants in on that. I told her she wasn't nearly fat enough to get on Channel 5 and unless she wanted to pick up some horrible ailment, it wasn't going to happen. But that's not what she has in mind. She wants to direct. Told her she'd have made a great director in the silent era but nowadays they generally want people who can talk.

I have a theory about LaFlambé. He was in all kinds of trouble. Drugs. Murder. Gangsters. Plagiarism. Maybe even Paul Daniels. Reckon he saw a way to get free of it all in one convenient swoop. Took to the stage as usual but left his assistant in a false-backed wardrobe when he unleashed the ultimate *Combustor* and made off. Get the picture? Faked his own death.

Laid low for a couple of years, just long enough for things to cool down. Literally. But the lure of the stage is strong. If you've trod the boards for thirty years, civilian life just doesn't cut it. Besides, in his two year sabbatical he'd developed the act further and taken it into new and more extreme territory. So he took on the name Pierre Covey and started again. It was tough being back at square one, and it didn't help that he had to wear a mask so that theatre owners wouldn't know he was the guy responsible for their astronomical insurance premiums.

Think about it. Covey. Little Cinders. 'One of the oldest men in Wester.' Which would mean Kevin could be...

At this point, Phillips returned. I hurriedly closed the journal and tucked it behind my back – unfortunate timing because I thought LaFlamme might have been about to expand on the word 'cute'.

Phillips beckoned me to the gate, lit a cigarette and handed it to me through the wicker bars. "What am I meant to do with this?" I asked. He took it back. Then he handed me a ladle filled with liquid. "What is it?" I asked.

"You're not very good at this, are you?" he said. "Haven't you ever been locked in a cage before?"

"No," I said, knowing that as an American he would be more familiar with the concept. "Wicker or otherwise."

"It's for your own safety. The troops are highly protective of the great one. Assassins are a threat to their livelihood."

"What makes you think I'm an assassin?" I said. "Apart from the bloodbath on the boat, which I've already told you is lipstick."

"There's an eyewitness," he replied.

"I only ordered two pints of Mount Titty Kaka and said she probably went like a steam train."

"You're a sick man, Boaks. But she's not the eyewitness, she only confirmed your identity."

"Then who's the eyewitness?"

"A guest on your boat. Goes by the name of McCorkadale."

"Who the hell's that?"

"Little guy. English."

"Corky?"

"Said you left the boat every night and stalked. He followed you. I'd say you're looking at life. Maybe longer." Oh great. I was to be the victim of a miscarriage of justice, and American justice at that. I was likely to fry in the chair before I was even sworn in. I took the ladle from Phillips and parked myself in a corner. At least my predicament allowed me a period of solitude in which to gather my thoughts and form a plan. Unfortunately this hope was also swiftly dashed as no sooner had Phillips left than two guards approached, untied the rope securing the cage and pushed a man with an alarming Afro inside.

"Afternoon," said Suave Gav.

"You again?" I said. "Are you an assassin too?"

"Certainly not," he replied. "But I do seem to have fallen foul of the authorities. Espionage, they said. Obviously nonsense, though frankly I'd welcome a bit of cold war right now. These temperatures are quite draining."

"So they caught you with microfilm or what?"

"You may jest Tony but the fact is I'd readily confess to the charge were it to bring me any closer to my goal. The Westerers have something we both crave and I may have mentioned that I believe my need to be greater than yours."

"Yes yes," I said. "But I still don't see why."

"Tony, how old do you think I am?" This was a question I always dreaded. If you overestimate, you cause offence. If you underestimate, the questioner becomes emboldened with notions of youthfulness, which all come out in the wash after they've thrown out a dozen mirrors they said were grey and baggy.

"I don't know," I said and, too tired to flatter or offend, offered my best guess. "Forty? Forty-five?"

He sighed. "Let me tell you a story." Anything to pass the time.

"During the First World War," he began, "Wester was in dispute with neighbouring Easterchessershire, or Easter as it's known, over the redrawing of the boundary between the two regions. You see, after the redrawing the only cemetery fell within the territorial limits of Easter. Well, the mayor of Wester at the time was incensed and refused point blank to allow burials until a new cemetery could be built in Wester. In the meantime he decreed it illegal to die. You could take ill and be as sick as you so desired, but death was strictly *verboten*."

"I imagine that would be a difficult one to prosecute," I said. "Did anyone try and break the law?"

"Surprisingly few and they were jailed. But most did their best not to extend beyond the boundaries of earthly life until the mayor acquired land and secured the necessary permits. Of course these things can take time. Getting planning permission to erect a fence alone can take months of trying to bribe your local councillor, so imagine how many favours it would take to grant a resting place for the deceased.

"Faced with this rather strict edict, the town elders – who were after all most likely to fall foul of it – found themselves forced to take the bull by the horns. Most had never broken the law in their lives and were reluctant to do so now. But the idea of dying and having to spend eternity in a prison cell was most daunting – something which, given your present predicament, I'm sure you can appreciate."

"Thanks for the reminder. So what happened?"

"They began extensive chemical experimentation with an eye to increasing longevity. One scholarly old boy, a botanist, insisted mother nature's larder held a cure for all ills and that man had so far merely scratched the surface of its unimaginable secrets. It was he who first made the discovery."

"Discovery?"

Suave Gav sighed again, somewhat impatiently this time.

"Tony," he said, fixing me with his piercing blue eyes, "I am not forty. Or even forty-five. I am one hundred and eight years old." I stuffed a finger into my ear and wriggled it rapidly. It was sweaty in there and I immediately regretted it.

"One hundred and eight," I said. "That's a lot of candles."

"I thought you knew."

"You'd be amazed at the things I don't know. But of all the things I don't know, it's safe to say that was the thing I didn't know most."

"I was born shortly after the dawn of the 20th century," he said, "and lived through two world wars. The first they called The Great War, but in truth neither was much fun."

This was getting altogether too hot and too freaky for my liking. I began to feel short of breath and started tugging at my collar. I was on the verge of a panic attack. "Are you all right, old chap?" said Suave Gav.

"I'm just not too sure what to say to a 108-year-old," I replied.

"You could start by saying I look well for my age."

"You're a miracle of nature," I said. "So are you telling me they found an elixir of life here in Wester?"

Suave Gav extended his arm, inviting me to take in the sight of the undergrowth surrounding us; the undergrowth that consisted mainly of short shrubby plants with distinctive maroon colouring at the base. "You yourself have sampled it," he said. "Do you not feel the better for it?"

"Blutwurz?"

"The potentilla erecta is a most miraculous and versatile organism. In its distilled form it has been found to increase longevity for an as yet unspecified duration – unspecified because the original discoverers are still among us." I recalled the blue flame beverage being served at the experimental chutney evening and the iced version Suave Gav produced on the boat. I remembered the unusual aroma, the medicinal flavour. I remembered the black teeth.

"But if Blutwurz is the elixir of life, then surely you already know the secret?"

"Oh yes," he said with a nonchalance I found maddening.

"So what are you searching for? Just what is it you want from the wizard LeSnide?" I had grown tired of explaining that LeSnide was an advocate and decided calling him a wizard would save time.

"Damn it man," he replied. "The elixir of life is child's play! I need a hangover cure!" He pressed his fingers to his spongy Afro with an expression of utmost despair. "Our Bavarian spring beverage is not merely an indulgence – it's medicinal. To stop the ageing process in its tracks, it's necessary to take daily doses and depending on one's age, these can be substantial. I am a slave to the law of diminishing returns and as a consequence my doses have reached epic heights. Add to this the unfortunate reality of morning-after symptoms intensifying over the years and you begin to see the problem – it's unlikely you will have experienced a hangover as bad as a 108-year-old."

"So when you say your need is greater, you mean..."

"Judging by your appearance, I'd say my need is seventy-five to eighty years greater than yours. I tell you Tony, I would sell my grandmother for an antidote, even though the poor old dear is almost a hundred and ninety."

I believe Suave Gav recognised I was having some difficulty with these revelations when I lifted the sleeve of my t-shirt and stretched it over my head. "It's not so bad, old bean," he said.

"I'll be fine," I said unconvincingly from beneath the sleeve.

"Here," said Suave Gav. "Take this." I uncovered just enough of my head to see what he was offering. It was a root or stem of some sort.

"I don't think this is an appropriate time for a thumping erection, do you?"

"No no," he replied. "This is valerian, a natural tranquilliser. I would never touch pharmaceutical sedatives, they're thoroughly tainted by other chemicals. And it goes without saying that I dislike doctors intensely."

"Don't you ever get sick?" I asked, taking the root.

"In 1952 I was diagnosed with a misaligned spinal column and the consultant insisted the only solution was a metal plate inserted into the base of my spine. Don't be ridiculous, I said. That would interfere with the bullet I'd had lodged there since Normandy. Surely we should remove the bullet, he said, but I explained that this would interfere with the magnet I swallowed as a child and had never been able to pass. Well of course he suggested removing the magnet. Probably not a good idea, I said. There's a metal pin in my elbow and the magnet's the only thing holding it in place. Remove it and the whole structure could collapse. By now the hapless quack was at the end of his rope and said so what are we going to do with this misaligned spinal column? I said if you let me step away from your confounded x-ray machine, the magnet would stop pulling my spine towards it. I only came here with athlete's foot."

I looked at Suave Gav with a mixture of disbelief and stupefaction. If this was his way of getting me to calm down, he was a very strange man indeed. But this was hardly news. I stuffed the root between my teeth and started gnawing.

"The point is Boaksy, as I've said time and again, nature is bountiful and has provided for us in ways that we are still discovering. Even a moderately adventurous gastrophile can work out how to balance the body's natural equilibrium. Go to a medic, on the other hand, and you'll have a metal plate in your backside before you can say 'Dr Shipman will see you now.'" Suave Gav may have exaggerated but I shared his distrust of the medical profession, as anyone who had encountered medical students in their college years would.

I may have felt a little silly gnawing on a tree root with an alarmingly Afroed 108-year-old man, but once the intended effect began to kick in I cursed myself for not having opened nature's larder sooner. I felt a warm glow as if having consumed a fine brandy and a new sense of being at one with my surroundings. This situation I found myself in wasn't something to fear, it was something to embrace. The people I had encountered on my journey may have been a bizarre assortment of freaks and weirdos, but they were *my* freaks and weirdos. This was what the 1960s culture of love, peace and happiness must have been like. I suddenly wanted to love everybody, take up the bongos and study transcendental meditation with a weird little Indian man. I wanted to renounce meat and eat only brown rice and other indigestible food.

Valerian not only had a calming effect on my mind, it also seemed to be having a mild anaesthetic effect on my mouth and the part of my hand clutching it. I was now sucking my thumb. It was far from dignified, but dignity wasn't really a big thing in the '60s. Dignity was what the stiffs were at pains to instil in the younger generation so they'd have successive rounds of insurance clerks and bank tellers through the '70s, '80s and '90s. They started their dignity indoctrination in secondary school, removing childhood prematurely and replacing it with a terminal mediocrity from which many would never recover. This wasn't a valerian revelation, by the way. Just personal experience.

But with this new clarity came the dawning realisation that Suave Gav stood to make a lot of money out of any cure, and if there's one thing bongo players don't like, it's money; more specifically, other people having money. "I admit," said Suave Gav, "when we first discussed a cure I was guarded about its development. I daresay whoever first brings a red-eye antidote to market will be a billionaire, such would be the demand for it. But the truth is Tony, should I ever be the one bestowed with such knowledge, I have decided I would simply gift it to the world as a symbol of my gratitude." There was desperation in Suave Gav's voice and I could understand why. A man who drinks and takes other mind-altering substances for medicinal reasons, but at the same time is generally intolerant of them, was in a no-win situation.

LaFlamme, returning from the compound to find me glassy-eyed and sucking my thumb, began shaking her head. "I don't want to know," she said. "Okay, so I arranged a meeting with the wizard."

"You did?" Suave Gav and I chimed, rising to our feet and clutching at the wicker bars.

"Yes, but Pip says the man's a genius, therefore it's likely he's also a fruitcake. So let's be realistic here. We've come a long way and should consider what we can reasonably hope to achieve from this meeting."

"What do you mean?" I asked.

"Well," she replied, "I want the secret of telepathic combustion."

"I want the secret of pain free overindulgence," said Suave Gav.

"I want paid," I said.

LaFlamme raised her wraparounds. "I said reasonable, Tony. Remember the man's deranged, and a lawyer, so it might not be possible to get your first wish. Besides, he's like the Queen – I don't think he deals in worldly goods anymore. Can't you just ask for a brain or something?"

"No," I said firmly. "This is a matter of principle. A man does an honest day's work and it's only fair that he be rewarded for his efforts. It's a matter of honour, a matter of respect..."

"*A matter of account reconciliation*," said LaFlamme in a whiny imitation of me.

"Exactly. Is it fair that I be tormented by bookkeeping imbalance whilst the architect of this most unjust situation is allowed to shed his responsibilities and go quietly nuts? What if we all did that? What if

I set myself up as a living god in an area where beards are not only acceptable but obligatory? You think the TV licence people haven't heard that one before? They'd be down here like a shot."

"They are terribly persistent," said Suave Gav.

"And there's something else you may be forgetting." I was on a roll now. "Our personal goals are secondary. It's not so much what we can reasonably hope to achieve as what we *must* achieve – if you recall, part of the deal is that we bring the wizard back to civilisation, even if it means the dart gun."

I tried to explain that other people's needs might occasionally be a consideration and that from time to time it was a good idea to recognise there was life beyond the front of your own nose. But by 8:00pm, this and other conversational dead ends had long since crashed and burned. The whole talking experiment had failed altogether and we'd been sitting in silence for well over an hour. Suave Gav spent much of this time chewing on a root, a picture of dharmic serenity. LaFlamme returned to scribbling in her journal and we sat back to back. I was on the inside of the wicker cage and she was on the outside.

I wondered if she found me any more appealing as a jailbird – if so, I might ask to stay a little longer. Even though we were practically stuck together I was at ease and the additional heat made me drowsy. I thought I could while away an hour or so like this by taking a nap, and did indeed drift off. But my plan backfired when I found myself in an extremely unpleasant dream.

I had no sooner dozed off than I was being chased through woods by a zombie Abraham Lincoln. He could really move for a zombie and I couldn't understand how his top hat could remain fixed on his head like that. Then a 108-year-old Donald Trump told me it was his birthday and asked me to help him with his re-election campaign. I said he didn't need me for that, as his record would show he'd been a notable president in so many regards. But he insisted.

I knew Trump had been taken over by body snatchers and was now a dangerous threat to civilisation. Unfortunately in my dream this was also the case. He was trying to convince me that a wall between the United States and Mexico was a good idea, his smirk frozen, his comb over gleaming and locked in place. I agreed that building a two thousand mile wall to keep out foreigners was a good use of taxpayer funds and said he should think even bigger. I suggested he build it around the entire perimeter of the US, bankrupt the country and thereby discourage any further international interest.

But it was clear the real Trump had left the building years ago. This bloated husk was all that remained and you could no more have a conversation with him than an eggplant. Not that that has stopped candidates in the past. There is nothing in the constitution to prevent eggplants taking office, as was demonstrated by the 43rd president.

Trump continued, telling me that although he considered socialised medicine an arm of the red menace, he had a great idea for a national health service. Rather than being funded by the government through collected taxes, it involved individuals paying large multinational insurance companies for cover. I said it sounded interesting but was clearly in its early stages.

Before I could ask for more detail he was handing me a gun, saying, "Welcome to America." It was at this point my dream became a nightmare. I was greeted by a marching parade as I stepped off the Ellis Island ferry. Somebody presented me with flowers and draped a garland around my neck. There were calls for a speech. Filled with terror, I stepped reluctantly onto a podium. "This is all happening a bit fast," I said in a stilted whimper. "I love your movies, and your dentistry is second to none, but I'm not sure I'm ready to settle here. When I look at some of the people you vote for and the insane things they say in order to get elected I get the fear. Your 45th choice was certainly interesting, but only in the way you might find anthrax interesting. I guess it was maybe just your turn to be an international laughing stock. Anyway I wouldn't feel too bad about it because the world has moved on to laughing about Britain. And being Scottish, I laugh along with them."

Excited at having a Scot amongst them, as anyone would be, the crowd began chanting, "One of us! One of us!" I turned and tried desperately to get back on the boat, but Trump had me by the legs and was clinging on for dear life. I was frozen to the spot, probably an extension of the cryogenic process that fixed his crazy grin and stiff mane.

"Boaks," said LaFlamme, nudging me with her elbow. "You're drooling again. Have you been at the Cryofreeze?"

"Oh thank God I'm only in prison," I said.

When the guards finally arrived to collect us for our wizard consultation, I felt a pang of loss – LaFlamme hopped to her feet and I could no longer revel in the sensation of her breathing close to me. We were marched up to the modernist complex where LeSnide was apparently hiding out. Floor to ceiling glass doors slid open and before us extended an imposing marble grounded hallway that was so long I thought the people at the far end must be Munchkins. Whilst it appeared to be a modest duplex from the outside, the interior was more of an auditorium.

"Wait here," said one of the guards as he turned and marched towards the hall's end. There a steep altar was flanked by flaming pillars and behind the altar was a vast tapestry with the ridiculous coat of arms I'd designed for LeSnide. It was far from my greatest work, but then a vulture that swallowed a fly wasn't particularly great source material.

The guard's footsteps echoed through the cavernous building and it was hard not to feel intimidated. Suave Gav and I cowered slightly behind LaFlamme, who had removed her wraparounds, probably in readiness to don her bug-eye glasses in an attempt at appearing studious.

"COME FORWARD!" called a booming voice from the direction of the altar. We advanced cautiously past numerous guards armed with long staffs, until we stood at the foot of the towering altar. Perched at the top was a prominent chin belonging to a man wearing a long flowing red gown. The chin was all that could be seen of his face, as a megaphone obscured the rest.

"I – AM – LESNIDE," called the megaphonic chin. "WHO – ARE – YOU?"

Suave Gav and I looked to LaFlamme and not unusually she took the initiative, cupping her hands to her mouth.

"I – AM – LAFLAMME," she called. "WHAT'S – IT – TO – YOU?" Suave Gav and I winced, unsure that this was the correct way to address a wizard.

"SILENCE!" he replied. "DO YOU DARE TO CHEEK THE GREAT LESNIDE?" The fiery pillars flared up in synchronisation with his raised voice. "WHAT DO YOU WANT OF ME?"

"You're a hard man to track down," said LaFlamme, "and now that I've found you I'm distinctly underwhelmed. But we've come this far so

I'm willing to give you a chance not to disappoint me. If it pleases your royal madness, and even if it doesn't, I am seeking my natural birthright, a recipe of sorts. I am a descendent of The Great LaFlambé, and the secret of telepathic combustion was his gift. It should have followed that this gift was bequeathed to *moi*, but to date I remain *sans flambé*."

"Is that...?" began LeSnide before remembering his megaphone. "IS – THAT – SO?"

LaFlamme cupped her hands. "YES – IT – IS," she replied.

"AND WHAT ABOUT YOU, MR SPECTOR?"

"Me?" said Suave Gav before remembering the unruly state of his hair. "If it pleases your grace," he continued, stepping forward, "I too am seeking a recipe. I have supped extensively from the fountain of youth and have become so dependent on it that my daylight hours pain me. If a cure for its brutal after-effects exists, it would surely exist in the region where the fountain's elixir was first developed. And it follows that the one most likely to know of it would be the grand vizier of the region. I ask only that you show mercy and help a suffering old man."

"I SEE. AND YOUR SHUFFLING FRIEND?" I wasn't aware I'd been shuffling until I shuffled in a more forwardly direction.

"If you recall," I began, "I did a little design work for you some time back. Before I got a chance to invoice, you had your little episode and ended up here. So if you could see your way to settling up before my IBS gets any worse, I'd appreciate it." LeSnide removed the megaphone from his mouth to scrutinise us, revealing an outlandish diamond and peacock feather headdress atop his dome.

"Boaks?" he said. "Is that you?" I waved and he stepped down from his throne, megaphone in hand. Descending the staircase that coiled its way around the pillars, he joined us at ground level. "Why the devil didn't you say so?"

I slipped a hand into my back pocket and produced a damp crumpled envelope that I'd been carrying for some time. "Here's the invoice," I said. "I just need a signature. It's the usual thirty day terms, but I trust you'll take into account the time it's taken to find you."

"You came all this way because of an unpaid bill?"

"Yes," I said. "And one other matter."

"Yes?"

"I'm following the instructions of Captain Pantless to bring you back to civilisation. I'm sure he'd appreciate if you packed your bags and joined us on the next litter home."

"Not so fast," said LeSnide, picking up his megaphone. "NOT – SO – FAST!" All three of us recoiled at the volume.

"Naturally, your splendid design work deserves recompense – I've had numerous compliments. But if you have been sent by old prissy-pants Pantling, you are merely another errand boy come to rein me in. And as so many of my foot soldiers can testify, Pantling's agents have a tendency to go native here in Wester." Several suspiciously lawyer-like guards nodded in agreement. "If I have not followed them back to your so-called civilisation and they have instead chosen to follow me, what makes you think you would be any more persuasive?"

"Frankly," said LaFlamme, "your foot soldiers don't look so bright. What if I were to tell you it wasn't so much a return to civilisation as a long term stay in a retreat for living gods?" The wizard sighed and removed his headdress.

"Actually," he said, "I am rather tired of it all. I was drawn to Wester by its abundance of legal practitioners, and therefore available lackeys. But returning to an area with such a rich theatrical tradition reawakened something deeper within me. As a youth I could think of nothing greater than to be a star of the stage. But in Northerchessershire where I grew up, it was the law that nothing pleasurable could ever be a legitimate profession. There were no indigenous stars of the stage in Norther as it was an offence punishable by imprisonment. I vowed to change this and studied for my LLB KnoB at the earliest possible opportunity – when I was ten."

"It's a lovely story," I said, "but I thought only politicians could change laws?"

"Don't be naïve, man," he replied. "Have you ever heard of a politician who wasn't already a lawyer? Anyway, I rose through the ranks of my profession at such a rapid rate that I never stopped to question the whole ridiculous nature of it."

"Law?"

"Work. As a trainee I was told 'the more you accomplish now, the more time you'll have to yourself later'. Now that I've reached the peak of my profession I find it's actually a case of 'the more you accomplish now, the more you'll see that work is one big swindle'. I don't mind telling you this realisation uncovered a void at the very heart of my existence. And I do not for one moment believe the void is likely to be filled by my continued presence here in the compound, or indeed at the faculty. I took pride in the role of Advocate For Self-Importance and indeed seemed well cut out for it. But in taking this advocacy to its logical conclusion, I inadvertently made a significant discovery."

"Work sucks? I could have told you that."

"Boaks, I do wish you wouldn't keep interrupting." He paused for no more than a heartbeat. "The self is important, of course. Without the artistic endeavours of key individuals throughout history, our world would be a very drab one. There's only one Van Gogh. Only Leonardo can paint a *Mona Lisa*. Cultural movements may appear to be group efforts but the truth is they depend on unique expressions of individuality, and artists must devote themselves to the supremely selfish act of committing these expressions to record if they are to be of any use to the wider world.

"My time spent here in this former hub for the dramatic arts has taught me that the importance of the self ends right there, with the universally enriching efforts of the creative. And alas, though I harboured artistic ambitions, these were frustrated by a combination of Norther law and a complete lack of talent. All of which brings me to a rather sobering conclusion:

"I believe I have lost all sense of self-importance."

Suave Gav appeared restless. "I don't mean to be impatient," he said, "but you do intend to grant our wishes, don't you? I've come rather a long way and although I'm quite happy to discuss art history with a wizard, I wouldn't normally do so without a libation."

"You have no idea how often I've been mistaken for a wizard," said LeSnide.

"Mistaken?" said Suave Gav.

"Given such an amorphous and little understood profession, it's understandable that it is assumed we perform magic." He clutched his red gown by the waist and stretched it out before him. "They even gave me this invisibility cloak, which makes me look like Demis Roussos. The only thing that's disappeared is my self-respect."

"I don't know what to say," said Suave Gav, close to tears.

"Come come man," said LeSnide. "That's not to say I cannot grant your wishes. First however, I wish to impart some simple words of wisdom to each of you." He stepped towards Suave Gav and clasped him by the shoulders.

"My friend," he began, "you say you have drunk heartily from the fountain of youth. It was inevitable then that you would seek to drink from a subsequent source in order to deal with its consequences, as it is the sad fate of those who attempt to cheat death to be tormented by the very thing that sustains them.

"The beauty of the rose lies not in its tender petals and distinctive scent, but in the inevitability of both fading. Only the vain or deluded would try to preserve a blossom in its full glory and ultimately they are bound to fail. As you have discovered, any cure brings with it complications. Soon you will require another fountain and then another, because the only fully effective cure for life is death.

"Nevertheless, I can assist you in the quest to ease your suffering. I believe you may have been trying so hard to find a solution that you cannot see one when it is right in front of you. Heed this, my friend: what you seek is an infusion. Just as a herbal infusion is the result of chemical compounds extracted from organic material in water, so too the infusion you seek requires extracting the essence of a profound truth from life and allowing it to steep over time. Do not overthink the matter and do not persist with your search. The solution will come to you."

He rummaged amongst some items on a table at the foot of the altar and produced an individually wrapped teabag. "As a token of these admonitions, take this organic ginger brew and wear it proudly at all times."

"Wear it?" said Suave Gav.

"And remember, my bewigged fellow, nothing that is worth knowing can be taught. Apart from how to yodel."

Suave Gav's facial expressions ran through a full range of emotions – a circle of delight, confusion and despair repeated several times – during the course of this unorthodox counselling. The Advocate for

Self-Importance had changed since I was first engaged as his logo interfacer. Yes, his mind was still very much on the wrong side of the sound/unsound divide, but his raving had taken on a philosophical tone reminiscent of that chubby Nepalese man who sits around telling everybody to chill. This was certainly a welcome development, as in the past LeSnide's words were less likely to result in enlightenment and more in a beating.

The former insufferable one turned his attention to LaFlamme.

"You my dear," he began. "You say the gift of telepathic combustion is your birthright. But what do you know of birthrights? Whilst you have been fortunate enough to be brought into this world in full health and with so many redeeming characteristics, there are others who know nothing but pain, suffering, poverty, sickness. And there but for the grace of the gods go you. What right do you have to demand more?

"What you have told me is that there is a void in your life. If you truly believe there is a void, there will always be a void. To jaundiced eyes all things look yellow, and yours are gazing out through dandelion coloured glasses. However, you appear determined to acquire the gift you believe to be rightfully yours and I intend to assist you.

"Fire is one of the earth's greatest mysteries. The ancients worshipped it, and with good reason. It gave them comfort, light and a means of making food more easily digestible. It saved them from an eternity of heartburn. But no man is impervious to fire. Its flames sear and its smoke asphyxiates. Use fire as you would your life – with care, attention, and avoiding accelerants. Taking too many precautions is one of life's most common pitfalls, but in your case a few might be no bad thing.

"Instead of focussing on the void, you must imagine a solid mass of possibility. This perceived emptiness must be transformed into a living breathing entity bursting with potential. Learn to achieve this and the world is your conflagration. But do not overthink the matter and do not continue to search. The solution will come to you."

LeSnide picked up a box of matches, emptied its contents on the table and gave the container to LaFlamme. She stared at it blankly. "You may need reminding of these words from time to time, therefore take this empty vessel and keep it near you at all times."

"Thank you?" said LaFlamme.

"And remember, my dear, turn your face toward the sun and the shadows will fall behind you. Just don't forget your sunglasses. And needless to say, it doesn't really work during an eclipse."

LeSnide turned to face me and laid his hands on my shoulders. "I don't think you have any wise words for me, Guy," I said. "I only want paid."

"You my friend," said LeSnide, "are the one *most* in need of wise words. Learning is a treasure that follows a man everywhere, but in your case it seems to have taken a wrong turn. You are looking for answers and they are not forthcoming. Have you ever thought it may be time to start asking the occasional question? You have taken the phrase 'if there were no losers, there could be no winners' to an extreme and consider your underachievement a service to the community. The secret to reaching your goals in life is not simply to aim low.

"You say you only want paid, but this particular wish concerns me. For in no other area has so much injustice been unleashed on so many by so few. The pursuit of wealth is one of mankind's most ignoble traits. It results in greed, exploitation and that particularly futile emotion, envy. Inequality divides communities and is responsible for most social upheaval throughout history. Should I grant your wish, do not take it as an endorsement of the system it perpetuates. For so long as the economic order continues to line the pockets of individuals whilst failing to provide for the whole of society, mankind can never progress.

"Be generous – remember that all the money in the world cannot buy you peace, and the key to happiness is not just being able to work the remote control. Despite your travelling companion's dearest wish, life is fleeting. And when its brief flame is extinguished, there is simply no point being the richest man in the mortuary."

LeSnide took my invoice, signed it, and scribbled something on another scrap of paper. "As a token of my good faith, accept this IOU and carry it proudly at all times. Do not overthink this matter and do not continue to search. Just reward will come to you.

"And finally, my design interfacer friend, here is a piece of advice that may stand you in good stead: never judge a book by its cover, unless it's by Jilly Cooper." LeSnide stepped back. LaFlamme, Suave Gav and I eyed each other quizzically. It's fair to say that at this moment we were united by a common bewilderment.

Phillips, the harlequinesque American, burst in. "Your majesty," he said with a sense of urgency, "another homicide has been reported, this time in the approach to the foothills."

"Good," I said before realising it may sound inappropriate. "I mean, that kind of rules me out as the Wester Ripper, doesn't it?" Phillips was unconvinced.

"You could have done it yesterday, Boaks," he replied.

"Phillips you cretin," said LeSnide, again taking care to pronounce it 'cree', "this man's no assassin. He hardly has the wherewithal to tie his own shoelaces." I was delighted by this affirmation of my innocence and agreed there was no way I was bright enough to kill.

"Either way sire," continued Phillips, "it's not safe for you to remain here. We must transport you to a safe house until such time as the perpetrator is caught."

"But I'm due at the festival shortly – the Litha of the summer solstice. The procession begins at 10:00pm and my appearance is the closest I will probably ever get to a live stage performance. No Phillips, I must insist. I will take my place at the procession, then afterwards we can secure safe passage from Wester."

"Very well majesty," said Phillips. "It goes against my better judgment but you will at least have a degree of anonymity under cover of night. I will escort you."

"My friends," said LeSnide, "you must excuse me. I will have Phillips arrange to reconvene with you afterwards."

It was almost fully dark by the time we left the compound and judging by the pounding drums and the glow from a neighbouring hilltop, Litha festivities were well under way. Our tokens in hand, we followed the drums and I could tell there was a sense of collective apprehension about the evening's impending revelry.

"What do they do at a Litha?" I asked, waving my IOU for no particular reason.

"They lithen to music," said LaFlamme, clutching her empty matchbox.

"Actually," said Suave Gav, pinning his ginger teabag to his lapel,

"Litha is an ancient pagan festival celebrating the summer solstice. The pagans believed that after the solstice, as the sun begins to slowly turn southwards, it allows evil spirits to roam freely – so they lit bonfires as a means of protection. They also believed that the golden flowering plants of midsummer, such as our precious tormentil, had healing properties. Much of it will be harvested tonight, therefore expect to see a fair number prancing around like Morrissey."

"As long as I don't have to," said LaFlamme.

"Some collect bones and dried herbs," he continued, "and burn them whilst reading magical rites. The released smoke permeates the air and is supposedly responsible for magical phenomena. Some perform mock weddings with fertility procedures, leaping through fire together to bring blessings to their lives. Others roll great wheels in a symbol of the southbound sun."

"It sounds like school sports day," I said.

"No no," said Suave Gav, "it's actually enjoyable."

We joined a stream of people heading up the path that spiralled its way towards the hilltop. There I could distinguish a large body of revellers concentrated around a central bonfire that raged furiously into the night sky. En route were many smaller satellite fires where individual groups of revellers huddled or joined hands in ritual. (With the sound of drums and the presence of so many beards, I imagined this was what it might be like at Glastonbury or one of those other festivals of not washing.) One group, stripped to the waist and painted with patterns of red and green ink, screamed past us rolling a man-sized wooden cartwheel down the hill. The cartwheel kept falling over and it took two people to lift and set on its way again. I wanted to tell them if they found a second wheel and stuck an axle between them it would solve a few problems – they could even hitch a ride at the same time. But this was probably not in keeping with the spirit of the proceedings, and besides they looked a bit ill-defined.

As the peak of the hill plateaued out around us, I became aware of three factors which in combination made me instinctively want to shield the sensitive eyes of Suave Gav: 1) the heat from the combined fires was intense; 2) the tribal drumming and gyrating bodies were distinctly pagan in their approach; and 3) live chickens ran around freely. It was all making me very nervous. I took the valerian root I'd stashed in my pocket and resumed gnawing.

The attendees appeared reasonably well oiled, and having never seen so many black teeth before, I had a fair idea what was their favoured tipple. "I say," said Suave Gav spotting this, "perhaps we should get a drink." He pointed towards an area that looked promising for refreshments. We made our way through the *melee* until reaching a makeshift bar with a straw roof and bark facade. Suave Gav rubbed the bark between his thumb and forefinger and touched both lightly to his tongue. (He was nothing if not an opportunist. I imagined in an emergency stimulant-free situation he might be found with his face glued to the bar, and not in the way that I sometimes might. Though I generally approved of exploiting nature's larder, I felt it could probably be put to better use than keeping notorious substance abusing centenarians off their faces.)

LaFlamme secured three plastic tumblers of the heady Blutwurz concoction and some ice from a cooler – in this heat it was important to go Bavarian spring and not Alpine winter, as a heated drink was likely to dissolve the head. I tried drinking from the plastic cup but was having difficulty due to the valerian. "You might have to take the thumb from your mouth first," said LaFlamme helpfully. I dribbled a response. She looked at me with pity.

An old woman with a painfully hunched back approached. She carried a cane basket and appeared to be selling something. "Roots," she said.

"Roots?" said Suave Gav, his eyes lighting up. "Perhaps something for the morning." The old woman uncovered her basket and revealed a selection of crops: beet, yam, parsnip and ginger, along with something she called 'herbal preparations', which looked rather like crude handmade cigarillos. Something was very pungent. I suspected it was neither the cigarillos nor the roots, but that in the true spirit of outdoor festivals the woman was refusing to wash. 'Good for her,' I thought in my valerian sedation. She stood very close to Suave Gav and despite his obvious distaste for the smell of old hunchback (he looked as if he had just sucked on a particularly tart lemon), he still felt inclined to purchase one of her herbal roll-ups and pushed it between his teeth.

"What do we do now?" I asked.

"Try and blend in," said LaFlamme. "Maybe we should set fire to something."

"Indeed," said Suave Gav, searching his pockets for a light but coming up empty-handed. He looked to LaFlamme, who could only hold up her empty matchbox and shake her head. He stopped several revellers but was surprisingly unable to find anyone with a match. "Of all the places to be short of a light," he said. Eventually a fresh-faced man who I recognised from our travels stepped towards the captain of The Inebriate, raised his hand and produced a flame. I didn't see any lighter – it looked like the flame had sprung from within his clenched fist. It was Kevin, the young man Corky had serenaded the night we were moored by the old charcoal narrowboat. Suave Gav accepted the light, puffed on his herbal preparation until it had a head of steam and thanked him. But once lit, our eyes remained on Kevin's hand.

"How did you do that?" I asked.

"What?" said Kevin.

"Show me your lighter." He opened his clenched fist revealing a yellow plastic igniter of the disposable kind. "Right," I said. "Sorry." It was another moment of confusion in a life practically defined by confusion, but seemed less so to LaFlamme. She stepped forward until her nose was inches from Kevin's.

"Little Cinders," she said finally. "What do you know about magic?" Kevin began to back up.

"Nothing," said a deep gravelly voice from within the shadowy thickets. An old man stepped forward, his skin coarse and leathery. He walked with a pronounced limp, leaning into a walking stick, which on closer inspection turned out to be an umbrella. "What are you looking for?" he said. LaFlamme shook her empty matchbox in his direction, knowing that had there been anything within, it would have made a satisfying rattle. "There's no magic here," he continued in an unmistakable French accent. "Nothing to see. Only illusions. If you want magic, read your *Harry Potter*."

"Grandad," said Kevin, "we should go."

"I don't expect you youngsters to understand," said the old man. Suave Gav shot me a sideways glance, flattered to be considered young.

"But as I'm sure you're aware, children who play with matches are likely to get their fingers burnt."

"I think I understand well enough," said LaFlamme. "I've seen your little boat, Claude." The old man flinched, as if he'd just been called a cheese-eating surrender monkey.

"I say," said Suave Gav, "do you chaps know each other?"

"The name's Covey," said the old man. "Pierre Covey."

"*Monsieur Covey*," said LaFlamme. "How's your burning sensation? It may interest you to know that although I have no connection to any Covey and in fact believe the Pierre variety to be a front, I am the great-niece of one Claude Balls LaFlambé, aka The Great LaFlambé. Should you be in a position to extend your conjuring capabilities into channelling the old boy, I'd very much like to have a word with him."

"But I thought LaFlambé faked his death," I said under my breath, trying to make sense of the fragments of information I'd gleaned. "Aren't he and Covey one and the same?" LaFlamme lowered her wraparounds and stared at me intently. I immediately realised my error – how could I have known this information unless I'd been reading her secret journal?

"*LaFlambé est mort*," said Covey, a touch aggressively. For a moment I thought we might have trouble on our hands as it looked like quite a sturdy umbrella. But then he softened a little and added, "I owe him a great deal, of course. And if you are who you say you are, you should be very proud of him."

"Were he present," said LaFlamme, "I could him tell him so myself." The old man's brittle face broke into a smile. I thought it might crack.

"Alas," said Covey, "that is not possible. The man you see before you is but a pale shadow of the great flame, and whatever talent he may have had has vanished in the mists of time. If you are looking for magic, *ma chère*, you are asking the wrong person." I wanted to click my heels and be shot of this whole situation, such was my mental exhaustion. But I reminded myself that Kansas was only one possible outcome and that I might be really unlucky and wind up in Texas.

This marginally ameriphobic reflection was interrupted when an unholy scream filled the air; a man's scream, piercing at first but trailing off into a pathetic resigned cry, as if having been punctured by a long needle and anaesthetised after the initial shock. Mr Covey and his grandson retreated to the shadows from whence they came, and as they gave way a cluster of indistinct figures beyond them dispersed – this was a scene nobody wanted to be associated with. Just one man remained at the satellite bonfire and he lay crumpled on a bed of straw – half a man, really. He was less than four feet tall.

I only knew one man of such stature. But this figure was stout and dressed in ragged trousers and cloth shirt, the shirt too tight across his midsection, its arms a couple of inches shy of the wrist. He had a tousled little beard that masked ruddy cheeks. Tears flowed from behind his bright blue eyes. I asked if he was all right but the question fell on deaf ears. Wooden ears actually, he was quite stiff. If this had been the source of the scream, it was a swan song. Suave Gav shook him gently by the shoulder and put an ear to his mouth, checking for signs of breathing. "Poor chap's been and gone," he said. "No more life in him than one of Tony's rambling stories."

A group of revellers surrounded us. "Wooh," said one in mock fearfulness. "Spooky." Another laughed hysterically, though I imagine if he'd been turned into a wooden man he might not laugh so hard.

The procession had been gathering around us for some time and as it finally began to wind along a cleared path through the hilltop scrublands, I was distracted by the sound of a Dixieland jazz ensemble leading the way. Normally this kind of band plays a jaunty style of music that wouldn't be out of place accompanying the Keystone Cops, but this was a funereal dirge; a lament, perhaps signifying the impending loss of the summer sun or the dying of the light. Groups of costumed dancers followed – not the peacock-feathered, vibrantly attired Mardi Gras performers you might expect from the genre. Their bodies were dark and muddy, plastered in earthy reds and terracottas. Their dances were elemental, primordial, as if from a time before dancing really existed.

Behind them were several floats, rickety-wheeled wooden constructions, their bases trussed together with rope, like rafts. Each had to be towed by a dozen men and carried what looked like dignitaries of the LeSnide community. From the abundance of wigs and gavels, I presumed they were judges – many seemed to be actually passing sentence as they travelled. The last and greatest of these carried a certain square-jawed gentleman being fanned by two flunkies either side of an ornamental gold pedestal. (I assumed these were paralegals as apparently they are the lowest form of legal life. Which is really saying something.) It was Guy LeSnide.

We followed in the wake of the floats, the front of the procession having completed a full circuit of the flattened hilltop before coming to rest by the great inferno. Here the drumming reached peak intensity, the dance building to a climax.

Despite the spectacle it was obvious three of us were feeling considerably less euphoric than the rest. Suave Gav became distant as any chance of a morning-after cure began to recede in his eyes. LaFlamme shook her empty matchbox from time to time, all too aware that it was unlikely to result in the gift of telepathic combustion. I was still clutching my IOU and held it above me, my arm fully extended and waving frantically – though I don't remember this method of getting paid ever having worked before. After an hour my arm was sore and I was still broke. I began to feel the situation was hopeless.

Sensing my failing arm if not my disillusionment, LaFlamme took the piece of paper and twisted it into a bow, tying it into a lock of hair just above my forehead. This was a further indignity as I now resembled a ten-year-old girl, albeit one with a heavy beard. But I had to admit this was minor on the scale of recent indignities and I was suitably buffeted by the valerian to think the look might help me blend in with the braided and crusted ones around me. Braided and crusted, that is, apart from a lone figure on the fringe of the proceedings, inappropriately attired in a black dinner suit and white bowtie. His face was obscured by shadows but I could hazard a guess as to his identity.

"Look," I said. "It's that crazy muppet."

"Donald Trump is here?" said LaFlamme.

"Corky," I replied. "But fully grown."

"Oh my," said Suave Gav. "I imagine a fully grown incarnation could be a bit of a handful. Perhaps we should steer clear."

"We have to stop him," I said in some ill-advised valerian inspired moment of bravado. I started towards the tuxedoed figure but was halted when a group of merrymakers rolled their confounded cartwheel directly in my path. When the cartwheel had gone, so had Corky. This didn't stop me running ahead to try and apprehend the monster, though what

I intended to do if I caught him was vague – possibly daub him with my drool-coated valerian stick or rub my hair ribbon into his chest. But the root had instilled such confidence in me that I lost all fear, all perspective, and after a few moments, separated from the crowd and disorientated, I found myself quite alone.

It was a clear night and on a hillside in a relatively unpopulated area like Wester that means stars. Hundreds of them. Tiny specks of light probably millions of miles away. Some might support other life forms. Some might support lawyers. Many of them formed constellations, patterns of stars in close proximity to one another. Ancient astrologers latched onto a dozen of them and called it a zodiac so that people like LaFlamme could get a job writing horoscopes for *Toady* magazine.

Stars.

Urban dwellers tend to forget they even exist. Light pollution obliterated them decades ago and took with it any curiosity the human race might have had about the possibility of other worlds beyond our own. That's a dangerous situation for a species as self-important as ours. If people could look out on a beautiful summer's night and see stars, they might stop arguing with neighbours about the size of their hedges.

Just when I was trying to make out if Orion's Belt had come undone, I was brought abruptly back to earth. "Looking for someone?" said a voice from behind a ragged thorn bush. The silhouette of a sharp suited man stepped out from behind the shrub. I made a retreat but he was nimble, following me to a point where I was hemmed in on three sides by bushes.

"I wouldn't bother running if I were you," he said, producing an open razor.

"What do you want?" I asked.

"What does anyone want?" replied Corky. The razor glinted as it caught a sudden flash of moonlight. "Time."

"Time?"

"You cannot cheat time. Nobody can."

"It looks like you've been cheating it for years."

"It's true, of course. But unfortunately those who choose to live in a place where nobody dies must forfeit the right to leave."

"What do you mean?"

"Let me tell you a story." He sighed heavily and I wondered what kind of story a newly restored man might want to tell. "I knew a chap," he began, "who had been alive for nearly two hundred years and had spent most of them here in Wester. One day he was struck with an overwhelming curiosity about his hometown and declared his intention to leave Wester in order to pay the town a visit. It would be a short visit, just long enough to take a look around and satisfy his interest. The villagers shook their heads and said 'no you mustn't, you will die'. But he was dogged in his determination and managed to talk them round. 'Very well,' they said finally, 'but you must take this horse, whom we call Ian…'"

"Ian?"

"Dramatic licence," he said. "'Take this horse called Ian and once outside Wester, it is vitally important that you never dismount.' The man said 'well, it's a most unusual name for a horse, and I might require some sort of traveller's companion tucked into my sock,' but he agreed and set off for his hometown. After several days of travelling he arrived at his destination and, finding the area he once loved, gradually became unsettled. The streets were virtually unrecognisable. The house he grew up in was gone. Everyone he had known was dead. Disorientated and distressed, he very quickly made the decision not to remain a moment longer and turned around.

"On his way out of town he encountered a raggedy old man by the roadside standing next to a horse and cart. The cart was loaded down with worn out shoes and apparently stuck in the mud.

"'Can you help me?' asked the old man. 'Alas, I cannot,' he replied. 'I cannot get down from my horse, Ian.' 'Please,' said the old man, 'I just need a little push.' 'No,' he replied, 'I cannot get down. Ian would never stand for it.' 'Look,' said the old man, 'soon it will be dark and I will be stranded. Without help, I could perish.'

"Finally, out of pity, he stepped down from his horse. And the minute his first foot touched the ground, the old man put a hand on his shoulder and said, 'At last I have you. I am Death. And these are all the shoes I have worn out trying to track you down. But I never gave up hope, because nobody escapes me.'"

Corky took a handkerchief and wiped his blade clean.

"I think I've heard it before," I said. "Don't remember Ian though, how did things work out for him?"

"Thought you might like it," said Corky. "The point is, everything is finite."

"So are you some kind of avenging angel?"

"I'm no angel," said Corky, breaking into one of his malevolent grins. "But I rather like the idea of being an avenger. If you'd witnessed a fraction of the horror I have, you might want to try it yourself." He looked up towards the hilltop where the distant sound of revellers filled the air. "Listen to them. They're pathetic. You think any one of those lives has any purpose, any real reason to exist? Particles of dust delaying their inevitable gathering on the earth's grimy floor. I'm merely providing a service. A cleansing, a sweeping up. I'm like a dust buster."

"You're like barking mad," I said. I knew it wasn't politically correct, but faced with true ill-definition only one word really nails it.

"Yes yes, I'm a monster," said Corky casually. "But you must admit I'm looking rather fine this evening."

"You've certainly sprouted. What did you do to Mr Beard?"

"I set him free," he said. "The poor man was never real to begin with."

"What are you talking about?"

"He was my creation. Don't you know I was the victim in that scenario?" As he spoke, light billows of grey smoke began to emerge from under his arms. "In this scenario however, I believe it's your turn." I was trying to alert him to the danger when his right arm burst into flames from elbow to shoulder. Corky panicked, flapping around and shrieking before dropping to the ground and rolling in the earth.

I hastily made my escape, hurtling recklessly back up towards the hilltop and eventually almost colliding with LaFlamme. She was alone, standing very still on the fringe of the ongoing celebration as if in the midst of some deep and profound contemplation.

I took a moment to catch my breath, resting my hands on my knees before finally giving voice to the only words that formed in my head:

"Did you do that?"

"Do what?" she replied.

16.
THE PROMISED LAND

"I must admit," said The Admiral, "you're looking well for your travels, at least now that you've shaved. The vagrant thing wasn't doing you any favours. In fact one might say you look a little younger than when you set off. Was it the Cryofreeze?"

"I don't think so," I said, "although I did use it to clean my teeth and remove my beard." The Admiral furrowed his brow as I continued my account of our voyage.

Having rounded up LeSnide, we retreated before things could get ugly and any litigation became truly vexatious. LeSnide, still fully kitted out in his procession costume, ordered his foot soldiers to hasten our safe passage from the Balding Hills and settled in for the journey. Counsel was subdued. He said he had the ennui and was ready to renounce his Advocate for Self-Importance title. He complained of not having had a decent game of tennis since he reached Wester. Apparently the balls were too furry.

"So it took you a week to get there and how long to get back?" said The Admiral.

"Six hours," I replied.

"I suppose it is only forty miles from the marina," said The Admiral. He suggested it might have something to do with the physics anomaly

Wester Mean Time and could even touch on Einstein's theory of relativity. But I didn't think today would be the day I took up particle physics. I was having enough trouble working the TV remote and gladly surrendered it to him.

"What happened to our friend Mr Armstrong?" said The Admiral, flicking channels, probably searching for *World Of Steam*.

"Armstrong?" I replied. "You mean Suave Gav."

"Terrible deviant."

"Yes," I said. "But not without charm."

It had been an emotional voyage of discovery for Suave Gav. Driven by a devastating condition which forced him to consume industrial quantities of the life extending elixir Blutwurz, he was consequently pushed to the edge of despair by chronic morning-after syndrome. He needed a cure for the cure. He knew he was not alone in his suffering and selflessly set out to find one, aware that it was such acts of bravery which made man a noble species.

Despite many setbacks, he never gave up hope and continued to quaff semi-lethal measures of bloodroot and various chasers that would have felled a lesser sort. He was an adventurer too; from willow bark to nitrous oxide, I never saw a man so dedicated to the art of indulgence. He said he did it out of a sense of duty to all the other inebriates, reprobates and deviants who one day might benefit from his efforts. There was no question about it – it was heroic.

"You're being terribly generous in your assessment," The Admiral interjected. "It's difficult to imagine the circumstances in which nitrous oxide could be considered a chaser." I told him he was spoiling the moment as usual and to let me finish.

Towards the end of our quest Suave Gav began to behave oddly. Or should I say more oddly. It may just have been the mescaline or the banana rinds but something was making him truly euphoric. He looked as if he might have seen the light at the end of a long bleary tunnel. Had he had an epiffly?

"An epiffly?" said The Admiral. I admitted I'd been without the *Collins Concise* for a while and was reverting to stupid form, but that this was no reason to keep interrupting.

When we reconvened at the approach to the staircase lock, about to begin the long and slow descent from the Balding Hills, Suave Gav took the ginger infusion given to him by LeSnide in one hand and a piece of gnawed bloodroot in the other. Slowly and deliberately he raised both hands as if greeting a heavenly host and uttered the words 'holy hell'. He said he'd had a vision of the promised land and that all he had to do was conjure it up in sufficient detail to get there.

"Did he get there?" asked the Admiral. I told him if he wasn't so impatient I could have wrapped this up ages ago and let him return to *Epic Rail Journeys* or whatever droning nonsense he was trying to hear on TV.

Suave Gav demanded LeSnide's guards take him to the nearest cocktail lounge. This would have been a tall order for the guards, as bars of any sort are scarce around the staircase lock. But as it turned out, it was a fleeting fancy. By the time we were halfway down the steps he'd also demanded trips to Real Foods, The Natural Kitchen and Planet Organic. I think he meant to stock up on supplies of root ginger, which after all is known for settling the stomach and relieving nausea. Perhaps in giving him a symbol of a morning-after cure, LeSnide actually led him to the additional ingredient he'd been missing all along. When he then asked to be taken to Boots, Poundstretchers and B&Q, I confess I had no idea what was going through his mind. It might not have been so much the places themselves that interested him as the idea of having minions willing to carry him around. In any case, he ultimately decided he wasn't leaving at all.

"He stayed in Wester?" asked The Admiral.

"He said the Balding Hills were the place for him." With the statue of LeSnide now somewhat redundant, it would only take some chin alteration to make it resemble him. I said some form of turret construction might be necessary to represent his alarming, and by now immaculate, Afro. A mere trifle, he replied. He would have his minions carry a few hundredweight of a particular limestone up the hill, Giza-style, and from thence a wire frame maquette like a hairnet could be filled with the stuff. I said maybe he could just get a haircut, but I could tell he preferred the limestone idea.

The only problem then was his boat The Inebriate, which had been his kitchen, laboratory, place of worship and of course bar. He couldn't be without it, and the arduous trek from the base of the staircase lock to the LeSnide compound was not one that could be made in a floating bungalow.

"He couldn't very well *Fitzcarraldo* it up the hill, could he?" said The Admiral. I smiled. The new Advocate for Self-Importance was a very powerful man.

The Admiral resumed flicking channels on the omnipresent television. I could have done without it but felt he'd paid his dues in terms of hearing me out – it was only fair he be allowed some viewing time in relative peace. In the absence of *World Of Steam*, he settled on the news.

We watched some vaguely familiar ministerial faces debate earnestly. One old duffer suggested the suspension of capital gains tax as a move to bolster the virtually terminal decline of the economy. What a great idea, I thought. That would surely be welcomed by those who would have to choose between heating and food this winter, as the tax on their second, third and fourth properties was crippling.

It seemed nothing had changed in my absence. Nothing ever changes. I think the vaguely familiar ministerial faces like it that way. Before we reached this chronic state of trundling along the economic floor, they took the last plane out and pulled the ladder up behind them. If you didn't have the money or connections to be on it, you'll be one of those breaking your back until you physically can't work anymore. You'll be one of those ending your days grateful that the modest home comforts that others consider bare essentials are there at all. You'll be one of those thinking 'things could always have been much worse.'

Other countries pretend they have a meritocracy. They say anyone, however lowly, can rise to the top through hard work and diligence. But that's just something they tell you to make you better slaves. You can't win against the house because the dice are loaded and it's not in their interests to play it straight.

In this country they don't even bother pretending. Go to the right school and you too can be a vaguely familiar ministerial face advocating tax breaks for the rich. And just when you think such an appallingly anachronistic system can't possibly continue in a modern civilised society, the ministerial faces introduce new employment laws that stop just short of allowing children to be sent back up chimneys.

Today I wasn't sure I had the stomach for it. I was ready to head home and return to my ball of string when I spotted amongst the faces a dapper-looking man with slicked back hair and a sharp suit. He stood slightly behind two others who were announcing some policy launch or other. One of them was LeSnide's tennis playing friend 'Dave', who I'd enjoyed insulting freely over the phone. Occasionally the man with the slicked back hair would prompt one of the others and then retreat to the shadows. From time to time his jacket sleeve would emit smoke. He would hurriedly pat it down with the palm of his hand before resuming an air of calm.

It seemed the thorn in the side of the Osborne brothers was still at liberty. Not only at liberty, but in a position of power. And why not? Nothing was ever proven due to lack of evidence. Even LaFlamme's footage showed a man two feet smaller than the accused and apparently made of wood. Another man was arrested and that pretty much put an end to it. Never underestimate the power of having friends in high places. Why the Osbornes and their ilk would welcome him back into their circle after his shameless behaviour was another matter. Perhaps it was like the old saying, 'keep your friends close and your enemies closer'. Even a murderous club member was preferable to a non-member. To them he'd always be one of us.

I would think of him whenever I heard 'Smack My Bitch Up'.

17.
I HEART DARKNESS

I was finding it difficult readjusting to civilian life. I'd been listless, agitated and unengaged for so long that I considered having it printed on my business cards. Work seemed futile. I had nothing but contempt for my clients at the best of times, but now I'd given up trying to hide it. I was openly dismissive of their ideas. I began overcharging to an outrageous extent. I wore pyjamas in meetings. I didn't know whose pyjamas they were, and I wore them on my head. I drank gin during client briefs. From a thermos. Clients would ask my opinion and I'd have to turn the TV down to hear them.

In other words I did everything I could to dissuade people from employing me. And yet they continued to call. I decided I must be a graphic designer of some merit, even genius, as now there was simply no other reason to keep returning.

My mood swings had become unmanageable. Friends talked me down from the roof one minute and were asked to rumba the next. I'd lost all sense of what was appropriate behaviour. One day I found I had concocted the perfect martini, only to be told by the bus driver that it was neither the time nor the place.

Needless to say I'd stopped washing and shaving. This may not be the worst outcome but I'd forgotten what the words even meant.

The reason for my decline was clear: the whole Wester trip had been a failure. Yes, I was recompensed for my work with the Advocate for Self-Importance. Handsomely, some would say, but probably only those who know what real work is. If I had to climb four-tier ladders in midwinter to fix broken roof tiles, or avoid being shot at by rabid mujahideen in blistering desert heat, I might think it was handsome too.

On paper you'd probably say everything worked out. I entered the office of Captain Pantling with my signed invoice and he settled the account immediately by BACS, a system that gives investment bankers only minutes to gamble with your money before they have to put it in your account. Then he brought me up to date. LeSnide had become a reformed character, hanging up his wig and starting a charity that provided shoes for poor children in Africa. Perhaps he didn't choose the best name for it – 'Shoddy' – but it sounded like a worthwhile cause. It was all good.

But what would happen the next time I was stiffed by a client? And the time after that? If experience had taught me anything, which was unlikely, one reformed character didn't cancel out all the millions of unreformed ones. There was always going to be a steady supply of bastards, and that's if I was lucky. Graphic designers all over the world are always desperate for clients. Some can only dream of the chance to be stiffed.

If chasing payment had been the primary motivation for the trip, the secondary had barely spoken to me since our return. The mere mention of LaFlamme caused me to wince. I'd developed a knot in my stomach that was now the size of a tangerine and the knot tightened whenever she crossed my mind. This meant I was in pain roughly every two minutes.

Despite my best efforts, I'd failed to win her over and I'm still not sure why. Yes, I had a lengthy beard which was often matted or crusted with the remnants of my last meal. Yes, I was often stupefied either by events or the bewildering array of concoctions that passed between my lips. Yes, the stifling Wester humidity meant my clothes never dried and dubious wet patches accumulated in unfortunate places. But was LaFlamme really that shallow? Surely she could see beyond the staining and dribbling to the real flesh and blood man. Sadly her last words to me, "Do you want me to lance that?" could hardly be considered encouraging.

Did she ever accomplish her goal of telepathic combustion, the sorcery she insisted was her natural birthright? I don't know. Certainly we never had any trouble lighting the cooker on the way home. And it was most fortunate that when I was on the verge of having my throat cut, the would-be assassin spontaneously burst into flames. It may have been that the symbolic empty matchbox given to LaFlamme by LeSnide focussed her mind in a way that allowed her to direct energy to any target of her choosing. Not sure I'll ever find out now. If she had discovered the secret of fire-raising without matches, it was likely she had taken it with her to pastures new.

I had to face it, I was miserable. This was not the way it was meant to be. If I wanted to be miserable I could have stayed with The Admiral and listened to his Gong records. I was going to have to do something about it.

I stepped into the shower. It had been a while and I had forgotten what to do. I shaved. Afterwards my beard did not resume the uncanny race to the floor that it had done in Wester. I hoped when it did return it would be soft, sporadic and altogether easier to control as it was before. I wasn't sure what to do with my clothes. A washing machine would have been useful but under the circumstances I decided an incinerator was best.

The whole process took several hours. Combing my hair alone took twenty minutes. Without the ingrained dirt, I felt much lighter. I was ready to face the world and indeed to tell LaFlamme I might be degenerating to Neanderthal status without her. I walked through the hallway practically squeaking with cleanliness, opened the front door and was confronted by a huge pair of bug-eyes. LaFlamme was clutching a set of books to her chest in a manner that suggested the unthinkable – she was about to join the world of the straights.

"I'm going to law school," she said from behind her thick glasses.

"No!" I said firmly. "You can't. You're the only hope I've got and if you join the straights, I'll have nothing left. I'd have to grow up. The world needs LaFlamme, it doesn't need another lawyer. And I need LaFlamme more than the world does."

"Only kidding," she sneered, removing the glasses and pushing past into the flat. She tossed the books aside and threw herself into the sofa. Surveying the chaos that several hours of intensive grooming had created, she said, "Maid's day off?"

"Actually," I replied, "my butler committed suicide last week."

The light was fading. In September, the early evening glow dies away rapidly and a chill can set in before you know it. But LaFlamme's radiance more than compensated for it. I stepped towards the window and was about to close the curtains when something caught my eye in the street below. A man was cradling a large potted plant, a shrub of some sort, in his arms like a child. It was stumpy and unattractive, also like a child, but it was a living thing and he obviously cared for it, shielding it from the breeze. I felt a tear form in my eye.

When we send our charges out into an uncaring world, we want them to be strong and have as many redeeming features as possible in order to withstand the many knocks they will undoubtedly take. That's why we nurture and care for our plants, our creative efforts and sometimes even our children. We shield them from the elements until they're fully grown so that once they venture out unaccompanied they have the courage to stand up and tell the world to get stuffed.

"So I've finished," said LaFlamme.

"Finished?" I said without turning around. "Finished what?"

"The film, Boaks, the film." LaFlamme told me how Channel 4 loved her fly on the wall story about a bunch of freaks trapped on a boat. "It was ages before they stopped fawning," she complained. "Only thing was the title. They weren't sure about *Beardy Goes Nutzoid* because they'd just done *Beardy Dwarfs*. So I suggested *I Heart Darkness*, with a little heart emoji."

"*I Heart Darkness*," I repeated distantly. LaFlamme's curiosity got the better of her and she joined me at the window.

"Are you okay?" she said, resting her hand on my shoulder. The man with the unprepossessing plant turned a corner and vanished into the early evening.

"I think so."

"Good," she said. "Because I brought some books."

"What kind of books?"
She leaned in closer and kissed me.
"Magic," she whispered.

THE END

THE UNBEARABLE STUPIDITY OF BEING (EXTRACT)

Editor's Note: The following journal was found amongst Tony Boaks' posses-
sions and is being published here with only minor corrections. Lots of them.
His spelling was terrible.

Boaks was a graphic designer, although his design work was largely
underused due to his mediocrity in the field and his unwillingness to work. He
was also clearly technophobic, a distinct disadvantage for someone in his line
of business, although I suspect this was more to do with his general disdain
for modern life rather than a singling out of any one objectionable aspect of it.

The journal is being published for the sheer depth of its author's haplessness
in the face of the world he was recording. I can hardly believe he was able to
locate a journal, let alone write one.

Monday

This morning I received a fax from The Admiral. It was unusual because I
don't have a fax machine. I picked myself up and made my way over to his
office a couple of streets away. It was a damp morning and I was pleased
I'd managed to avoid much of it. People going about their everyday business. Cars. Guys on bikes. Joggers. I hate that stuff. I raised the collar of
my jacket and tried to pretend it wasn't really happening. The five-minute
walk seemed an eternity.

The Admiral's office, in common with my own, was the kitchen of his
already too-small flat and was littered with the tools of our trade: discarded
pieces of computer hardware, manuals, cuttings from magazines clipped
in the interests of providing much needed inspiration. Today there was a
dismantled fax machine in the corner. Unlike my own office I could see
no empty bottles, but I attributed this to The Admiral's fastidiousness. (I
was all too aware of his fondness for industrial strength ale, as befits a man
who wears a cardigan.)

I found him in typical pose, hunched over some miniscule technical
device, poking and prodding, his milk bottle glasses thicker than ever. I
made coffee and pulled up a chair by the ex-boardroom table. Only then
could I see that this wasn't another piece of his electronic fiddling. He was

texting, and the miniscule device was in fact a phone. It was difficult to see how this gadget could be dialled by anyone outside Lilliput and this gave rise to my theory that either phones were shrinking or my hands were expanding.

I wondered how a form of typing could ever have become so popular. If texting were taught in schools, it would surely become a minority pursuit like algebra. The fact it's not taught in schools probably helps ensure its continued popularity.

I felt sorry for anyone who had taken the trouble to learn to type properly, only to see the practice made obsolete by the superfast motion of twin thumbs. It's bound to be the evolutionary legacy of our generation – lightning digits. It seemed a shame in the Admiral's case because he could type with all ten fingers and possibly write several documents at once.

"I'm not typing," he said. "I'm tweeting." Even though he was using a phone rather than a keyboard, I still felt he was essentially typing. But he took issue with this, insisting he was neither typing nor texting.

"Tweeting?" I said. "Not typing?"

"Mm."

"Not texting?"

"That's right. It's when you describe in 140 characters or less what you are doing."

"I know what tweeting is."

"Let me give you an example." He began thumbing the device. "Going to meet my colleague, the eminent psychologist Lydia Pine-Coffin." He looked pleased with this.

"You're still typing."

"Well yes, but you're missing the point. This is about social networking, about micro blogging."

"It's about typing." I took the device and punched in the following letters: 'hav just stuffd my armdillo and now thinkng tacos for brekfst.' I showed him this marvellous piece of prose. "Typing."

"You're being childish now," he scolded. "Deliberately obtuse."

"Bum bum bum," I retaliated, deciding to stick with childish rather than have to look up obtuse. "You don't need 140 characters to describe what you're doing. Just write 'typing.'"

But it seems The Admiral is far from alone. Most people's list of pastimes would be headed with 'typing' if they dared admit it. Maybe it was like going to the bathroom – you might enjoy your rest breaks but you wouldn't necessarily class them as a hobby.